SEBASTIAN

THUNDER VALLEY MC

SUSAN LOWER

Time Glider
Books

SEBASTIAN

Book three in the Thunder Valley MC Series

By Susan Lower

Copyright © 2024 by Susan Lower

Published by Time Glider Books LLC

ISBN: 978-1-945274-12-1

SEBASTIAN

For Roberta
Thanks for always being there.

1

Sebastian parked his motorcycle beside the shed in the rear lot of the vintage white church. He'd arrived twenty minutes early. Maybe he should just circle around the block again so he wouldn't seem too anxious. He took down criminals for a living for years. Teaching people to ride their motorcycles safely sounded like a breeze when his high school buddy requested the favor. Asking Yeats to check on Sebastian's family had been a mistake, as was letting Yeats talk him into coming back here to check on them himself. And somewhere in the conversation, Sebastian ended up as the one doing the favor.

Thomas Yeats had a way of negotiating to ensure he always got the better end of the deal.

He removed his helmet, slid down, and sat on the ground beside the Honda Rebel, carefully avoiding the hot pipes—one leg bent, the other out straight. Sebastian scanned the area. There were a few access roads and play equipment on the other side of the churchyard.

The sound of a motorcycle caught his attention. The rider pulled in on a shining silver Yamaha, curvaceous and sleek like the rider. After parking, the rider swung a long leg over the seat.

Catching sight of the custom paint on the tank, Sebastian rose, whistling low. It took a talented artist to make it look like the metal was tearing away to aqua blue with blurred skulls beneath. He tore his gaze away from the artwork as the rider pulled off her helmet. The woman shook out long, shiny black tresses that cascaded down past her shoulders. She kept her back to him, taking care of her gear. Reaching inside a saddle-bag, she pulled out a clipboard and some other papers. The view of her backside wasn't all that bad, and when she turned, Sebastian met her sunglass-covered gaze. He anticipated their removal.

"Sign-in isn't for another hour."

"I'm not here to register," Sebastian said, amused by the way her lips turned down. "I'm a rider coach. You must be Cortés. I'm Daniels—Daniel Jones."

No matter how many times he practiced it, the alias always rolled off his tongue as awkward as it sounded. Awkward for him, anyway, because how would this woman know that wasn't his name at birth?

Her brows furrowed between eyes he wished he could see. "Thomas never mentioned a fill-in. My schedule says Davis, not Daniel."

"The last name is Jones." He needed to get used to using this new name and accept his new identity before he blew it. Someone else he cared about might get hurt if he didn't.

She walked past him, pulling out keys from her pocket and slapping the clipboard to his chest as she approached. She unlocked the shed full of motorcycles. "He offered me the position. It's my understanding the other guy isn't coming back."

"Thomas told you that?"

"That's what he said when he hired me." He and Yeats went way back. While Sebastian headed off for the police academy, Thomas Yeats joined the army and became a ranger. Thomas returned home years ago, while Sebastian worked undercover in Johnstown.

"We'll see." She pulled out a cell phone, keeping her gaze locked on him. "Call Thomas Yeats." Her phone responded, and she lifted it to her ear as it rang. She lifted her slender brow as she spoke. "Did you replace Davis?"

No hello? A direct woman was someone to be admired.

"Okay. Thanks." She slipped her phone back into her jean pocket and turned toward him.

"Looks like you're legit. Have you ever taught before?"

"No." He tried not to get offended by her brisk manner. No one called Yeats *Thomas* unless they wanted to get under his skin or didn't know him personally. What had he gotten into?

She took the clipboard away from him. "You have your certification?"

"Yes, I took the course and passed the test."

She nodded. "Fine. We have ten riders for each session today. We only take twelve riders, so there might be walk-ins or no-shows for the morning."

"Just tell me what you want me to do." He kept his gaze on her face. Most men probably only ever ogled her the first time they crossed her path.

"Once we have the course set up, I'll let you observe while I demonstrate it. These are beginner riders, and some need more instruction than others."

"As you wish," he said.

She glanced back at him. Her expression was unreadable through the sunglasses. He envisioned the options of her eye color with her Hispanic heritage.

They worked together for the next half hour, starting up motorcycles, pulling them from the shed, and ensuring they all had enough gas. She gave the orders, and he obeyed, something he learned to do while working in law enforcement.

When the first rider came, Sebastian tensed. His hand went through his hair. *Remember, you signed up for this.* What were the chances someone recognized him? He didn't know any of the men approaching. Sebastian stood behind the table, prepared to check their registrations. As each student came, he relaxed more. His presence went unnoticed. None of them wore cuts with patches in association with a biker club. They had one no-show, and four people showed up to fill in, so they had to send one potential rider away. The extra rider had come in with her boyfriend on a single motorcycle, so she had to stay on the side during the four-hour morning session.

The morning passed quickly. Cortés mounted her Yamaha and demonstrated the course by weaving through cones laid out on the asphalt. Soon, the others followed her lead. She said little to him as they watched the men and women ride the course. She spoke to him only when she needed him to move the cones or help a rider. The morning stretched out while the asphalt grew hot beneath his boots. At lunch, the group left, and they prepared for the next round.

They'd both packed lunches. She chose an apple and a granola bar while he ate half a sub and a bag of chips from last night's deli run.

"Not bad for your first time. You did good." She sat in the shade at the far end of the shed where grass provided cool relief from the hot asphalt.

He sat beside her and offered her a baked cheddar chip. "Does this mean I passed the test?"

She didn't give him a direct answer. "You handled the guy with the Harley well. I admit, out of all of them, I figured he would be the one to drop his ride. There is usually always one rider who drops his bike, but this afternoon is full of experienced riders. I should warn you, most of them are Ghosts. They come more for fun than for the learning aspect, and they'll likely give you a hard time."

"Is that so?" His eyebrow rose. She'd finally spoken to him.

She'd probably wanted the other guy to show up so she could get rid of Sebastian. Or maybe she wished he'd get bored and decide the job wasn't for him. "I think I can handle it. You said they're Ghosts?"

"Ghost Riders." She drank from a thermos probably filled with water. "They're the local motorcycle gang around here. Their clubhouse is in the more populated section of town. Since you ride, they may try to recruit you."

"No, thanks." He had been there, done that, and vowed he wouldn't go there again. Sebastian knew he would encounter motorcycle club members with this kind of job and hoped it didn't bring him any more trouble. He reached up to push his sweat-dampened hair from his brow.

"You sound like you know them pretty well." Sebastian wanted to get to know her better. Alarms rang in his head to stop. Memories of Audra in those last moments of her life churned his stomach.

"That's because they consider me one of their own." Her voice conveyed a sense of wistfulness or defeat. "Once a Ghost Rider, always a Ghost Rider."

In his experience with biker clubs, most women had old men—boyfriends or husbands—who claimed them. This was another reason for him to keep his involvement with her professional.

"I ride alone," he said, deciding not to butt in her business. Her affiliation to them was not his concern.

Caitlyn Cortés pushed her sunglasses up in her hair, and for the first time that day, he caught the color of her eyes— liquid amber, like when tea in a jar caught the sunlight on a hot day. It had been worth his wait.

The sun beat down on him. Sebastian rose and cleaned up his lunch. It looked like he had enough time to take a walk before the next session. Maybe he should reconsider this gig and stay somewhere close enough to watch over his family.

The law enforcer inside him scanned the area again. No,

he wouldn't leave her alone and unprotected. A few hours with her, and all he cared about was her safety. *Not again.* Maybe this was a bad idea. He couldn't do this again.

He failed too many times, and his shoulder ached as a reminder. The sooner he got this gig over with, the sooner he could distance himself from the curvy, long-legged coach.

By the afternoon session, Caitlyn had shed her leathers and applied another coat of sunscreen across her nose and cheeks. She adjusted the bill of the ball cap to keep the sun from her face and walked out amongst the bad boys of the Ghost Riders, who came to give her a hard time.

Antonio, her brother and VP of the Ghosts, sent them to spy on her. Like Pops, many believed that a woman should be by her man's side, caring for him and raising a family. This is why Caitlyn showed the members of the Ghost Riders that she could hold her own, with or without a man.

Antonio disowned her father when the club stripped him of his position as president, and her husband, Silas, nearly cost the club everything.

Grover and Blue were the first to show. They thought of her as Silas's old lady. The divorce. The fact he went to prison. Neither made a difference. No man in a hundred miles would dare ask her out. She belonged to the Ghosts and Silas. Her testimony helped put him in prison, and she prayed he stayed there a very long time.

"You'll need a helmet for the course," she told Blue. Bald beneath the blue and red Yankees bandana, the large, muscled man grunted at her.

"No helmet, no ride on my course," she said.

"His head is hard as granite," Grover vouched for him.

"You know I don't wear a helmet," Blue said.

Caitlyn shrugged. Blue carried too many points on his

driver's license to risk walking away from the class. "Not my rules. If you want to take the course, you wear a helmet. I can look in the shed and see if I have a spare."

"And I'll crack it in half before my head ever splits," said Blue.

"That's the point," Caitlyn said.

Blue's face turned from all-knowing to confusion. "You are telling me I can't take part in this sissy parade without a helmet?" Blue clenched his hands into a fist. The left one had BLUE written across his knuckles.

"Grover does," Caitlyn pointed out as Daniel returned from his walk. Although nice, he exuded a simmering intensity. Unlike her prior partner, Daniel approached the motorcycle course with a seriousness that bordered on brooding. Not quite a scowl, but a permanent furrow etched between his brows while dealing with the riders. His presence crackled with tension, which intrigued and unsettled her, leaving her wanting to see what laid hidden beneath that serious exterior.

"Grover has Jello for brains," Blue said.

"Then it's a good thing he wears a helmet," she said.

"Where is Davis? He'll put an end to this," Blue said.

"He's not here. I need to sign in more people for us to start on time." She pointed a pen at him. "Helmet."

"No way," Blue growled.

Caitlyn's heart hammered a frantic rhythm against her ribs. Blue towered over her, his sneer deepening. Out of nowhere, a figure materialized beside her. Caitlyn flinched, whirling around to find Daniel's broad shoulder, blocking some of Blue's imposing presence. He wasn't Blue's size, but he held himself with a quiet confidence that sparked a flicker of hope in Caitlyn's chest.

"If the lady says you need a helmet, then you wear a helmet." Daniel stepped alongside her behind the table.

"Who are you?" Blue scoffed, his gaze flickering between them.

Caitlyn's mind scrambled. What was Daniel doing? Did he know the trouble he was wading into?

"New guy," Caitlyn said as a hesitant warmth that might have been gratitude seeped inside her.

"Is that right?" Blue sneered.

"The others are on their way." Grover lifted his chin.

Instead of taking it as a threat, Daniel said, "Good. Looking forward to meeting them."

Begrudgingly, Blue took the helmet she offered him. He leaned in close to her. "Wouldn't want to do anything that might get somebody hurt now, would we?"

Caitlyn glanced at Daniel from the side.

She refused to look at Blue. Holding her breath from his sour stench, she focused on Daniel's blonde scruff, where he missed a spot shaving. It was several shades lighter than his hair.

Daniel's jaw twitched, but he kept his gaze held on Blue. Caitlyn looked away, heat climbing her neck from the growing humidity. Definitely not from the fact that Daniel might have caught her checking him out.

"You good?" Daniel raised his brows.

"We Ghosts look out for our own." Grover gave Blue a nudge to step away from the next person waiting in line to sign in

"Caitlyn?" Daniel said when Grover answered him instead of her.

She forced a tight smile, the effort a strain on her already taut face. Her gaze flickered to Blue. "I'm good," she rasped, the word catching in her dry throat. Her mind raced with the terrible possibilities of the Ghosts' wrath. "I got this."

A glance at Blue made her fingers tremble. She almost dropped the pen she picked up for the next rider to sign the waivers to participate in the class.

The rider coach program ran through the state Department of Transportation. Those who wanted to get their license or refresh their skills after meeting citations took the courses. Of course, Blue and Grover would be amongst them, but half the class wore Ghost Rider patches today.

Butch and his old lady, Zelda, showed up. Zelda's hair was flaming green, and she'd gotten a new piercing in her nose. She rode on the back of his touring bike. Zelda settled near the shed, laying out her jacket and going to business on filing down her nails—she wouldn't be taking the class, but she brought everything she needed for both a manicure and a pedicure while she watched the others. Butch and Zelda have been inseparable, especially since last year when Zelda got diagnosed with ovarian cancer. Most of the Ghost Rider men were over-protective of their women.

The rest of the Ghost Riders arrived with Butch to take the class. No women had signed up for the course this afternoon. Usually, she and Davis had an agreement. She did the demonstration, and he stayed out of her way. Mainly because the guy was lazy and looking for easy pay.

"Your turn. Do you think you can handle showing these boys the ropes this time around?"

"I can do that. Which exercise are we starting with?"

She pulled out the cards and showed them to him. She pointed to a simple pattern of weaving through cones.

"I can do that." He headed toward his bike.

"Use one of the student bikes. Less wear and tear on yours."

He looked between his bike and one of the student's bikes. Students had a choice of riding their own or one provided for them. Most liked to ride their own—they were more comfortable handling it. She preferred her own motorcycle, but Daniel didn't remark on it. He headed for one of the student bikes.

Daniel weaved through the cones with surprising smoothness, considering it was his first try. The moment his feet hit the pavement as the motorcycle came to a halt, Blue blurted, "Whoa there, slowpoke!"

Grover chimed in, "Pretty sure a sloth could move faster than that!"

"Yeah, seriously." Blue chuckled, holding his motorcycle up, waiting to take his turn. "You make it look harder than it is, newbie. You ride like my old lady. Maybe you should take the back seat and let Cat show us how it's done."

Caitlyn bit the inside of her cheek. Blue and Grover narrowed their eyes at Daniel. As she was about to intervene, she took a breath when Butch rode up behind Blue. "Knock it off or go back to the clubhouse."

Blue scowled and mumbled something under his breath.

Daniel smirked, a hint of amusement dancing in his eyes. "Maybe next time you can be the coach and teach me a few tricks."

"Now you're talking, Newbie," Blue said.

"Don't encourage them," Caitlyn hissed at Daniel. "Our goal is to teach safety, not promote competition."

Daniel made a big act of sighing. "You heard the lady. No stunts. Guess we'll have to do it the slowpoke way. Who's up first?"

2

Chum stood in Denny's, bewildered. He watched men with black leather cuts and crosses in their patches arguing with their old ladies over what eggs they wanted or French toast and pancakes. Pathetic. What kind of biker club went out for breakfast and let their women order for them?

The eldest, a man with short white hair, laughed as the woman beside him wagged her finger and reminded him about his salt intake.

What made him think he could find what he was looking for here? It was hard for him to believe that the club had no place to gather, and none of their old ladies prepared meals for their monthly meetings.

Someone would have to teach them how to hold church. These old timers had lost it in more ways than one.

But he didn't come here to show them the error of their ways. Chum scanned the faces. There. A few seats down sat Haden Patterson. After the fire last November, he took over Charlie Brooks' motorcycle shop while his buddy, Daniels, the undercover cop, led them to believe he wanted to join the Sharks using the road name Beast.

But hiding Beast's motorcycle while the cop fooled them all?

Haden was lucky. All the Sharks did was burn down Brooks' shop. Chum never met Haden personally, but Pike complained about the Brooks and their interference with his business plenty enough times for Chum to recognize him.

Beside Haden sat his old lady, Holly, a dark-haired woman with an agenda out across the table and a sweet smile that made his stomach ache. Opposite them, a face he recognized gazed at the baby she held. Her hair was darker, her face less round, but looking into her eyes would make his heart bleed with familiarity. But the woman he saw was dead, and the child in her arms should have been his.

He knew several of these people, but none of them knew him. He looked nothing like his brother Pike, and until Beast betrayed him, he had no reason to interact with the holy rollers on their mission to help others. Do-gooders—until they got involved in people's lives and took them away.

They messed with the wrong guy this time.

Never again would Chum allow another brother to steal from him. *Thou shall not steal.* He did not miss the irony. Chum grew up living by the bro code, the law of all bikers—so much different from the ones held by the people sitting around this table arguing about eggs and pancakes.

Haden was the first to notice Chum's presence. He got up from his seat and approached Chum. "You look lost, bro. Can I help you?"

"Maybe."

"You looking for breakfast, or the Thunder Valley Motorcycle Club?" Haden stood a few inches taller, but he wasn't as broad and he shielded his woman from Chum. He respected a man who guarded his woman. Too bad the man associated with the very Beast he hunted.

"Both?" Chum peered again at the baby in the woman's arms. He'd heard Audra's sister had named the baby Isaac.

The dark-haired little boy chewed on his fist. What would he have done to have that little boy grow up and call him Daddy? Audra's loss burned in his gut. She should have been his. He spotted her first, took her to the club, and introduced her to Pike. They were traitors—all of them. First Pike, then Beast, but never his beloved Audra.

His gut twisted thinking of all the months Beast hid Audra from Pike after he tried to kill her and dispose of their kid in the trash. It made him sick. Beast could have protected her and saved the baby, but he let Audra die.

Haden slightly turned to follow Chum's gaze. Quickly, he averted his gaze and glanced over all the other members. "I heard this place is non-judgmental and has no membership requirements."

"The only requirement is to abide by the bylaws and acknowledge Christ as our savior."

An older man joined them. Taller than Chum, with a thick waist and deep lines etched into the older man's face, he stuck out his hand to Chum. "I'm Larry."

The hardy grip did nothing to intimidate him. Smiling faces greeted him—all except for Haden. He kept his mouth in a pressed line. Chum avoided paying him any more attention than the others. He would fit in. He would get the information he needed. It didn't matter if Hayden or any of the rest of them liked him. The opportunity to see Audra's son, *his* son, elated him.

They seated him near the old white-haired man, intentionally far from the woman and baby. He gritted his teeth, listening, smiling, and ordering runny eggs to top his pancakes.

The waitress who brought his order reached over to fill his coffee. He got a good eyeful of her service and winked when she moved on to the next table. Larry frowned. The man was whipped by his old lady.

When Chum dug into his cakes, a guy named Max stood to lead them all in prayer. Chum chewed through half the words and swallowed in time to mutter amen. By then, he had caught the attention of every old lady's gaze. He lifted his brows and shrugged. Whatever they held against him lifted, and conversations flowed while they ate.

"How did you find us?" a woman named Tina asked him.

"Let the man eat," said the man beside her. "Can't you see he's starved?"

"I just asked," Tina huffed.

"Beast." Those words made half the table go quiet.

"You know Sebastian?" the woman with the sugary smile asked.

"Is that a problem?" Chum stabbed his fork down into the remaining pieces of his pancakes.

"No." Larry shook his head, glancing down at the table. "We didn't know *Beast* had many friends."

The woman lost her smile and glanced away.

"We used to ride together," Chum said, gauging their reaction.

A few seats down, Haden's eyes narrowed. "You're a Shark."

Chum grinned and quickly deflected his reaction. "No, man. No Shark. Not anymore. Didn't you hear? They are all gone."

"But you were a Shark?" the woman beside him asked. The one with the baby held the little one closer. Her name was Emma, the lawyer and the baby momma's sister. He remembered the way Audra used to talk about her sister. She'd married the trash man who found the baby.

"Nope." Chum put his fork down. "I tried. Just like Beast, it wasn't for me."

"Why aren't you in prison like the rest of them?" a man in his late forties asked. His cut said Vince, and his long hair pulled back to reveal the scuff on his jaw below his hollow cheeks.

Larry bumped into the man. "We don't judge here." He

looked directly at Vince. The man scowled, tossing down his napkin and leaning back.

"It's alright," Chum addressed Vince. "I hear you, man. Most of the Sharks are dead or in prison, but I was a prospect, and I kept my nose clean."

Larry cleared his throat. "I think we best get started. There is no pressure to join. You're welcome here. Our membership is a test."

"The paper kind," Tina said with an uncertain smile. Although she had every reason not to trust him, she accepted him at their little breakfast meeting.

"If it was good enough for Beast, it's good for me," Chum said. He listened through their meeting. He attended church plenty of times, listening to club business. The Devil Demise would hoot and holler when he told them about his experience with the Thunder Valley MC. Maybe he would join. It couldn't hurt to get to know them. They might open up and give him the information he needed faster than a fellow member.

After the meeting, Chum took his time. His Harley sat by a blue Honda with sparkling chrome. Haden held the helmet while Holly situated her bag with what Chum figured were a few notepads and a calendar book. He had never seen a woman who needed to document everything in numerous books. She took the helmet from Haden, and he helped her buckle the strap. He tweaked her nose and kissed her, and Chum stared for a minute too long.

"You think you'll come back?" the woman asked, glancing over at him.

"You want me to come back?" he asked, curious by her inquiry.

Haden stepped in front of her. "Watch it, man—Hols helps plan the annual rally. My girl here will put you to work."

Holly was the daughter of the former president of the

Thunder Valley Riders, Charlie Brooks, who had offered to help his sweet Audra in times of trouble.

"I'm not afraid of grunt work. Beast and I had our share. You haven't seen him lately, have you?" Maybe that was pushing. Patience wore thin after months of coming up with no signs of the traitor cop.

Haden wrapped his arm around his woman. "If you know him like you say you do, then you know he's gone."

"I figured, being a cop and all, he would come back." Chum had promised the Devil Demise he could deliver. They collected the bounty on the first cop without delay.

"Beast is gone."

"He's not dead," Chum said.

"Maybe he is. Maybe he isn't." Haden shrugged.

Holly glanced at him, clearly desiring to talk, but Haden silenced her with a headshake. Her lips pressed together in a thin line, and the frustration mirrored in Chum's gut. There went his chance at a decent answer.

"You mentioned Beast told you about us. When?"

"When we were both with the Sharks," Chum said.

"It's been months. What took you so long?" Holly asked.

"I don't believe you." Haden motioned for his woman to move toward the motorcycle.

His sweet Audra helped Holly escape when the Sharks kidnapped her. Chum tried to warn her not to trust these people. He should have known Beast would get involved and try to steal his woman.

If what they said about God and free will was true, no one could have stopped the events from unfolding. It was fortunate that Chum had different religious views about "church" than these individuals.

"And he wouldn't befriend a guy like me," Chum said.

"No. That's…" She looked at Haden and frowned. "I didn't mean…"

Chum held up his hand. "It's okay. I get it. The thing is, I don't know why he talked to me either. We were cool. If it wasn't for him, I wouldn't be here."

"Looks like he kept you out of jail." Haden swung his leg over his bike. "Hols, babe. We gotta go."

She gave Chum one last look. "It was nice meeting you. Chum, right?"

"Yep."

"Road name?"

"Shark name."

"We don't go by road names here. Since there are no Sharks, use your given name. We're neutral. Don't let this grump keep you from joining us again."

"Next month?" he asked.

"We go for ice cream over at Little Sprinkles on Friday nights." Holly laid her hand on Haden's shoulder.

"I know the place."

"Good. Maybe we'll see you there." Holly took hold of Haden's shoulder to swing up on the motorcycle.

"Chris." He grinned. "My name is Chris."

3

The clock on the stove screamed 3:58 pm, the red digital numbers pulsing like an accusation. Caitlyn slammed the oven door, a hiss escaping as the preheated air met the cool metal. Today's training session at the range ran longer than usual with the new guy, Daniels—Daniel Jones. Technically, it wasn't his fault—it was his first time processing all the paperwork—but the extra hour gnawed at Caitlyn's tight window for getting ready for her second job and spending time with Owen.

Caitlyn glanced at the sink, a battlefield of greasy pans and crusted plates. The mountain seemed to mock her. Dishes rose higher each time she came home. The money she clipped to the curtain was missing—most likely taken by Pops—and the dishes still sat dirty. There went trying to bribe her kid to do kitchen chores. A mother could hope, but Owen wouldn't be of any help, lost in his usual video game.

She stuck a sticky note on the fridge with a list of emergency numbers. She'd need to grab some tape to make it more permanent so she didn't have to stick up a new one every weekend.

Trusting Pops with Owen was a gamble since Owen

clearly cared more for Pops than the old man looked out for her boy.

"Alright, Owen." Caitlyn knelt beside the lanky form sprawled on the living room floor. Owen, headphones jammed on his head, was a tangle of limbs and controller buttons.

Not looking up, he said something to the person on the other side of the headset.

"Remember the drill tonight? Veggies are chopped in the crisper, and the lasagna is cooling on the stove. You and Pops." Her gaze flickered to the recliner where Pops sat, eyes shut. Was he sleeping or pretending?

Maybe he didn't hear her. Caitlyn tapped the top of his headphones. He tilted his head and scowled at her. He ripped off one side of the headset, revealing a red ear from the tight fit. "Pops can take care of himself," he muttered, his voice filled with as much impatience flowing through Caitlyn, knowing she might end up late to work.

"That's not the point," she said, her voice low. "There are emergency numbers on the fridge. Try not to lose them this time. Understand?"

Owen stared at her, a flicker of something, annoyance, maybe a hint of fear, crossing his face before he mumbled another "K" and slammed the headphones back on.

"Veggies. Snack. Lasagna supper. On the stove." Caitlyn raised a brow, waiting for him to acknowledge that he understood.

He rolled his eyes in response and went back to his game.

Caitlyn straightened, the knot of tension in her stomach tightening. She ruffled Owen's hair, but he swatted her hand away. A familiar wave of frustration washed over her.

Brushing it off, she announced, "I'm heading out, Pops."

Pops didn't even crack an eye open. In the flickering light of the television, she saw a tremor run through his fist and thanked God for another day of her father's sobriety. Pops, known as Welder, used to lead the Ghost Riders but was no longer welcomed. Her brother rarely visited, blaming her and their father for the past events involving the club, her, and Silas.

Standing there, waiting for some acknowledgment, Caitlyn sighed. "Food is out. Owen's playing games. Don't..." She hesitated, the words catching in her throat, "Thanks for keeping an eye on my boy tonight."

Pops mumbled something suspiciously like, "leave the kid alone," but Caitlyn didn't stay to hear it. She hurried out the door, afraid of becoming later than she already was, and prayed for a veil of protection over her father and son.

———

Nothing and everything had changed.

Sebastian stood outside the stables, inhaling the scents of horses and sunbaked hay, cooling with the setting sun. On the hill overlooking the stables, the stone farmhouse frowned upon him. He lost count of the years he avoided this place. Avoided his family. Avoided his twin sister. Sebastian let them all down. Let *her* down.

And it hadn't changed.

Just like the candles his mother kept in the windows and the old farmhouse he grew up in, they kept everything original because his father liked it that way. His parents claimed it was good for tourism. People enjoyed going back to the past. It was funny how people seemed attracted to the dead, enamored with history. If only the past would stay behind him. Sebastian became a police officer to protect and see justice served, but he failed one too many times to uphold his vow.

A truck drove down the lane and pulled up alongside the stables. Sebastian hunched down near a rusted tractor to keep out of view. He had parked his motorcycle a block away next to another driveway shielded by a line of trees.

A man in a ball cap exited the truck. "Sam."

Sebastian's twin sister, Samantha, emerged from the stables, and she embraced the man. She grabbed the man's face and kissed his cheek. His mom had emailed that they'd gone on a cruise and planned to travel for the next few months. They left Samantha behind to run the stables and lead the horseback tours through the battlefields, but she wasn't alone, to his relief. The man wrapped his arm around Samantha, and she tilted her head back, laughing at something the man said.

She must have let go of most of the staff early today. His family often hired a couple of hands and an extra guide for the busy season. Plus, they hired a few teens for the summer who needed a place to go to stay out of trouble.

Sebastian waited. When the sun disappeared and dusk took over, their shadows lengthened in the barn. Getting closer would risk being spotted out in the open distance between the tractor and the house. If someone caught him, they might call the police, and then his family would find out he returned. It wasn't a risk he was willing to take.

With the first camera installed inside the tractor, Sebastian waited. Not long after the man arrived, Samantha led him toward the house. His father had security cameras inside the barn to check on the horses. Sebastian had helped his father install them before he left to become a cop. He kept to the darkness, slipping into the barn, grateful they never locked the barn doors. He needed more time to finish adding his security system on the property.

It wasn't the homecoming he envisioned, but how could he face his father after failing to protect Sam for the second time?

Their father understood Sebastian's need to get away, but Sam—not so much. With his departure, there was little else to be said between them. She wrote him emails and sent him texts until he stopped giving them his new number. Would she even want to see him?

While the police chief back in Johnstown assured him it

was safe to return to work, Sebastian lived with the Sharks for almost two years, and his gut twisted at the thought of them coming after him and his family. And they would if they thought it'd help them get revenge for taking them down. The club broke up. Some members had gone to prison, and some were dead, but Sebastian couldn't shake the gnawing feeling in his belly that one of them could come after him. Some wouldn't remain in prison for long.

It was better he kept his distance from Sam.

Sebastian returned to his motorcycle, his jaw clenched. Though he wished to conceal his return, he detested having to leave again. He didn't plan to go far this time, and he had the cameras and Yeats to ensure his family stayed safe.

4

"Order up!"

Caitlyn shoved another large pizza with the works in a box and moved on to the next order. The back door stood propped open, and the air conditioner stuck in the wall hummed, but neither kept the sweat from rolling down her forehead.

She took a moment to step outside, pull off her bandana, and pat her face. Sweat from the heat of the ovens inside the kitchen flushed her skin and dampened her hairline. Leaning against the wall, she took a deep breath, regretting not grabbing a bottle of water when she stepped out. Exhaustion clung to her, but despite the familiar chaos brought by the business of her shift, Caitlyn welcomed the bite of the brick against her back.

The safety course had run smoothly earlier that day. Beyond the satisfaction of surviving the safety course without one of the Ghosts coming to give them a rough time, partnering with Daniel had been...unexpected. Daniel's calm demeanor and simple instructions balanced her detailed and in-depth approach. Over the past two days, she'd found it easier to banter with him, and she liked how he pulled his weight on the range with the motorcycles and the riders.

The image of Daniel silhouetted against the early morning sun, his face creased in a genuine smile, lingered in her mind. "No more guys on motorcycles," she muttered, and the phone in her pocket vibrated. She pulled it out, answering automatically at the sight of the number flashing on her screen. "What's up?"

"Mom?"

She held the bandana against the side of her face. "Owen, what's wrong?"

"Old men came, and Pops went with them."

Caitlyn took a deep breath to stay calm. "Do you know where they were going?"

"The Pub inside the hotel here on Main Street, but I don't know how long he's been gone."

Caitlyn stuffed the bandana into her mouth for a moment to silence the scream curling up her throat.

"Mom?"

She removed the bandana and said, "Thanks, buddy. Go back to playing your game, and I'll take care of Pops."

On the other end of the phone, Owen paused, then said, "I'm sorry, Mom."

"Lock the doors and keep the phone close. I love you, bud." And she hung up.

Sober one hundred and twelve days. What a waste.

Stepping back into the hot kitchen, she found the manager, Regina.

"I'm sorry, I need to go. I'll be back as soon as I can."

Regina planted her hand on her hip. Sweat beaded on her brow. The older woman bit her lip for a moment. "We're short tonight without Leo. I need you to come back."

"I'm sorry," Caitlyn apologized again. Regina was among the few who supported her after Silas. After Pops hit rock bottom. After her brother Antonio disowned them as members of his family. She needed this job. Teaching motorcycle safety on the weekends supplemented what she didn't earn here. Without the income, they would lose the house, her business aspirations, and the stability she worked hard to achieve for Owen.

Regina grabbed a pizza wheel, grimacing as she turned back toward the red brick oven in the wall. "Just get there and get back."

Caitlyn worked for Regina's family off and on since she graduated from high school. No one else would allow her to flex time like this, not in a million years, but she grew up in this town, and pity always won people over.

"*Gracias*, Regina." Chucking her apron in the bin and grabbing her keys, she headed for the Gettysburg Hotel.

Once she was inside the hotel's pub, Caitlyn took a moment to allow her eyes to adjust to the dim interior. Her father sat at the bar with his old pals Terry and Lucas.

Why they chose the Gettysburg Hotel was beyond her. Usually, they went farther out of town and found a dive or one of their regular hangouts, where they drank and relived their old glory biker days. Since the Ghost Riders stripped Pops of his patch, Butch no longer allowed him in the Ghost Riders' Tavern. Where else would the three amigos have to go without leaving town? Battlefield Tavern on the other side of town?

Terry, once the road captain, and Lucas, one of her father's favorite enforcers, fled the club with Pops' banishment. Whenever they came to town, they liked to stir up trouble.

One of them must have given Pops a ride. One too many DUIs, and her father lost his driver's license. She'd taken the keys to his Roadster and hid them.

Yellow globe lights strung across the ceiling inside the dimly lit bar area. The dark wood wainscoting and burgundy walls gave off a burlesque feel. It wasn't hard to spot the three men at the bar, their tattooed arms and unshaven jaws out of place amongst the more refined patrons. On the floor, the reflection of the yellow light gleamed. Almost every table held occupants drinking, talking, and eating. A server with blonde hair and a perky smile headed toward a table of men with a tray full of fries, burgers, and wings.

"Figures," she muttered. Pops would have to cause trouble during the dinner hour.

Caitlyn moved toward Pops when someone stepped in front of her. A solid chest blocked her way, and she smacked right into it. She bounced back away, and a set of hands grabbed her shoulders to steady her. Panic flared like a lit match close to her skin.

"Whoa there." With rusty brown hair and a nick on his chin, likely from a recent shave, Daniel murmured an apology. What was *he* doing here?

The last thing she needed was to run into the rookie rider coach around town. Before she knew it, word would get around, and if the Ghost Riders thought she was dating him, they might come knocking on her door. She swore after Silas to keep her distance and keep her son safe. Why did everything in her life have to be complicated? A slick of sweat glazed her arms. Not wanting to cause any more attention than Pops had created with his buddies, she tried to play it cool. She smiled, but Daniel took one look at her with those sinfully blue eyes and cut through several layers of her defense.

The softness of his gaze stilled the anxiety in her chest for the moment.

"I'm fine," she said, stepping back to keep space between them.

Daniel cleared his throat, dropping his hands from her shoulders. "You sure?"

Amongst all the malted beverages and fried food, she swore she smelled fresh-cut grass on a warm day and a hint of bacon. Or maybe the bacon came from her and the last order she prepared before leaving the kitchen at La Rosa's.

An outburst erupted from Pops at the bartender. "Fill 'er up now!"

Pops' amigo, Lucas, smirked at the bartender. This wouldn't go down well. Caitlyn rolled her shoulders back. "If you'll excuse me," she said, trying to remain calm.

Pulling up those invisible shields she'd gotten so good at constructing, Caitlyn wiped her hands down the side of her worn jeans. The entire place smelled of various brews and smoke, and she wanted to get out of here pronto. She blinked to keep her eyes from watering. The sting of the smoke caused her irritation the closer she approached the bar.

Daniel stepped out of her way, distracted by her father yelling at another man joining the bartender behind the bar. She kept from looking back at Daniel, even though she wanted to, despite knowing it would bring her more trouble. Men were trouble, and she had enough trouble on her own.

"Pops," she said, staying far enough out of his reach. When he did not acknowledge her, she said louder, "Welder."

Her father swiveled around. His lips curled up in a sneer. "What are you doing here?"

Caitlyn licked her lips, careful to choose her next words. So far, she'd avoided attracting additional attention in the hotel's bar. Daniel stayed nearby. Cringing inside, she tried to will him away, not wanting the man she worked with to see this part of her life. Not when those eyes of his softened in a way that borderlined pity. She had enough of that stored away from everyone else in this town. The idea of Daniel seeing her the same as the locals did unsettled her. She needed to take her father home and return to La Rosa's, since they were already shorthanded. Regina might not give her a next time when an actual emergency arose.

"I'm on break. Wouldn't you like to go somewhere else? I can drive you," she offered. *Don't make this difficult.* But he would. He always did.

Pops shook his head, his dark hair peppered with grey.

While he'd once been an attractive man, the drink had tinted his skin a sickly grey and sunk into his once-ruddy cheeks.

"If we wanted to leave, I'd have taken him." Lucas glared at her. His leather ties swung under his arms.

"Go away. Go back to your work." Pops waved her away. "*Lejos contigo.*"

Her lips thinned as she pressed them together. Lucas hadn't taken his gaze off her in a challenging sort of way. He shared the same opinion as her father, but she was strong and stubborn, like her sister. Just not as smart, according to Antonio. Too stupid to know when to leave enough alone. Too stupid to pick up her son and run far away. Too stupid to find somewhere else to go. No. Not stupid. Caitlyn's sister Isabella fled from their father. Her own sister wouldn't offer to help her, and Caitlyn couldn't bring herself to ask.

The bartender took several steps back from the bar.

"The night's young." Terry beat on his chest. Long white hair fell around the old timer's shoulders. "We're just getting started."

The bartender, a college-aged guy—barely old enough to serve alcohol by the looks of him—seemed desperate to escape the three old men. The younger man's eyes widened as Lucas leaned forward to mutter something to the bartender. Caitlyn took a deep breath. Another man wearing a suit and a tie moved closer to the bartender.

"Why don't you, Terry, and Lucas, hang out at the house?" She could call Regina and see if she could bring Owen in to work with her for a few hours. Calling off would only get her fired. "I'll grab some pies, and it will be like old times."

"I'm staying here," Terry grumbled.

Lucas waved her off. Gritting her teeth as to keep back the unsavory words lying at the tip of her tongue, she placed her hands on her hips. How could they? How could he? She ground her teeth against the irritation of them coming to town and screwing up his sobriety.

"Why not go to Battlefield Tavern across town? I'm sure you haven't been there yet," she said.

At the mention of the new Ghost Riders' president's name, Lucas tightened his hand around a half-empty glass.

"Kicked us out," her father snarled. "Wouldn't give me a drink!" He pointed to his chest. Her father going along with them wasn't part of her plan. He knew better than to show up at Butch's place. The Battlefield Tavern was the club's hangout, and they often held church in the back room.

"Well, that explains it," she muttered, throwing up a silent thanks to God that Butch sent him away with no other consequences.

"Don't you got someplace to be?" Terry turned, steeling those beady eyes on her.

Too angry to allow his unspoken threat to cause her fear, Caitlyn snapped back at him. "Yeah, I do, and as soon as you all clear out of here, I can get back there."

Glancing over her shoulder, she saw Daniel standing at a distance, watching. Silent. His arms crossed and his feet shoulder-width apart, he stood like a guard at her back. She wanted him to leave. Heat burned in her cheeks at his intense gaze. Not daring to look back at him, she felt his stare on the three men more than her. The muscles in her back loosened, but not much. She both appreciated his presence and loathed it at the same time. Deciding to push those worries away for later, she crossed her arms like Daniel.

"I'm staying here," Terry said.

"We've got rooms for the weekend. I'm taking your rider course tomorrow night and Saturday," Lucas said.

"You can take it when you return to Florida. They've got them down there too," Caitlyn said, inching closer. "Come on, Pops. You promised you'd stay with Owen."

"The kid's old enough to take care of himself. Now be off!" Pops waved his hand, knocking Caitlyn back. She met two hands again to steady her.

"Where's my drink?" Pops demanded.

She glanced back at Daniel, about to tell him she had this. He shook his head—not at her, but at the bartender, who held up his hands for accountability.

"We're done serving you for the night," the man in the suit said.

"What? Is my suit not fancy enough for you? I told you boys we should have gone across town," Pops said. "Why are we meeting here again?"

"You wanted to walk," Lucas said.

So, Caitlyn had assumed correctly.

"We're staying here while in town," Terry said.

Fury radiated down her bones at her father's old riding buddies. They knew her father was working on staying sober. A little after seven in the evening, her father was *ebria*. Caitlyn started her shift at four after finishing the paperwork for the rider coach course registrations for the upcoming weekend and spending a few minutes with her son. She should have paid more attention to the names on the forms. She barely had enough time to check on Owen and prepare for her shift at La Rosa's.

How long after she left for work had Terry and Lucas come calling at the house? Or had her father called them? And on a Thursday. Caitlyn tried to draw in all her emotions, tucking them away for later. She drew up her frame, standing tall near Daniel. His presence brought an unwelcome comfort.

"I'll drink if I want to drink!" Pops slapped his hand down on the bar.

And that's when the pub went quiet, and Caitlyn froze. Her father's death glare landed on her. *I'm not afraid. I'm not afraid.* Daniel must have felt her slight twitch, for he stepped in front of her.

"You won't get it here," Daniel said.

The man in the suit stepped closer to the bar between them. "No more," he confirmed. "You have reached your limit at this establishment. Please leave."

"You heard the manager, Pops. Let's go. I have to get back to work, and you left Owen alone."

5

Pops' unfocused gaze landed on Sebastian. "What are you looking at?"

An old man who lost his soul to bad choices and an alcohol addiction, but Daniel said, "Nothing." Wise man.

Her father's gaze shifted away from Daniel to meet Caitlyn's. "You know him?"

"No." It wasn't a lie. They weren't friends, and beyond having worked with him on the course for two days, she didn't know him enough to admit it. His brows gathered together. She ignored him, not needing to see the judgment in his gaze.

"Come on, let's get out of here. This place is boring." Pops vacated the bar stool. A stout man at one time, his skin clung to thick bones. He stood several inches shorter than Daniel, but was at the right height to stare directly at Caitlyn. Her father wavered, reaching for his stool to hold the world still as he motioned for his buddies to follow. She waited, keeping her hands at her sides rather than assist him. She stayed frozen as he launched himself toward the door. Waiting for a heartbeat, then two, Terry and Lucas looked at one another. Both of them shrugged and let Pops lead the way, but not without Lucas making a noise in his throat as he passed her.

Those in the bar returned to their drinks and conversation, the noise a dull roar fading into the background. Caitlyn let out a shaky breath. She squeezed her eyes shut, a silent plea escaping her lips. *Please, God, change Antonio's and Isabella's hearts.* Having her siblings here, estranged as they were, felt like a fragile chance. Maybe, just maybe, their hearts could soften toward Pops with God's intervention. The support she craved wasn't just a shared burden of dealing with their father. She yearned for a united front and a listening ear in her battle to keep their father from losing to his demons.

As she headed toward her father, Daniel caught her by the arm. "Hey," he said soft enough for only her to hear. "You need help?"

It sounded like a statement, but she saw the question in his eyes. No one ever cared to inquire. If she wasn't careful, he would break the invisible shield she had built long ago. If the man was wise, he would mind his business and keep far away from her.

"I've got this." She moved to the exit, trying to keep an eye on Pops.

But Daniel held on. "I'll follow you."

"Why?" She glanced between him and her father, afraid he might jump on Lucas or Terry's motorcycle, making her have to hunt him down. Craning her neck, she kept her father in sight.

Daniel searched her face and relaxed his grip. "You're afraid of him."

"He's my father," she said, as if that was enough explanation for him to move on. Strangely, she wanted him to hold on, but she needed him to let go.

Daniel slid his hand inside his pocket. "I have a father, too. He might have tried to scare me a few times into doing what was good for me, but he never made me tremble with fear, and neither should you."

She placed a hand over the spot vacated by his hold,

trying to trap the comfort it gave her, even if it was fast fleeting. "You need to learn to mind your own business."

He lowered his chin, bringing his gaze level with hers. She took a step back, needing to go. Where was Pops? She had lost sight of him. She moved to go out the door. Terry and Lucas blocked her view, but Pops' voice kept her calm. She hadn't lost him.

"What are you doing here, anyway?" she asked Daniel.

Someone called his name, "Daniel," and the bartender slid a bag with takeout carriers along the counter in search of a face. Daniel waved and stepped aside from her. "It's wing night, and I heard the ones they serve here are sweet and spicy." He winked and pulled his wallet from his jeans.

Caitlyn froze, giving Pops a minute to say goodbye to his amigos before she made him leave and kept them from getting into any worse trouble. Counting to ten, she held her breath and approached Pops, feeling Daniel following several steps behind her.

Welder Cortés wasn't a big man, but when he drank, he got meaner than a wet tomcat. Having Daniel involved in one of her father's episodes made her cringe inwardly. She had to work with him on the weekends. What would he think of her? What did it matter?

She hurried to catch Pops before one of them convinced him to get on and ride along with one of them. Lucas had a sidecar on his motorcycle; she wouldn't put it past Pops to join them in his current state.

"You coming?" Terry called to Pops.

"We'll meet you there," she said, not bothering to ask which way they intended to go. Nothing could make her happier than seeing them drive away and leave her father alone for good.

Pops cussed up a storm at her. Stumbling onto the street, he staggered past the parked motorcycles to where Caitlyn's

Escape waited. Hurriedly, she unlocked the door before he busted it, yanking too hard on the door handle.

Once the old man was in the vehicle, she got in on his other side. She spotted Daniel sliding into an old Chevy pickup with a few takeout boxes. Huh, that was Yeats' truck.

"What you looking at, girl?"

Snap out of it. "Buckle up." She had no business watching Daniel and shook off her disappointment at not seeing him with his Honda Rebel. It was a nice ride. Daniel Jones gave off a more subtle vibe than the members of the Ghost Riders. If Daniel belonged to a club, he must have a reason not to wear a cut or make his association known. He might be one of those guys who ride for the joy of it, but Caitlyn didn't think so. He had that bad-boy look, from his short hair to his black boots. And maybe that's where she'd gone wrong. She always fell for the wrong kinds of men.

"You don't tell me what to do," Pops grumped. Hopefully, she caught him in time before he turned angry. How long would he make it this time?

"Your rule, not mine." She waited for Pops to put on his seat belt before turning on the engine. She needed to get back to work and have her mind back on what mattered. Her son. Her father. She'd sworn off men. The Ghosts made it impossible to do otherwise.

From her rearview mirror, she spotted Daniel pulling away from the curb, heading in the same direction as them. His white-knight attitude wasn't welcome in her world. She bit her lip, concentrating on driving. It unnerved her to have Daniel following her. They worked together—nothing more. There was no place in her life for heroes.

Especially ones she knew very little about.

Pops muttered under his breath, and she pressed her lips together to keep from saying anything that would put him in a rage. His eyes drooped the closer they got to home. When the

Escape rattled from a bump in the road, he asked, "Where's the boy?"

"You should know. I left him with you."

Now that they sat inside her vehicle, shut in by the doors and closed windows, the stench of alcohol and body odor filled the interior. All the while she drove, Caitlyn tried to figure out how to keep her father home and her son safe.

Pops' old drinking pals ignored her warnings. They weaved down the road ahead of her. Regina might say nothing about Owen sitting at a back booth and playing his handheld video games until her shift ended, at least until she found an alternative to keep him safe.

No alcohol in the house. No alcohol around Owen. No drinking buddies in the house, but she'd slipped up and invited them there, trying to keep the peace, trying to hold it all together. Tossing her father out of his own home wasn't an option, and she couldn't find another place she could afford with a garage. It took everything she had to keep this place running.

"Was it Lucas?" Caitlyn asked.

"It's none of your business."

"Did they just show up?" Caitlyn focused on the road and the truck in front of her. Pretty soon, Daniel would turn off and head toward his place—away from her, away from seeing the place she lived.

"Where'd they go?" Pops asked.

"Who?"

"Don't play that game with me!" He slammed his fist down on the dash.

So Pops noticed the motorcycles weren't in front of them anymore. They turned off at the next right ahead. She kept quiet. They probably headed to another bar without him. Her father's eyes got a wild look. Soon the desperation would change to anger thanks to the alcohol. Lucas and Terry brought trouble to their door. They provoked her father and encouraged him to go down this path. Look where it got them all.

"I thought Terry moved to Florida?"

"Terry's granddaughter graduated. He came up to celebrate. You're like your mother. You can't be happy unless a man's miserable."

Not in the mood to have her father rub her life in her face, she pressed her lips together and kept one eye on the man in the truck following her.

———

Sebastian pulled into the gravel driveway behind Caitlyn. He slid out of the vehicle and paused halfway, waiting for Caitlyn to exit her SUV first. Her black hair draped over her shoulders, and the scowl on her face was sharp enough to slice a man in half.

"Why are you following me?" Caitlyn waved him off. "Go home. This isn't your business."

Because of the high pitch of her voice, Sebastian slowed his steps toward her as he assessed the situation. Upsetting her wasn't his intention.

Pops got out of the SUV, and Caitlyn moved to assist him, but he jerked his arm away and weaved his way to the porch. She shrank back, keeping her distance.

Sebastian's gut tightened. He resisted closing his eyes and kept his gaze on Caitlyn, a sickening feeling rising in his throat. Every muscle in his body tightened.

"Where'd they go? You tricked me!" Pops curled his fist, and Sebastian instinctively put himself in the middle. The old man would have to go through him first.

"Stay out of this," she said, moving out from around him. Her brow furrowed. Those amber eyes turned to a dark maple. "Owen!"

Caitlyn waved her hand to catch his attention. "What are you looking at?"

"You," he said.

She looked—well, pissed. He didn't get it. What had he done to her? Her eyes, more narrowed than wide, glared at him, but her stance said she'd flee at a moment's notice. Couldn't she see he wanted to help? Wanted—not needed—to protect her.

A kid that couldn't have been older than ten poked his head out the door, eyes wide and wary. Sebastian's stomach lurched. Years on the beat had left him with a hair trigger for anything that smacked of neglect. The sight of the kid alone with a belligerent drunk like Pops sent an icy dread down his spine.

"You need to go," Caitlyn motioned dismissively. "I've got to get back to work."

Sebastian hesitated, his gave flickering between the woman and the child. The straightforward answer was to leave, like she said. But the kid's nervous stare, the echo of countless past cases, held him rooted in place. "You're going to leave him here?" His voice came out rougher than intended, laced with tension.

"I ain't watching him," Pops grunted as he passed.

Owen looked at Caitlyn with a questioning glance. She placed her hand on the boy's shoulder. "Go grab your hand-held game and get in the car."

Owen glanced around at Sebastian. The kid had his mother's eyes and a dark mop of hair on his head. "Who are you?"

"A friend of your mother's."

Owen snorted. "Yeah, right." He headed after the old man.

"Hey!" Caitlyn called. "Manners."

"What did I say?" Owen asked.

"You good taking him to work?" How many times had he been called to a domestic dispute or seen kids like Owen abused? "I'm headed over to Yeats' place. The kid could come hang with us until your shift's done."

"We're good. If I return soon, my shift won't last much longer. But I need to get back."

Sebastian pushed his hands into his pockets. Owen and the old man disappeared into the house.

"You leave him here alone often?"

Caitlyn moved off the porch toward her vehicle. "He's been fine with Pops."

He wanted to believe her. Sebastian saw the gloss in the old man's eyes, his stagger as he lifted one foot and then the other to climb the stairs on the porch. In his experience, there were two types of drunks: the mean and the depressed. By the snark in his comments to Caitlyn, Sebastian doubted it was the latter. For both their sakes, he wanted to be wrong.

"If you're sure." He cupped the back of his neck. *It's not your place. Don't get involved.*

Audra's face, her arms battered and bruised, caused a wave of nausea. *"Help me,"* her voice pleaded. *Big tears rolled down her eyes. She cradled her stomach, and the staunch of blood nearly made him vomit. "Pike's been here." Not a question. Tiger sent him to this address. He knew what Pike was looking for. "Find her," Tiger said.*

Sebastian squeezed the back of his neck, the pressure grounding him to the present. It wasn't until after he watched them bury Audra and saw Pike dead that Tiger's intentions registered.

"I'm sure," Caitlyn said.

To the right of the house, an oversized two-car garage rose from cement blocks. Several old cars, a truck without a bed, and a few motorcycles littered the yard. The old house porch leaned toward the rusted lawn ornaments.

The grass in the yard stood a foot high. Maybe she expected the kid to mow it. As his father would say, they could bale hay from the height of the grass in the front yard alone.

He glanced around, expecting to see Caitlyn's silver

motorcycle. She must keep it locked in the garage, away from thieves and prying eyes.

Sebastian let his hand slip away from his neck.

Her brow arched, and her lips pressed out. They'd be sweeter than tea, he imagined. And that nearly had him sweating with panic. Fighting for the fist of control he kept over his emotions, Sebastian focused on the boy.

Caitlyn called out to Owen, returning outside and telling him, "*Vamanos.*"

There was no arguing with that. "You'll be okay?"

"You don't need to worry about me. I've been taking care of my father for a long time." The fire in those amber eyes dimmed. Her shoulders sagged a little as she said, "He's not as scary as he looks, okay?"

"Sure," Sebastian said, not wanting to set her off again.

"Did something happen to your Rebel?" she asked, her gaze flicking pointedly between him and the landscaping truck. "That's Yeats' landscaping truck."

"I'm working there during the week."

Her lips twitched upward in what could have been a smile, but the tension in her shoulders and how she kept glancing at the house told a different story.

He didn't want to pry. It wasn't his place to get involved. Yet, the struggle in her eyes settled a new understanding in his gut. "I won't keep you." He offered gently. "I know you can handle this, but I wanted to offer you backup if needed."

"This isn't the range, and I don't need you to do anything for me outside of work." Caitlyn glanced at the house. Owen skipped down off the porch. "You need to go. I'll see you on the course in a few days."

"Sure." He held onto his truck keys, unable to convince his hips to swivel and to turn to leave. She reached up, pulled her hair into a messy bun, and held it with a thin black band from her pocket.

She walked up to the porch and peered inside momentarily before wrapping her arm around Owen's shoulders and leading him to her vehicle.

"Not your problem," he muttered to himself. *Not going to get involved with another woman and her problems.*

Yet, he just did.

6

"Have you thought about what you want to do?" Yeats asked Sebastian. "Maybe it's time you think about joining another club, since you plan on being here for a while. You're not going to stop keeping an eye on your family anytime soon, right?"

He had family back in Johnstown—the members of the Thunder Valley Riders were his brothers and sisters, even if it wasn't by blood. After all these years, moving to another club didn't feel right. Technically, Sebastian never withdrew his membership from Thunder Valley. Transferring to another Christian Motorcycle Club seemed like a betrayal. He was done with getting involved in motorcycle clubs and their business.

He took the rider coach gig for Yeats, swallowing his pride. The pay wouldn't equate to what he made as a cop, but a nest egg was a distant dream. He hadn't exactly been clocking in forty-hour weeks back on the force, not with the Sharks surrounding him day and night. Working around another motorcycle club was a bitter pill, but quitting wasn't an option.

"Is that why you insisted I help you with the range and offered me a place to stay?"

Yeats snorted, but Sebastian was unconvinced. He owed him a favor. He took the motorcycle safety coach position to fulfill it. "We had a deal to keep my location on the down low, especially from my parents and Sam, if I agreed to take the rider coach job."

Once his family figured out where he was, his father would pull him into the family business, drawing in the wrong kind of attention and threatening their safety.

"We still need to complete the paperwork for you to become a partner in the landscaping business."

"I told you I don't need a partnership agreement to work for your family. No more extra paperwork to complicate things."

"Because you're trying to hide behind an alias."

"I'm not hiding. I can't risk anyone associating me with your business or my family."

"Our business. No one is going to mess with you here. Didn't you say the Sharks are back in Johnstown and the club is no longer running?"

"It doesn't matter. Some of the members won't stay in jail forever, and I'll always be looking behind me." Sebastian rolled his shoulders back. "If I go home, I could bring danger to their doorstep."

His aching shoulder throbbed. The gunshot echoed from memory in his ears. He closed his eyes briefly against the phantom twitch of his body as he relived it. The nightmares still came regularly. Audra's trust-filled eyes would haunt him for the rest of his life. He never told his parents what happened, and he almost let the feds rope him into changing his identity, despite his old police chief assuring him it wouldn't be forever.

Sebastian couldn't allow his parents and twin to think him dead. Nor did Sebastian have any right to come back to Adams County and invade his twin sister's life. He couldn't protect her back then, just like he couldn't protect Audra from

Pike. What would happen to his twin when his past caught up to him? To his family?

And it would.

The best thing for him to do was to keep his distance. He couldn't risk anyone else getting hurt. "I'll take you up on the offer of the place to stay, but I'm not getting involved with another club."

"Fair enough." Yeats shrugged off his leather jacket. "Sooner or later, you should let your family know you're alive. How long has it been since you spoke to them?"

"I send emails." He never gave them his phone number after he went undercover. Even the cell in his pocket was his third burner phone this month.

"My parents left for a cruise to Alaska last week. My mom will post pictures online when they get back." The last time he got a phone call or text from his parents was when his last case went down the toilet, and he switched to using burner phones. He hadn't told his parents about getting shot or having to leave Johnstown. His mother would still worry, even if he was thirty-two.

Yeats scratched his chin. "Sam will be upset if you don't tell her you're near."

"You've been watching out for her?" Why should this surprise him?

Yeats grinned. "She's dating some teacher that moved here last year. He goes to church with her on Sundays, and I hear he helps her out at the stables when your parents are gone."

Sebastian went to the old teal-colored fridge and pulled out a bottle of water. There wasn't much else inside besides a few takeout cartons of Chinese food and a half gallon of milk.

His sister deserved happiness after what happened to her in high school. Seeing her wrapped in a man's arms caused a mix of emotions, but it was relief that hit him the most. At first, it shocked him that his parents would take a cruise and leave Sammy to run the horseback tours during the busy season. After witnessing her with this teacher guy she was dating, he understood his parents must have approved. The fact Sammy trusted this guy enough to allow their parents to leave her alone with him spoke volumes.

"You didn't have to do that," Sebastian said.

"I know people," Yeats said. "That's what friends are for."

Sebastian eased down into a chair at the kitchen table. His legs and his lower back ached. He knew Yeats from high school, and even back then, Sebastian knew his friend had an eye for his sister. Sebastian warned, not threatened, Yeats to steer clear of his twin, but it had been Yeats who found her violated the night of their senior prom. And it had been Yeats who talked him down from killing the jock who hurt his sister.

Sebastian guzzled down the water, trying to flush the memories away. Razek, his former chief of police in Johnstown, still held his badge and offered to help him relocate to another police force. He refused to run, but he refused to be a sitting duck. He knew someone from the Sharks put a hit on Tiger, the other undercover cop working the case, and took him out. What would stop them from ordering one on Sebastian?

He touched his shoulder—the ache was mental more than physical.

"Your shoulder still bothering you?" Yeats spun a chair around, took a seat, and leaned against the back of it with his arms propped on top. "Maybe I shouldn't have talked Davis into switching sites and given you more time to heal."

"It's not the shoulder." Sebastian had a hole inside him, so big, gaping, and painful that he doubted it would ever heal. He stuffed it with regrets for the past year. Crawling into that hole and hiding away, just like he said he wouldn't. He lied. Nothing would ever fill the huge, hollow emptiness inside him. He wasn't a cop anymore, nor did he deserve to get involved in other people's lives. He could endanger them all.

This is why Chief Razek urged him to accept the alias

they had given him. Daniel Jones didn't fit him, but Razek assured him it wasn't forever. That stubborn streak his mother claimed he got from her would get him killed. He needed to go far away and stay there. Instead, after almost a half-year of roaming and sulking, he called Yeats, his old buddy from high school, and hauled his butt farther away from the Sharks and the haunting memories of the woman he couldn't save.

Why? Every night, he asked that question. Why did Audra have to die? His mind reminded him that every time he closed his eyes to replay the nightmare and analyze everything he should have done differently. Where was God when he needed Him?

His mother taught him to believe in God. To trust in God's purpose and plan for his life. Yeats wanted him to transfer to another Christian motorcycle club, but how could he? Leaving the Thunder Valley MC stabbed at him like a betrayal.

"Listen, man. I figured this was a good fit for you, but if the job is too much, then say the word. I'll find someone else."

"It's not the job." Sebastian twisted his empty water bottle. Spilling his guts to Yeats would get his old friend in trouble. Haden, his friend and club brother back in Johnstown, knew too much, and Sebastian hated cutting ties with him.

He couldn't get close to people. Not anymore, or they would get hurt. He fisted his hand around the crushed plastic. No one else was going to watch over them. The responsibility was his alone. Because of Sebastian's part in the takedown of the Sharks, his family was in danger.

"Is it Caitlyn?"

Sebastian dropped the crumpled bottle on the table. "Cortés?"

Yeats grinned. "I should have known she would call to verify you."

Sebastian's chest tightened. "She calls you 'Thomas,' you know that?"

"Yep." Yeats' grin broadened.

"What did you tell her?" He tried not to eavesdrop during her call.

"The truth." Yeats lifted a shoulder. "I told her Davis took another job and moved too far to return on weekends."

"That's it?" Sebastian asked.

"Don't fall for the good looks. Caitlyn's pretty, but she's not worth taking a bullet to the head. You got by with a shoulder wound, but her old man, Silas, will go for the kill."

"She's married?" Sebastian got up and started pacing. What was he doing, asking about her, anyway? She wasn't his business. The fact she had an old man should have come as a relief. The Ghost had made it known she was one of them, and he didn't need to get involved—not again.

"Divorced, but the Ghosts don't believe in divorce. They're not the worst club in the county, but Welder holds his beliefs as law."

"Welder?"

"Cat's father. He's the former president of the Ghosts."

"Former?"

"You're not the only one who had stuff go down," Yeats said.

"And you paired me to work with her?" Sebastian's jaw clenched. Working with someone who could get him targeted by another outlaw motorcycle club? Brilliant. Friend or no friend, Sebastian couldn't tell Yeats the whole truth. He left the force, and Yeats knew something from his last case made him leave. He wouldn't talk about it, and Yeats didn't ask. It was better this way for both of them.

"Just stick to your plan, man. Hang for the summer. You got nothing to worry about."

No women. No clubs. No getting involved with the law.

And stay away from family.

If he could do that, Sebastian might have a chance to keep his family safe.

"I'm heading to Hanover to grab the mulch for the Lehman job. Would you like to come along?" Yeats shoved his foot into a boot. "It's that, or you sit around here all day waiting for trouble to come. Otherwise, I would feel responsible."

Sebastian snorted. "I don't need you to babysit me."

"I don't need to come home and find you dead, either." Yeats sat back and looked up at him. Yeats tilted up his chin, almost as a challenge.

"That, or you don't want me here. I can leave. I never expected you to put me up at your place. I don't want to put you in danger." Sebastian ran his hands down over his face to wipe away reminiscences of a sleepless night, staring at the ceiling, unable to get Caitlyn, her father, or her boy from his mind. They kept the nightmares at bay, filling his mind with something else to distract it.

In his experiences, he learned that run-down houses, over-grown lawns, and dirty garage windows either indicated no one cared or they were too busy trying to keep their heads above water. He got the impression that Caitlyn was a woman too proud to ask for help or admit she couldn't do it all on her own. Why hadn't anyone in her club come to help with the upkeep of her home?

"Do I look scared?" Yeats stood and rolled back his shoulders. While they matched in height, Yeats held a good fifty pounds on Sebastian, all of which came from the width of his shoulders and the thickness of his frame. Sebastian could run down a perp in the alley, but Yeats was the blockade no one could pass. All those years in the Army trained him well.

"You're stupid," Sebastian muttered. A man built like a tank should have some fear in his bones. Everyone knew Yeats —the guy who'd give you the shirt off his back. Since coming home from the army, he'd dedicated himself to the commu-nity center. Hurting him wouldn't just be wrong, it'd be a terrible gamble. If someone came after Sebastian, they'd use

Yeats as leverage. Sure, Yeats could handle himself, but that wouldn't protect Sebastian from the fallout.

Yeats grinned, and they were back to the immature bickering. "You've got no idea what you've gotten yourself into by agreeing to stay here."

Maybe he understood exactly what he was getting himself into. Maybe that was why he'd spent a sleepless night thinking about it. "I am here, am I not?"

"The silent partner returns." Yeats held out his fist. "I had faith in you, man. I knew you'd come back."

"For a time." Sebastian bumped his fist with Yeats and grinned back. "What's the plan, then?" The sooner he got immersed in his new life, the sooner he could gain control over this one.

"I'll drop you off at the shed. You can take the company truck and load up the mower and weed eater for the day. The range needs to be cleaned up, and while you're there, take care of the church lawn. I'll be over later with some mulch to fix the side beds."

Sebastian laughed, following Yeats outside the house. "You want me to get all that done in one day?"

Yeats hefted a duffle bag with tools over his shoulder. "What's the matter? You don't know how to get your hands dirty anymore? Or is it sweat? Because if you can't handle it, I can leave you at the store with Ma to answer the phone."

Sebastian shook his head but kept smiling. "Alright, alright." He stretched. His mind would take him to other places if he didn't keep moving. Going without sleep wasn't foreign to him. Maybe he needed to keep his backpedaling thoughts at bay by breaking a sweat and doing some work.

"Then that makes you the dumb one." Yeats chuckled, and something lifted between the two of them, and the tension in Sebastian's shoulders cleared.

Yeats tossed him the keys to the company truck. "Grab the mower and weed eater at the shed. You can use the big mower if you hook up the trailer, and remember to take a gas can to fill for later."

Sebastian pocketed the keys and opened Yeats' truck's passenger side door. "Anything else?"

Yeats paused as if considering something, then shook his head as if deciding against it before finally settling on a single command: "Don't get killed."

"That's what I'm working on," Sebastian muttered.

Yeats climbed in and started dialing numbers on his phone.

With a sigh, Sebastian leaned back in the seat and closed his eyes against another random thought that involved Caitlyn.

A dumb thought. One he shouldn't entertain. Yeats warned him not to get killed. Would Caitlyn harm him for what he had in mind?

"When are you going to hire some extra help?"

"I did. I've got you. Both on the range and now back in business."

Oh yeah, Sebastian was the dumb one.

When they were teens, Yeats and Sebastian started mowing lawns for extra cash. Yeats bought his first truck, and Sebastian bought his first motorcycle—an Indian Scout. The motorcycle was now charred to a crisp, thanks to his last assignment. He spent summers working to buy it and spent time with his uncle getting parts and repairing it. It was ironic that he would end up back where he started.

Yeats dropped Sebastian off at the company shed a few miles down the road. No one would have thought a big, gruff guy like Yeats would hang flower baskets on the end of a pillared shed of his landscaping business.

For the entire morning, Sebastian mowed the churchyard, weeded along the hedges, and made sure the range looked good for the next weekend's class. At lunch, he entered La Rosa's for a quick sub. He scanned the menu board, stomach grumbling as he spotted Caitlyn wiping down tables. She moved with confident grace from one table to the next. He hadn't pictured her waiting tables outside of the motorcycle range.

A smile tugged at his lips, igniting a flicker of warmth in his chest. She looked good in those jeans. He watched her a moment longer than he should, mesmerized by the way her ponytail swished with each passing moment.

A sharp cough drew his attention. The woman behind the counter stood with raised eyebrows. "Ready to order?"

"Uh, yeah, Italian sub on rye."

As he waited for his order, Sebastian stole a glance back. Caitlyn was laughing with a customer. A familiar warmth bloomed in his chest, pursued by a pang of panic.

"That'll be eight-fifty," the woman at the counter announced. Sebastian paid quickly, mumbled, "Thank you," and grabbed his food, practically bolted out the door. He took a deep breath, a strange mix of disappointment and relief washing over him. Maybe he'd find a way to say hello without making it weird next time.

He texted Yeats to let him know he would return later after a last-minute task he needed to do. Twenty minutes later, Sebastian pulled in front of the rundown two-story house with tall grass and a grimy window garage. To the side, a set of stairs led up to a door, and below it sat a couple of motorcycles and an old Ford Fiesta.

Sebastian unloaded the mower and the screen door swung closed on the house. Caitlyn's son walked out on the porch. He crossed his arms and tilted up his chin. "Who are you? What do you want?"

"I work with your mom. Remember? I followed her home the other day."

"Stalker?" Owen asked.

"Friend."

"My mom's not here. Go away."

"You shouldn't tell people that." Sebastian stepped off the mower and kept his hands where the kid could see them. He didn't want the boy to think him more of a threat than the kid already assumed. What kind of trouble came knocking here?

"Pops is here. He doesn't like strangers. Neither do I."

"Good thing I'm not a stranger. You ever drive a mower like this?"

Owen tilted his head, narrowed his eyes, and shook his head.

"Well, I'm going to mow the grass. You want to help and get it done before your mom comes home?"

Owen looked over his shoulder, then back at Sebastian. "Who sent you?"

"Your mom puts in a lot of hours. She's been a great help at the range where we coach motorcycle safety. I know it's difficult taking on a new partner. This is my way of saying thank you." Sebastian swept his hand out to the yard.

No word in return came from Caitlyn's son. The boy appeared to be deep in thought. Sebastian left him to decide to while he got to work. Caitlyn taught her son well for not trusting strangers. He put on the safety goggles and started up the mower.

"I can help!"

Sebastian raised an eyebrow, surprised by the small voice offering assistance. This wasn't something he'd expected from the skinny kid perched on the porch railing. Few kids these days were willing to lend a hand. A smile tugged at his lips.

"You sure about that, bud?" Seeing the determined nod, Sebastian continued, "Well, then you start by gathering up some bigger branches and twigs, so I don't have to mow around them. That would be a big help."

Owen nodded again and set off to do his task. He went around the lawn, picking up the fallen branches and carrying them to a pile away from the mower. He worked diligently and purposefully.

At one point, Caitlyn's father came out on the porch, looked around, spotted the boy, and returned inside.

Once Owen finished his task, he returned to Sebastian and asked, "What else can I do?"

Sebastian handed him a smaller tool. "You can edge the lawn for me," he said. "It'll help the mower get a clean cut."

Owen watched while Sebastian demonstrated how to use the edger. He accepted the tool and went to work. Owen edged the lawn carefully, keeping it even and straight.

Sebastian mowed in long, steady strokes, the noise from the machine filling the air as the boy watched in fascination. When he was done, he surveyed his work with a satisfied smile, proud of the job he and Caitlyn's son had done.

The sound of a car engine startled Sebastian, momentarily breaking his focus on the task at hand. He realized with a jolt that he'd lost track of time. It was only now, as the sun was setting, that he realized just how late it had gotten.

He turned to the boy, panic in the kid's eyes. "Your mom's home," he said. "Help me load up and get out of here."

"What's your name?" the kid said.

"Daniel." Sebastian held his hand out to the boy.

They shook hands, and Sebastian said, "Quick, you can take all the credit."

Owen's eyes widened as the slam of Caitlyn's SUV door echoed from the other side of the driveway.

7

"He mowed my grass, Thomas." He then took off before she could confront him. Owen scampered into the house, back to his video games. When she tried to question him, her son pretended not to know what she was talking about. Traitor.

Caitlyn waved the cash in front of Thomas.

"Keep your money, Cat."

Caitlyn replayed what he said in her head, dissected each word, and searched for a hidden meaning. Her hands clenched and unclenched at her sides, she said, "Since when do you mow lawns for free?"

"You should know better than to ask," he said.

"I'm not one of your community service projects. You don't need to send your guys out to care for my lawn."

"I know that," Yeats said.

A bittersweet sigh escaped Caitlyn's lips as she lowered her arm. His gesture warmed a place deep in her chest, a flicker of hope battling with the fear of appearing too vulnerable. She forced a smile and held out the cash again. "Then take the cash."

Thomas shook his head. "I'm not the one who mowed your lawn."

"But he works for you. It was your truck pulling out of my driveway," she said.

Thomas shrugged casually. "Technically, we're partners."

"And he works for you on the range."

"Yep, and he wanted to do something nice for you. I didn't know he did until he finished and returned the equipment to the store."

Caitlyn nodded slowly, unsure how to respond to that information. Thomas continued before she could say anything else. "Keep your cash, Cat. Accept it for what it was: a friendly gesture." He grinned. The smugness in his expression annoyed her.

Caitlyn looked away, tears prickling in her eyes. She wasn't one of his charity cases. She wasn't. Had he felt obligated as her friend? Or her co-worker? In either case, she was thankful. One more thing off her ever-piling list. She asked Pops to handle it, but since he could no longer order one of the Ghost Riders to do his bidding, nothing got done unless Caitlyn did it herself.

Whatever Daniel said to her son motivated him to help mow the lawn. It must have been a bribe to get Owen away from his video games. Caitlyn felt guilty for suspecting they had orchestrated the whole thing together. "What's his story, anyway?" Caitlyn pressed. "Please tell me he's not one of your charity cases, and you put him on the range with me."

"Stop." Thomas held up his hands in surrender, as if sensing her conflicting thoughts. "I know him. He's one of the good guys."

Caitlyn's brow furrowed slightly, but a flicker of curiosity replaced her suspicion. "He's one of your ranger buddies, isn't he?"

Thomas shrugged casually. "Sometimes, a change of pace is good for everyone. You could say Daniels has… seen things from another perspective." He paused, a cryptic smile playing on his lips.

She stared at Thomas, her mind spinning with questions. Since when was Thomas Yeats vague with her? Was it just a coincidence that Daniel showed up on her property out of the blue, or was there more to the story? She took a deep breath and looked into his eyes to get some answers. "Did my brother put you up to this?"

Thomas shook his head in confusion. "I don't understand."

"Seriously?" Caitlyn crumpled the money in her hand and let out a frustrated sigh. "Antonio swore us off, but I wouldn't put it past my brother to have arranged with you for someone to keep an eye on me. You understand how the Ghost Riders work. I know he sends guys to take the course and spy on me. Was it my brother's idea or yours to replace Davis? I know it wasn't my father's."

Thomas raised his hands defensively as if trying to allay Caitlyn's fears about what he had done behind the scenes. "No one put me up to anything," he said earnestly. "I wouldn't do anything like that without your consent."

Caitlyn studied Thomas, searching for any hint that he was being less than honest. But all she found was sincerity in his expression and a willingness to tell her the truth. She had been right not to allow her fear to take over. Whatever Daniel's motivations were, they had nothing to do with Thomas.

Relieved, Caitlyn relaxed and nodded understandingly at Thomas' words. "I appreciate you telling me the truth."

"It's okay to let people help you. Sometimes helping others is a blessing to the one giving the help," Thomas said as he stood up from his chair. "And you can be the one to tell him not to mow your grass anymore. I'm sure it won't go over well with your son."

Caitlyn laughed at Thomas' suggestion before catching herself and nodding in agreement. "You're right," she said, suddenly grateful that Daniel showed up for them in such an unexpected way. "No more mowing my lawn for free."

Thomas smiled at her response before getting to his feet and exiting. He paused before leaving, however, turning back to Caitlyn with a thoughtful expression. "I know it seems like you don't need protection," he began slowly, "but I think it would be wise to keep Daniel close by...for both your sakes."

Caitlyn's mind raced as she mulled over Thomas' words. Had he meant her and Owen? Or by helping her, did it help Daniel? Daniel Jones didn't come across as a man who would demand a favor for a favor. Not like Silas, her ex.

With the Ghosts monitoring her, the news would travel back to Antonio and maybe even Silas. Her brother walked away from their family and held their father accountable for more. All the while, her father allowed Silas to corrupt the dealings of the club. It tainted their meetings and the minds of their members. Yet, Antonio looked out for her and Owen. At Christmas, Owen received a new Xbox with games delivered to their front porch.

She suspected Yeats had reported to Antonio, which made her assume Yeats had sent Daniel to mow her grass. Why else would a man like Daniel show up and clean up her yard?

She glanced at Thomas and saw him observing her. His eyes filled with understanding and compassion. In all the years she had known Yeats, the way he seemed to read people still spooked her.

"I'm not a charity case."

"No," Thomas agreed.

———

Chris sat outside Beast's last known address for hours, and there was still no sign of the mysterious cop. He watched the passersby warily, sweeping the street for any sign of Beast. Eventually, the man responsible for his brother's and his girlfriend's death would come home. He figured Beast would show, thanks to a tip from one of the Thunder Valley Rider's old ladies. What kind of man skipped out on their brother's wedding? Unlike the Sharks, these people did not ascribe any meaning to blood. Blood was thicker than water. Blood tied you to family debts and inheritance. He should have stepped into Pike's role as president. Too bad Beast was responsible for Audra's death. He might have made him VP. They'd been friends. Chums. Chris got his road name, Chum, from Pike, and the hurt and the pain sunk in deeper than a hook. Friendship. No. Foolishness. Not anymore.

After he proved he could tie up loose ends, no one would push him aside or underestimate him anymore.

His gaze darted across the street, searching for signs of activity. The leather of his Thunder Valley Christian Motor-cycle Club jacket weighed heavy on his shoulders, with its large back patch a beacon in the twilight. He wasn't a stranger in this part of town. One wrong move, one person recognizing him, and all his carefully laid out plans could come crashing down.

He still couldn't believe his luck. The Thunder Valley MC welcomed him into the club without first making him a prospect, and he was still trying to gain some stance amongst them. The members of this motorcycle club took their church literally. He never met men who prayed or women who spoke their opinions. The wives sat alongside their husbands. No one treated their old ladies like property.

But they couldn't fool him with their talks of brotherly love and helping others, and he almost choked at the thought of every time they prayed over a decision. What would Pike or their father think? The members of the Thunder Valley Riders talked about family. After what Beast had done to his family, Chris would make them pay, starting with Sebastian Daniels.

But first, he had to find him—which proved more difficult

than he had hoped. Sebastian might have changed his road name so "Beast" could vanish without a trace. Despite Sebastian's efforts, Chris would track him down. Hanging out with Beast's biker brothers and joining the club helped Chris get close to the ones Beast loved. Eventually, one of them would tell him where Beast went. They slipped and gave him the information about the upcoming wedding. Someone knew where to find him. But Chris was still trying to process their hospitality. He vowed never to forget why he was there. Audra. Her death sent him into a deep freeze, but now, in the thaw of her passing, he needed justice.

If Beast hadn't killed his brother, Audra wouldn't be dead, and Chum's nephew would be his son, not Pike's. He couldn't let Beast get away with his crimes. Even cops needed to know they were not above the law. And Chris was the new enforcer. He settled into his seat.

It was a warm night, and Chris felt sweat bead on his forehead as he waited. His heart was pounding, and he was on edge.

Suddenly, a figure came around the corner. He tensed, and his heart raced as a vehicle came down the street. He watched as it parked outside the house. A man and a woman got out and disappeared inside.

He pounded his fist on the steering wheel and shouted an expletive.

He stared at the house. Already, he spent too much time with the goodie-goodie club. The longer it took to find a missing person, the slimmer the chances of success. He might have failed to live up to his brother's expectations or help Audra escape Pike alive, but this time, he wouldn't fail. Couldn't fail. He made a deal with another MC moving into the Shark's old territory, and if he didn't keep his end of the bargain, not getting patched was the least of his worries.

Chris stepped out of the car, phone in hand. He checked his watch for the time. Lights came on inside the house. He didn't care that it was after ten o'clock. He marched up to the door and rang the bell. Biting the inside of his cheek, he listened for footsteps. About to knock a second time, the door opened. A man close to his age glared at Chris.

"Hey, man, I'm sorry to disturb you so late. I'm looking for Beast."

The man shook his head, like he was trying to comprehend Chris' words. He frowned and blinked a moment before responding. "Listen, whatever you're on, take it somewhere else. There are no beasts here." He moved to close the door. Chris persisted. "I must have the wrong address." He rattled off the address, knowing all too well this was the right one.

"Right address, wrong place. Now, I would appreciate it if you leave, or I'll call the police."

"Funny thing," Chris tried to smile. "My buddy Beast, who lives here, is a cop. He said if I ever needed anything, to come find him. Do you know where he is?"

The man wiped a hand down his face. "I don't know anyone by that name. We bought the place several months ago. Now, if you don't mind, it's late, and I need to set the security alarm. You have a minute to get off my porch."

"Yeah, sure." Chris backed away. He glanced down at his concert t-shirt, the chain from his belt to his pocket with his wallet, and his worn boots. The vest with the patch might have misled the guy. He thought anyone seeing a cross on the club patch wouldn't see him as a threat.

The man yawned, and Chris stepped off the porch. He hoped it wouldn't come to this, but a man needed to use all his resources, and he had plenty. Chris started dialing his phone as he returned to his car. Bringing his motorcycle to stake the place out wouldn't have been comfortable and too suspicious.

"Hello? Who is this?"

"It's Chum," Chris said. "Remember me?"

"Yeah. What do you want?"

"Information."

8

With the sweltering heat reflecting off the blacktop, Sebastian wondered who would melt first, him or Caitlyn's kid. She brought the boy with her this morning. Poor little dude looked blurry-eyed while curled against the motorcycle shed with his backpack as a pillow. He slept a little, then worked with a scowl on his face. Sebastian couldn't blame the kid. He'd rather have slept in on a Saturday, too, but this was his regular gig now. He let Yeats teach in the classroom on Friday nights, and Sebastian worked the course with Caitlyn on Saturdays and Sundays.

He watched as Caitlyn strolled around the blacktop in her way-too-snug jeans and those laced-up black boots. She'd braided her hair, letting it swing over her shoulder as she marked off on her clipboard for another participant to complete this part of the course.

She glanced at Owen for what must have been the hundredth time. It didn't escape Sebastian's attention how the mother kept her son in her line of vision. It made him edgy, like something was about to go down. But what?

Sebastian slid off his leather jacket when the sun burned away the morning chill in the air. He wore long sleeves to protect his arms and applied a good ration of sunblock to his nose. Hats were never his thing.

They had a small class—seven riders—and none of them seemed to harass Caitlyn or give either of them a hard time. No one dropped motorcycles or incurred any injuries. Sebastian cupped the back of his hot neck. He didn't miss the tense standoffs and suspicious glances exchanged between club members. Here, laughter filled the air as a student fumbled to right a tipped motorcycle. Sebastian chuckled, a genuine sound he hadn't experienced in a long time. He reached for a bottle of sunscreen, the afternoon sun already warming against his skin. A stark contrast to the bulletproof vests and stifling anonymity of his previous life.

Shaking his head, he walked over to Owen, the kid's hand-held video game console still going strong. Did those things still run on batteries, or did they need to be plugged in to charge?

A sweat drip ran down the boy's face, his lip caught between his teeth in concentration. Sebastian reckoned they'd move to the other side of the shed in another hour. He reached for his water and caught Owen looking at him from the corner of his eye.

"Alright, everyone, that's it for this morning's class. You can park the motorcycle over by the shed. Great job!"

Maybe in another week or two, she might feel comfortable letting him take the lead on more of the sessions, but sometimes, a woman liked to feel they were in control. Caitlyn gave him that vibe.

She thanked him for mowing her grass but warned him not to do it again in the next breath. Behind those dark, sunglass-covered eyes was a soul haunted by a traumatic past. She could act like she didn't need him. He shouldn't care or want to help her. The last thing he wanted was another female thinking they could rely on him. So why did it matter so much to him if Caitlyn brushed off his attempts to get to know her?

The buzz of the phone in his back pocket sent a jolt through Sebastian. It'd happened three times this morning. Only a handful of those he trusted had access to this number. A wave of nausea washed over him. He went through a new phone every few weeks, paranoid and determined not to do anything foolish. The Sharks, a once-powerful club, broke apart because of his actions. But loyalty ran deep in that world, and vengeance was deeper still. Every unknown number, every unexpected knock on the door, was a potential storm cloud on the horizon.

The phone in Sebastian's pocket buzzed a fourth time that morning, the insistent vibration a counterpoint to the rumble of motorcycles in the distance. He curled his hand around the phone, shoving it deeper into his pocket. Fear coiled in his gut like a cold serpent, but this wasn't the place nor the time.

Across the training yard, Caitlyn stood with her clipboard, her sharp gaze fixed on a rider parked awkwardly in the center. A knot of sympathy tightened for the guy. Sebastian recognized the crestfallen poster, the hangdog expression. He'd worn that same look plenty of times himself, back when mistakes meant more than just a gentle redirection.

Caitlyn pointed toward the designated parking area near the shed, her voice clipped but not unkind. The rider flinched, a flicker of embarrassment flitting across his face before he mumbled an apology and maneuvered his motorcycle.

Sebastian walked around to the other side of the shed. The phone in his pocket stopped buzzing.

Owen looked up at him. His scowl relaxed and soon turned into a deep frown. Several granola bar wrappers littered the pavement. Across the street, the light blinked on for the ice cream stand.

Sebastian forced a smile, hoping to project optimism toward the boy. "Hey, kid, why don't you get some ice cream?"

Owen's dark eyes softened as a wicked grin spread across his lips. The kid would have all the girls' hearts in a trap in a few years. What he did with them worried Sebastian. Caitlyn insisted Sebastian do all the demonstrations for the class. He couldn't let go of the unease crawling between his shoulder blades. She must not have wanted to leave the boy with her father. He'd dealt with his share of drunks in the past. It was clear Caitlyn was a good mother. She tried to raise the boy with good manners and respect. Sometimes he wondered if his own mother had been strict enough, but in the end, he couldn't change the past. Laura Daniels wasn't below giving him a good kick where it counted to get him to stop making excuses.

Owen stood up. Sebastian pulled out his wallet and handed the kid some cash. "There and back. Don't get me in trouble with your mother."

Owen's eyes widened, big and brown. They lit up, taking the cash.

"There and back," Sebastian repeated.

"Yes, sir." Owen saluted him before taking off across the parking lot.

Caitlyn came out from around the shed.

"Where is Owen?"

Sebastian nodded toward the little ice cream shop across the street. "I gave him a few bucks. He deserved it after sitting in this heat all morning."

Caitlyn bristled. She slapped her hip. "You might be part-ners with me today to teach these classes, but you have no say over my son." She pulled out cash, and Sebastian held up his hands.

He should have seen this coming. "It's my treat."

Panic fluttered in her eyes. Her chest rose with quick breaths. He spoke to keep her distracted, hoping it would calm her. "Besides, I owe him. Little dude cleaned up those flower beds over by the church last week." Owen came back into view. Sebastian pointed. "See. He's there."

The scolding look she gave him could have burned rubber

on the hot pavement. Owen licked a cone, dripping chocolate ice cream. In the boy's other hand was a cup with another scoop inside, which he held out to Caitlyn. Scowling at him, she planted her other hand on her hip. She went into "mad mother mode." Sebastian shrugged, giving the kid a sheepish look. He couldn't seem to do right around this woman. She spoke to him in Spanish, rattling off so fast that he couldn't pick up the words, even if he could recognize a few of them.

Caitlyn took the cup of ice cream, still glaring at the boy. He walked past his mother, looked at Sebastian with a sly grin on his face, and said, "You didn't want any, did you?"

Sebastian shook his head, ruffling the kid's hair as Owen headed back to his spot under the tree. Over the past couple of weeks, Owen'd slowly warmed up to Sebastian. The boy did minor jobs for him while they were on site. He tried to encourage the boy to help his mother more. Ice cream and slipping him a few bucks worked as a good motivator.

Sebastian grabbed his water bottle and went to his bike to grab the protein bar he packed. Seeing a shadow stretched out beyond him, he tensed. His blood pumped. His hand dropped from the protein bar, reaching for under his jacket to his back.

"Don't do that again," she said.

All at once, the tension let loose. He wiped his sweaty palm down the back of his leg. Glancing over his shoulder, he watched her take a bite of soft-serve ice cream.

"I won't without asking. I'm sorry. I should have figured it would scare you not to know where he was." Only he expected it. Thinking that hunch itching at him all morning was never wrong.

Her eyes widened slightly. She dragged the spoon from between her lips. His attention drifted to the action.

"Why would you think I was scared?"

He shed his jacket, feeling too hot under the sun. His t-shirt stuck to the center of his back. Relief came in a small chill against his sweat-slick skin. Pivoting, he tossed the jacket over his motorcycle. The protein bar was on the ground by the motorcycle's rear wheel.

Patiently, he grabbed it while he thought about how to respond. She was like a crouched tiger about to pounce.

"My mother liked to always know where her kids were. I figured it was a mom thing."

Partial truth.

The unease didn't lessen in her stance. She played with her ice cream. "You should eat that before it melts." He opened his water bottle, guzzling a good portion down. The cool liquid refreshed his insides but curled and froze in his gut as a little nagging suspicion tugged at him.

The law enforcer part of him kicked in, wanting to protect her, protect Owen. Sebastian doused some water over his head, hoping to come to his senses. The heat, not this woman and her son, had gotten to him.

"I'm not sharing."

"I'm not a vanilla kind of guy." He winked and headed toward the shade and Owen. The kid hadn't taken his eyes off Sebastian since he slunk at the tree's base. Suddenly, he took an interest in Owen's game. Caitlyn stood over them, her lips wrapped around a spoonful of ice cream while her gaze zeroed in on him.

"Here, you try." Owen handed him the game.

"You know how to drive, right?"

The kid smirked at him, actually smirked. Sebastian chuckled and leaned back against the shed. He played while the boy licked his ice cream methodically, holding the cone straight, eyes squinted in concentration as he worked his way around. Sweat trickled down Sebastian's neck.

Looking up while he waited for the game to restart, Sebastian watched Caitlyn's tongue dart out, catching every drip as she licked off the spoon. His heart thumped against his chest, and he averted his gaze and forced himself to focus on the game in his hand.

Owen grinned as if he knew something Sebastian didn't. It was enough to rouse Sebastian's curiosity and take his mind off Caitlyn. He spent the next few minutes trying to discover what was so exciting. It seemed like a relatively simple game—drive around a track and score points by collecting items—but it kept Owen occupied.

Finally, he figured it out. Every time he collected an item, Owen let out a contagious sound of delight—even Caitlyn couldn't help but smile at it. She had gone quiet since they'd started playing, content to watch them from afar while she finished her ice cream.

Now that he'd seen her actual reaction—not just the one she felt obligated to put on for him—he smiled at her before turning his attention back to Owen's game. Sebastian joined in the boy's joyous screams whenever they scored points or picked up bonus items along the way.

Caitlyn finished her ice cream, and Owen took back his game. She walked inside the shed. Sebastian patted Owen on the shoulder. "I have to get ready for the next class. Make sure you drink water. Do you need more snacks?"

Owen lifted his bag to show he had a few, and Sebastian gave him a thumbs-up before heading around to the front of the shed to find Caitlyn.

"So, what is your plan?"

"My plan?" She stood inside, flipping through the pages of her clipboard. "The class will begin in ten minutes. We should have thirteen this time."

"Anything I should know?"

"Same as the first class."

He stared at her, waiting to see if she'd tell him anything else.

"You want something, Jones?"

"Are you doing okay?" He ignored the fact that she called him by his last name, leaned against the doorjamb, and peered out at a motorcycle with custom pipes approaching.

"You think you have a right to ask?"

He shrugged, not able to let it go. He saw the invisible armor she wore reappear.

Caitlyn rolled her eyes. "Listen, my family, my problem. I don't need your nose in my business. I appreciate you helping Owen mow the grass and don't think I don't know. It's you who put him up to clean the garage windows. Whatever you're bribing him with, stop. I like my garage windows dirty. People don't look in them if they can't see."

"Hiding something?"

Caitlyn tossed her ponytail off her shoulder. "Listen, I appreciate you wanting to help, but it's unnecessary. I can manage."

Her gaze flickered across his face. "It's important that no one in the Ghosts has any reason to be interested in what I do and who I work with. Maybe it's best if you don't get involved in my personal life, okay?"

"Is there something I should know?"

Caitlyn hesitated, then shook her head. "Trust me. Keeping things separate is better for everyone involved, especially you."

Especially him? What was that supposed to mean?

She tried to step around him, but Sebastian caught her by the arm. Her eyes landed on his fingers. "Caitlyn." The slight edge in his voice brought Caitlyn's chin up.

"How about we focus on the job and keep things professional?"

Sebastian glanced at the boy. He lay on his belly, the game in his hands. His eyes looked from Sebastian to Caitlyn. His eyebrows wrinkled as if he, too, picked up the subtle undercurrent between them. Not wanting to argue in front of the boy, Sebastian said, "Yeats has me here at the site until the end of the season."

"Lucky you," Caitlyn said.

More sounds of motorcycles coming into the parking lot

entered his ears. "You plan to bring Owen with you every weekend?"

His question caught her off guard. Good. He planned to defuse her attitude before the next group of riders arrived. She bit her lip and glared at him.

"I'm asking to ensure his safety. Any Ghost Riders joining us today?"

"No one will mess with my son, especially a Ghost." She planted her hands on her hips. She looked beautiful when she was in defensive momma mode.

He ran his hands through his hair. "Yeats might find some landscaping to keep him safe and out of trouble."

"Don't worry about it. I've arranged for him to stay with a close friend at Grace Meadows."

Sebastian's breath hitched at the mention of his family's horse farm. He forced a nonchalant shrug, scratching his neck as a bead of sweat trickled down his spine.

"That some kind of daycare?" His voice sounded rougher than usual, trying to mask the turmoil churning within.

"It's a horse farm. They give tours of the battlefield on horseback." Caitlyn's explanation was clipped, her eyes locked on him.

He schooled his features. Her gaze, dark and sharp, held a hint of suspicion. It could cut a man's heart if he still had one whole.

"You know the owners?" Sebastian swallowed hard, his throat suddenly dry as sandpaper. Feigning ignorance was his only option, no matter how much it twisted his gut.

"Samantha Daniels," Caitlyn continued, oblivious. "I've known her since high school," Caitlyn said, glancing over to check on Owen as another motorcycle drove into the parking lot.

Sebastian's parents had always been passionate about helping troubled teens, and the farm offered them a summer program working with the horses. It was how his sister met

Alex the summer before their senior year. The memory brought a pang of longing and regret he hadn't experienced in a long time.

Knowing his sister, Sam, would help Caitlyn with Owen. Her generous and forgiving heart never stopped caring or loving, despite all that happened to her. Something Sebastian lived with all these years, having been unable to prevent it. Alex had fooled them both. It was a mistake Sebastian never intended to make again and failed. Audra's desperate voice continued to haunt him at night.

More riders pulled into the lot. Owen continued to play his game, likely oblivious to their conversation. Caitlyn watched him as the riders approached. He owed her no explanation and didn't know how much Yeats spilled to her about his life. He couldn't afford for too many people to know the truth.

Sebastian met her gaze, a silent question hanging in the air. As she looked away, a barely perceptible frown creased her brow.

"Here for the intermediate rider course?" she said after a moment of awkward silence between them before turning toward the men walking their way.

She signed in the men for the class, and a strange sense of separation swept through him. Hopefully, with time, they could become friends. He prayed to God that she would never come to trust him. Women who trusted him always ended up hurt—or worse, dead.

9

Caitlyn had work in an hour. Where was her other shoe? Someone banged on the door. Owen never budged from his video game.

Finding her shoe, she hopped to the door. Wrenching it open, she dropped the shoe and tried to wiggle her foot inside.

"Honey, I'm home." Silas held his arms wide.

Caitlyn's legs weakened at the sight of her ex-husband. Dark blue jeans with black biker boots and a stained wife-beater shirt. He loomed in the doorway. Knowing better than to step back or show him any signs of weakness, Caitlyn's fingers tightened around the doorknob. "What are you doing here?"

"Can't a man come home to his wife?"

Dread swirled around in her stomach like soured milk. Swallowing down the bile rising in her throat, Caitlyn crossed her arms to make it clear she wouldn't fall into any of Silas's schemes. "I'm not your wife, Silas."

"A piece of paper means nothing," Silas said, moving closer. "You wore my cut. You bore my son. You. Are. Mine."

She tried not to roll her eyes at his disgusting remark.

"Funny, since you haven't been around for years. What are you doing here? Aren't you supposed to be in jail?"

"Parole, baby." Silas lowered his arms, but then he lifted them higher again. "Off early for good behavior. And now I'm home. It's good to see you kept the shop waiting for me. That was some trick you played." He wagged his finger at her. "But don't worry, I've had time to think of how you can make it up to me." He winked. "Where is Pops? I need to see him."

Caitlyn's stomach rolled. "No one notified me of your release."

A sly grin spread across Silas's face. "Been keeping tabs on me. See? You do care."

Panic clawed at her throat. Images of Owen engrossed in his video games in the other room filled her mind. Pops was tinkering in the garage, trying to replace the parts she took off his motorcycle to keep him from driving off on it.

Silas's eyes twinkled with an unsettling glint. The carefully groomed beard couldn't mask the broadness of his chin, a feature that used to send shivers down her spine. Nausea churned in her gut. "If you don't leave, I'll call the police."

Was her restraining order still good? Did such things need to be renewed? He wasn't supposed to get out of prison this soon.

A tense silence stretched between them. Caitlyn forced herself to meet his gaze, hoping the threat held a sliver of believability. Maybe, just maybe, a reminder of the law would be enough to scare him off.

"You can't keep me away from my son, Kitty Cat," Silas finally drawled, a mocking smile playing on his lips. "And last time I checked, I still owned half the business."

"There is no business. The shop has been closed for over a year. Besides, I bought you out a long time ago. Remember all those legal fees? The lawyer? The divorce?"

Silas's expression blanked. Caitlyn stiffened, knowing that dead look he got before the storm hit. Instead, he smiled, his ice-blue eyes sending their frosty chill to the pit of her stomach.

"You always did like to dig your claws in deep," he said, taking another step toward her. Caitlyn reached out to hold the door frame. She wouldn't budge—not for him. She wouldn't allow him to intimidate her ever again, no matter what he said or did.

"I recently saw a sweet ride with lightning painted over the tanks. I'd know my wife's artistic style anywhere."

"I did that a long time ago." Her heart hammered in her chest.

"I asked the guy." Silas's gaze fell below her neck, then up to meet her eyes again. "He said it was custom. By appointment only. He got it done last month."

Caitlyn tried to breathe out her nose and steady her nerves. "It's not your business."

He stared, his steel eyes narrowed and assessing. A trickle of sweat ran down her back. He pulled his shoulders back. His arms remained toned and well-muscled, just as she had observed the day they took him away in the courtroom.

"Where's the boy? It's been a while since I saw him."

"He's not here," she lied.

"I have my rights, Kitty Cat. Now tell me where he is." Silas leaned toward her.

Caitlyn leaned back, her throat tightening. "He's not here."

"Then I'll wait." Silas stepped back. "I've got time. Is the apartment above the garage still empty?"

Their old apartment. He would try to move back in with them again, force his way back into their lives. *Not with a protective order.* She planned to call the lawyer, find out what happened to get him out, and get the name of his parole officer.

"No. It's rented," she lied again. A mutual friend of theirs, Pete, went through a divorce. Needing a place to live, Caitlyn offered him work in the garage to help her out that first year Silas went to prison. He wasn't as good as Pops with mechanics, but Pops lost interest in the shop when the drink ruled him. For a long time, she blamed Silas. Pops lost his leadership of the Ghost Riders for his part in allowing Silas to direct the club's path. It ruined their business. It aged and destroyed her father. And Pete found another woman to move in with and left the garage apartment empty last year.

Now, Caitlyn did custom paint jobs to earn extra cash between the pizza shop and the motor coach gig during the off season without having time to find a new tenant or wanting to deal with one.

"Ole Pipper is still around. I'm sure he won't mind me crashing for a while," Silas said.

Pipper was Pete's biker name. They'd called him the Pied Piper for all the pies his wife baked and brought to the Ghost Riders' meetings. He had a half-dozen kids, and his ex-wife suspected a few others he hid from her through their years together.

Exasperated, Caitlyn said, "Whatever trouble you're in, we don't want it. I'm not about to let you near Owen again. You'll find some way to use him in one of your schemes."

"You're right, I will." Silas's grin widened. "You always knew me best. My wild Kitty Cat." He took a step closer, his hand reaching out as if to cup her cheek, but Caitlyn turned her face away.

He dropped his hand away from her. "I never could hide the truth from you."

Caitlyn recoiled, her stomach twisting with a sickening mix of fear and loathing. "Don't touch me. And I mean it." Did she? Would she call the police? The memory of the restraining order was hazy, and dealing with the authorities again filled her with a renewed dread. But what choice did she have? "Stay away from us. Stay off this property. If I have to, I swear, Silas, I'll call the cops!" Her voice wavered slightly, a tremor of uncertainty she desperately hoped he wouldn't notice.

Silas chuckled, a low, humorless sound. "You do that, sweetheart. And while you're at it, ask them if they have a guy named Sebastian Daniels on the force."

"Who?" The name slammed into her like a physical blow. So much for a clean break. Her carefully constructed life teetered on the edge like a house of cards.

Silas stepped back, a predatory glint in his eyes, and perched himself on the porch post. The air crackled with unspoken tension, thick enough to choke on. Caitlyn kept hold of the door like a lifeline. A silent prayer escaped her lips, a plea for strength and guidance.

"Sebastian Daniels," he drawled, each word slow and deliberate, like an icy blade scraping against bone.

"I thought I heard Owen mention you had a friend named Daniels," Silas continued, a sly smile playing on his lips. "Sandy or Sandra, I think?" He clicked his tongue in mock contemplation. "Ah yes, Sammy! A strange name for a girl, wouldn't you say?"

Caitlyn's mind reeled. But Owen couldn't have mentioned her. He was three when the police arrested Silas. Who else could have revealed it? Her gaze darted toward the garage, a knot tightening in her stomach, deepening her dread. Several Ghost Riders' members kept in touch with Silas, even after his incarceration. Had one of them been keeping more of a watch on her than she realized?

"What about her?" she managed, her voice barely a whisper. A faint rustling sound came from inside the house. Panic once more pressed into her throat.

"She got a brother?"

"How should I know?" Caitlyn listened, hoping Owen would stay inside, but the footfalls came closer. Sammy talked about her twin brother often in the first few years of their friendship. Lately, life kept Caitlyn from seeing Sammy for more than a quick hug on Sunday mornings. Sammy was proud of her brother. A cop.

"Just tell me what I need to know. She's your friend... or was," Silas said, leveling his gaze upon her. "I may have been in prison, but I still heard gossip about my wife and our son."

Caitlyn clenched her jaw. With everything he had done, she couldn't allow him around Owen. Silas wasn't the man she had once fallen in love with long ago. He used her. He needed her to help him move up the ranks of the Ghost Riders by marrying the president's daughter. They called him Shadow because he'd do anything, even if it meant carrying out their dangerous orders. Her father didn't understand. None of the Ghosts did.

Silas flexed his muscled arms, showing off tattoos she used to love, running her fingertips along his back when she believed in him and thought he differed from the other Ghost Riders. Now, they were just a reminder of a past she wanted desperately to forget.

"Why should I help you?" she replied coldly, keeping her insides from trembling. Silas made these kinds of inquiries for one reason. *Dear Lord, please let me be wrong.* "Why does Sammy having a brother matter?"

The hopes, the dreams—all lies.

According to her father and Silas, it was all a way to protect her and Owen. Her heart no longer ached for the pain this man caused her and her son. Eventually, with the support of her friend Sammy, she survived the trial, but the erratic jump in her pulse reminded her of the fear she didn't think would ever go away.

"You'll help me, Kitty Cat, because I say so."

"Get out of here, Silas," she forced out, her voice a low growl.

"Sure, babe. As soon as I see my son." He waltzed up to her, his steps deliberate and predatory. The toothy grin that used to hold a hint of charm now only sent shivers skating across her arms.

"Don't even think about coming near us, Silas." Caitlyn spat, her voice laced with a desperation that both surprised and terrified her. He sneered, his entire demeanor shifting. Cold, calculating eyes locked with her gaze. He leaned in, and his voice dropped to a rough tone. "Or what? Still going to call the cops on me, Kitty Cat? Go ahead. Make sure it's Daniels. It would make my job much easier."

Caitlyn stared back at him, the faint sound of Owen's game behind her. Fear warred with a surge of defiance. She silently prayed Owen kept his headphones on with the volume up loud so that he wouldn't be able to hear his father's voice.

She opened her mouth to speak, but no sound came out. Would she call the police? Could she risk the consequences of Silas's retribution if it turned out the restraining order wasn't valid anymore? Or was there another way out of this? A way to protect Owen without escalating the situation further?

Caitlyn's heart pounded in her chest, knowing the answer before she asked the question. "What job are you talking about?"

He didn't give her a straight answer, causing the drumbeat of her heart to still.

"When I opened the shop, I thought I was doing right by both of you, ensuring that both of you were provided for. How could you destroy our son's future like this? Was it because you hated me that much?"

Caitlyn's heart resumed its pounding against her ribs. Fury threatened to boil over, but she forced it down. She shook her head furiously.

"I protected our son," she spat. "Do you think I would want him to grow up and follow in your footsteps? You used the shop as a cover. It was never about providing for us. And here you are, tracking someone down. You'll be back in jail soon enough."

Silas's face contorted in rage. In a lightning-fast move, he grabbed her face roughly, strong enough to cause a gasp to escape her lips. A primal fear shot through her, momentarily paralyzing her. She held his gaze, a steely glint mirroring her own.

"I know what you did, babe," he rasped, his voice tight with barely controlled fury. A slight flicker of madness in his eyes sent a fresh wave of terror rocking through her.

His fingers tightened against her jaw. "And I know you'll make it up to me."

Silas stepped closer, the stale smoke from vaping on his breath. "Sooner or later, Daniels will come home, and you'll help me get my reward."

Caitlyn swallowed hard, taking a small step back and leaning against the door. "There can be no reward for doing the devil's work."

"You never complained about the cash, babe. You're as guilty as I am. We both know you snitched to save your own hide. Don't lie, and say it was for the boy's sake."

Lifting her chin and averting her gaze from him, Caitlyn clutched her hands at her sides.

Voice full of contempt, he shoved one hand against the door near her head. "Look at me."

His fingers bit into her soft skin, but she remained still and met his gaze. His lips curled into a sneer, and those cold mud-colored eyes of his fell to her lips. Her stomach twisted in knots, and she silently prayed that Owen stayed in his room, out of sight.

"You're going to help me find Daniels. He may still go by the name 'Beast,'" Silas said as his hand slid across her jaw to her neck, where it lingered. "You'll get me the information I need."

Caitlyn's mind raced, trying to rationalize why Silas would be after someone like Sebastian Daniels. The man didn't live here anymore, but someone must have wanted him dead. She needed to warn Sammy. Knowing Silas, the payout must have been significant to put him on the man's trail. What else could Silas want with him?

"And if I don't?" Despite the fear coursing through her veins, she made no move to force him off.

Silas lowered his voice, his hot breath on her face. "The old man has an accident, and our son discovers the truth." He paused for a moment as he loosened his grip on her neck. She winced and tried to pull away from him, but he tightened his grip again.

"And what truth is that?" Caitlyn whispered.

Silas reached with his other hand and pulled her hair from its messy bun, twisting it in his finger. "That Mommy lied, and then he'll come with me, and you'll never see him again." He released her hair and touched his forehead against hers, their noses touching. "Did you miss me?"

Tears welled up in her eyes. Caitlyn jerked her face from him, but Silas's hand tightened around her neck. Squeezed. Her hand flew up to cover his. "Silas."

"Did my son?"

The sound of feet running and music playing drew nearer. The door opened with a creak, and Owen came sprinting around the corner, her phone clutched firmly in his hands. "You almost forgot your phone... Are you late?" Owen paused abruptly when his gaze met Silas's. Those wide, innocent eyes looked between them, then filled with fear as he glanced back at Caitlyn.

Silas released her neck and stepped back, breaking their eye contact. His voice was heavy with emotion when he finally spoke. "Hey, kid."

Owen stared at him warily before turning to answer his mother's anxious question. "You okay, Mom?" Her damp cheeks glistened with relief as she breathed deeply once more.

Silas smiled slightly and composed himself before posing a

tentative query to the young boy. "Your mom's happy to see me. Are you?"

The silence stretched between them before Owen finally shrugged and acknowledged his father for the first time in years. "You've gotten big since I've seen you." He gave one last hesitant glance at Caitlyn before scurrying back inside and shutting the door behind him.

"He doesn't know his own father," Silas growled.

"He doesn't remember you. He was three the last time he saw you."

"Whose fault is that?" Silas shoved past her. He paused in the doorway, effectively trapping her between him and the solid wood. "I'm going to get to know my son."

Her sweet, innocent Owen. No. She didn't want Silas anywhere near their son. But what else could she do?

Her hand curled around her phone, her thumb swiping to open it. One word, and it would dial the police. Silas hooked his finger under her chin to get her attention. He wanted this. He *wanted* her to call the police.

"And you, Kitty Cat, are going to ask your friend where her brother is."

Releasing her, Silas went into the house. With a trembling hand, Caitlyn dialed the number of La Rosa's. "Hey, Regina," she began, trying to keep her voice calm and controlled. "There's been a family emergency... I won't be able to come in today..."

The act of not telling the whole truth tasted like ash in her mouth, but having Silas near their son was a far more bitter pill to swallow. Caitlyn watched Silas talking with Owen inside the house, trapped between the fear for her son and the potential consequences of losing her job. Tears escaped and ran down her face.

"I am sorry," Caitlyn said, not paying attention to anything Regina said on the other end of the phone. *Lord, what have I gotten myself into this time?*

10

Sebastian's phone vibrated on the coffee table, a shrill notification jarring amidst the roar of the virtual race car engine on his screen. He glanced down, momentarily distracted. It was the live feed from the security camera he'd rigged near the barn at Grace Meadows.

He muted the game audio and snatched up his phone. The screen displayed Samantha reaching toward the camera with her face etched with worry. Her agitation clawed at him, twisting his gut. Would she recognize the difference between their father's security cameras and the ones he hooked into the system? What was she doing that close to the camera?

A tuft of black fur smeared against the screen. It came down with a blur of a shirt sleeve, then refocused again to show the back section of the barn. Frantic energy filled him. He scrolled down, checking the other cameras, finding the one showing Sam holding a kitten and shaking her finger at it before handing it off to a teenage girl in jeans and a flannel shirt hanging off her shoulders. Sebastian let out a breath. A cat. The tension seeped out of his shoulders, replaced with amusement. He could almost hear Samantha scolding the feline intruder. The image on the screen was far from the nightmare he'd conjured in his mind.

After checking the other cameras, satisfied all was well, Sebastian didn't linger, watching Samantha as she worked in the barn. He missed his sister. He hadn't realized how much until coming this close to home without being home. Before he dwelled on it too long, he went back to the game. Leaning to the right as his on-screen car swerved and curved around obstacles, Sebastian tried to catch up to Owen on the virtual racetrack. Caitlyn's kid hooked him on the video game, and he seemed content with a controller in his hands. As Sebastian got caught up in the thrill of racing, he heard Owen's voice come back online.

"Hey little dude, all good?"

"Dan."

Startled out of his reverie, Sebastian crashed his car on the screen.

"What's wrong?"

"There's a man here, and I think he's threatening my mom."

Sebastian stood up from the couch, setting the controller on the coffee table. His heavy work boots clunked against the hardwood floor as he paced around the room. "Where's Welder?"

"I don't know. He's not here." A familiar panic sent a jolt through Sebastian. It mirrored the frantic calls he used to get from back in the day, the kind that never ended well.

"Is your mom okay?" he managed, his voice tight. Scaring Owen wouldn't help, but the question hung heavy in the air.

"I dunno," Owen mumbled, fear thick in his voice. "He's yelling at her, and she doesn't look happy." Sebastian gritted his teeth.

"Dan?" Owen said, and Sebastian realized he must have been silent for too long. "Dan? Are you still there?"

Sebastian flinched at the urgency in Owen's voice. "Yeah. I'm still with you."

A cold sweat prickled Sebastian's skin as static crackled through the headset. Owen's voice wavered through their connection. "What do I do?"

Sebastian ran a hand through his hair. Caitlyn asked him to stay out of her personal business. But the memory of Audra's tearful face, the fear shaking in Owen's voice, warred against him.

"Do you know the guy, O?" Sebastian asked, shortening the boy's name the way another online player might.

"No."

"Has he hurt your mom?" A surge of adrenaline went through him. God forgive him if the man laid his hands on Caitlyn or Owen before he got there.

"I dunno."

The safety of their online game world shattered, replaced by urgency. "I'm coming over," Sebastian said, feeling this time was different. This time, he wouldn't fail.

"No, wait!" Owen pleaded desperately. "That dude just came inside!"

"I'm on my way," Sebastian said, throwing his headphones on the coffee table.

Grabbing his phone, wallet, and keys, he sprinted out of the house, a silent prayer escaping his lips. Shocking him because, after all this time, he'd found a reason to pray again.

He sent a quick text to Yeats, who was going off to meet a woman for dinner and the movies. He glanced at the company truck and then at the Rebel motorcycle. Sebastian grabbed his helmet and mounted the bike.

He picked up a secondhand gunmetal grey Honda a few days ago. It was a plain, anonymous bike with no distinguishing features. Just what he needed for his new life. The tan leather seat, however, reminded him of the Indian Scout he had left behind in Johnstown. The fire, which destroyed his motorcycle and several others at Brooks' Motorcycle Shop, still rose in his mind like a wall, and he shuddered as he remembered what he had done—what he'd had to do—to protect his brothers and sisters. He couldn't stay in Johnstown now, not after everything that had happened. He was no longer Sebastian Daniels, the cop. The woman he hadn't been able to save the night before her death saw to that.

The low rumble of Sebastian's motorcycle echoed through the quiet evening as he parked on the street across from Caitlyn's house. He scanned the street for any sign of additional vehicles—a black pickup, a Harley with chrome accents. Either might belong to any of the Ghost Riders. His gut clenched, the engine ticking as it cooled. A tense silence followed, broken only by a passing car on the street.

Steeling himself, he considered the best course of action. He dismounted his Rebel and strode toward Caitlyn's house. Bursting in without warning could escalate things. Why hadn't he told the kid to call 911 and let the police handle it? Because for a moment, he forgot he wasn't a cop anymore. Then, a sound—a muffled clatter from inside Caitlyn's house—lengthened his stride. He jogged to the porch, and the door flew open. Caitlyn stood there with a look of shock that quickly shifted to confusion. "Daniel? What are you doing here?"

Behind her, Owen rushed up, shaking his head back and forth.

Gritting his teeth, forcing a smile, Sebastian said, "Hey bud, came to check on your game. It's not working, right?"

Owen tilted his head, his eyes widening. Smart kid. "Totally. I mean, it wasn't, but it's good now. I'm sorry."

Sebastian spun a tale about playing Mad Dash online with Owen when the boy's system crashed, so Sebastian offered to come over to help fix it and finish their Mad Dash match. The explanation sounded flimsy, even to his own ears. It wasn't far from the truth. They had been playing, but Owen's fear of the strange man had crashed their game. Lying came easily to him over the years of keeping his cover, but lying to Caitlyn made him uncomfortable.

A nervous tick played out in her jaw as she chewed on a thumbnail, her gaze flickering repeatedly toward the back of the house. Sebastian followed her line of sight, catching nothing but a glimpse of a hallway before it disappeared from his view. He glanced back at Owen, whose shoulders slumped farther in Sebastian's presence.

"You good, bud?" Sebastian asked, trying to sound casual. He gave Owen credit for not panicking after their earlier exchange, but seeing Caitlyn unharmed and a little rattled made him doubt the situation was as intense as Owen had made it. Or had he assumed it?

"Yeah," Owen mumbled, kicking at the floor with his foot. The playful glint in his eyes was missing, replaced by a wary uncertainty.

"You should have asked me first." Owen flinched at the harshness of Caitlyn's voice. He'd hoped to deflect from the situation, but his presence was clearly unwelcome. And there was no sign of another man in their home. He scanned the room, searching for anything out of place, any evidence of a struggle. But there was nothing. Did Caitlyn know the man Owen mentioned? Was the guy here on some legitimate business, like getting his motorcycle painted?

"You know you can't have people over when I'm not here." Caitlyn's hand flew to her cheek, her fingers brushing away a smudge that hadn't been there before. Color flooded back into her pale face, a telltale sign of tears quickly wiped away.

Sebastian couldn't help but notice how her full lips parted slightly when she finished. He chuckled and gave her a crooked smile as the tension between them built further. Their gazes locked, and time seemed to stand still. He wiped his sweaty hands on his jeans and swallowed hard, knowing this was more than just a staring contest.

"But you are here," Owen piped up, oblivious to the undercurrents. A hint of defiance in his voice.

Her gaze, filled with raw vulnerability, left Sebastian speechless. Fear flickered like a trapped flame in her depths, a stark contrast to the defiance she projected. For a fleeting moment, he glimpsed Audra and remembered how she confided in him—trusted in him.

The playful banter he'd planned died on his tongue. This wasn't about finishing a video game. Or even Audra. This was about Caitlyn and her son. Protecting them. But apprehension lingered within him. He still didn't know who the stranger was, and Caitlyn clearly didn't want him involved.

"Are we finishing the game or what?" Owen's voice cut through the tension.

Caitlyn's gaze lifted toward him, breaking their intense connection. She turned to Owen; her voice was tight. "I called off, so I'll let it go for tonight." Her voice softened. "This once." Her gaze moved to Owen. "But only until Pops returns."

Relief flooded Owen's face. He did a fist pump and grinned. "Come on, Dan!"

"Be there in a minute," Sebastian mumbled, watching Owen retreat towards the living room. He needed a moment. His cop training screamed at him to investigate, to find out who the stranger was and why Caitlyn seemed on edge. "Your father's not here?"

A flash of alarm fluttered over her face. "He's out with one of his old pals." Caitlyn huffed, about to move away, when Sebastian reached out, his hand hovering hesitantly near her arm. He stopped himself before making contact. "You, okay? Did one of your father's friends do something?"

Her face twisted into something that wasn't quite a scowl, but close enough. "Did Owen tell you? Is that why you came?" The hitch in her voice betrayed her bravado. "I don't need you coming around here and making things worse for us."

Sebastian held up his hands in surrender, taking a slow step back. "Hey, I came to play video games with Owen. We're buds, right, kiddo?" he called out, hoping to lighten the mood.

Caitlyn's knuckles turned white as she gripped her hips. "You can't keep coming around here, Daniel. We work together, nothing more." Her voice was laced with desperation that lit him with anger inside.

"Is it because of the Ghost Riders?" he asked. "Or your father?"

"We work together. Nothing more," she repeated.

"Yeah," he said. "I'm just here to hang with the kid," Sebastian lied, his heart heavy. Getting involved deeper was a roadmap for disaster, but the thought of leaving them vulnerable bothered him more.

11

Owen leaned against the passenger door of Caitlyn's vehicle, arms crossed and eyes burning. No headphones, no handheld video game—just a sullen silence. When they arrived at Grace Meadows, he got out without a word and slammed the door behind him. She called after him but thought better of it—he was still angry about her ultimatum: either come to work with her or go to Grace Meadows with Sam. Either option didn't include staying at the house with Pops or going across the yard to where Silas monitored them from above the garage. The other night's encounter with Daniel coming to the house had been a close call.

"Go." Owen waved her off as she got out of the car. "You don't want to be late for work."

"Hey. Watch the tone."

"Whatever," he muttered, turning away from her.

Frustration bubbled in Caitlyn's chest, hot and unwelcome. She put her hands on his shoulders, forcing him to turn around and look at her. "We talked about this," she said, her voice firm but laced with a tremor she couldn't disguise. Was it anger at his disregard for her boundaries or relief that he'd shown up concerned about Owen?

His gaze held hers, a silent apology warring. "You can't keep punishing me because of something I asked you to do."

"It's not fair. I want to hang with Dan."

Caitlyn let her eyes flutter closed for a moment. She asked Daniel not to come by without calling first. Boundaries were important, as a shield she'd carefully constructed to ensure neither of them got hurt. Seeing him there after her encounter with Silas chipped away at her barriers. A ghost of a smile played on her lips.

"You'll like working with Sammy and the horses."

Owen scrunched up his nose at her and stomped off toward the barn, his initial defiance waning at the mention of horses. He mumbled a noncommittal response and stomped off toward the barn, a hint of curiosity battling his usual resistance.

She followed him and caught up just as he stepped through the entranceway. The smell of hay and horse filled her nostrils as Sammy emerged from an adjacent room, carrying a cup of coffee and a warm smile on her face. Normalcy. That was what Caitlyn craved most right now.

"Hey, Owen," Sammy said with a friendly smile. "You want to head out back with Cole? He's saddling up for the next tour group."

Owen stood there, like he was unsure of what to do. He glanced at his mother before finally speaking up. "You want me to ride a horse?" he asked, his voice cracking as he spoke.

Sammy leaned back against the wall and shrugged, her hands cupping her coffee mug. "I don't see why not," she said casually, her eyes glowing with amusement. Owen attempted a smile in return, but it came out as more of a grimace, and he glanced away. With a last nod, he walked away, leaving Caitlyn and Sammy alone in the barn.

The silence was palpable as they both stood there, neither speaking nor looking at one another. Caitlyn swallowed, the familiar ache in her chest tightening. It wasn't fair. Life had become a relentless tug-of-war between work, Owen, and keeping Pops sober. The last thing she wanted to do was burden Sammy, who was always there with a smile and a helping hand, never a complaint.

Sammy had on a well-worn Grace Meadows t-shirt under a button-up and a baseball cap holding her hair in a messy ponytail. Her high cheekbones and uncanny blue eyes sent a chill through Caitlyn. She'd seen them hundreds of times, and yet today, they seemed overly familiar.

They'd texted, arranging Owen's visit while Caitlyn worked. The convenience of it gnawed at her. How long had it been since they'd truly spoken, confided in each other? Sammy, ever the patient one, sipped her coffee, waiting.

Caitlyn's gaze snagged on the glint of a new ring on Sammy's left hand. A pang of something indefinable shot through her, a mix of joy for her friend and a flicker of... longing. She cleared her throat. The sound echoing in the sudden silence. "So," she began, searching for where to start. "What have you been up to lately?"

Sam paused momentarily, her brow furrowing ever so slightly before answering. "Just trying to stay afloat, I guess... it's been hectic this season."

"I'm sorry I've had to add Owen to your responsibilities," Caitlyn replied.

"Owen is no burden." Sammy smiled. "I haven't seen him in so long. We've missed you at church." When Sammy said "we," she meant her and Cole. "It's hard to believe how quickly he's growing up." Sammy paused momentarily; her eyes filled with a warmth that tugged at Caitlyn's heart. "I've been thinking about you so much recently, Cat," she admitted quietly. "I'm glad you called. I've missed you."

"I...I missed you too, Sammy," Caitlyn stammered. She desperately wanted to ask about Sammy's brother. To warn her, to warn him. But the words were like a physical barrier in her throat.

She couldn't do this. Caught between loyalty to her friend and fear for Owen's safety, a wave of guilt and grief washed over her. What would Sammy think of her showing up after all these months of sparse communication and asking questions about her estranged twin brother? She didn't even know his name. Was it Sebastian?

When Caitlyn needed someone to confide in, Sammy became close as a sister. If she could just confide in her now. What if it was Sammy's brother? She knew he was a cop. Is that why Silas was hunting him?

What did she say? *Hey Sammy, isn't your brother's name Sebastian? I think someone might be looking for him.* But if Sammy's brother lived far away or if Sammy didn't know where her brother was, she couldn't tell Silas. He would find another way to get the information that might involve hurting Sammy.

"I am forever in your debt."

Sammy watched her thoughtfully and took a sip of her coffee. "Is there something else you're not telling me?"

Caitlyn sighed and rubbed her temples. "It's not something I can talk about." There, she'd said it. Maybe Sammy could pray for her and pray for a way for her to find a safe solution to her situation for everyone—including the man Silas was hunting.

Sam rubbed her finger over the rim of her cup and waited patiently, giving Caitlyn the time she needed to collect her thoughts. After a few moments of silence, Caitlyn finally spoke.

"It's Silas." Caitlyn told Sammy about Silas showing up on her porch, about him moving in above the garage, and roping Pops back into starting the restoration business in the garage again. She left out the parts about Silas hunting a man named Sebastian Daniels or the fact Silas threatened her.

"They let him out early on parole." Sammy glanced down at the end of the barn at the man strolling toward them.

Caitlyn's chest fluttered. She hadn't expected Sammy to know.

"Is he yours?" Cole walked up behind Sammy and wrapped an arm around her waist. He planted a kiss on Sammy's cheek, making her grin back at him.

"Hard to believe he's getting so tall, right?" Sammy asked.

Cole lifted the ball cap on his head and resettled it. "Big enough to watch Sparrow and Titus while I grab a new girth strap." Cole stepped away from Sammy, a playful grin splitting his face. "You two ladies take your time catching up. Owen and I have the work covered. Besides, someone needs to make sure these two goofballs don't get tangled in the reins."

Sammy tilted her head and laughed, a light, joyous sound that warmed Caitlyn. "I guess it helps. This morning's ride is a private party of two." Then she looked at Caitlyn, her blue eyes sparkling. "Newlyweds."

A genuine smile bloomed on her lips. Sammy's happiness was contagious. "That will be you soon," Caitlyn said, her voice filled with a wistful longing she couldn't quite mask.

"One day, if Cole will ever agree on a wedding date."

"I'm sure you two will figure it out," Caitlyn said, sticking her hands in her back pockets. Her gaze flitted to Owen, who was peering around the corner of the barn at them, a mischievous glint in his eye. A flicker of hope ignited with her. Maybe Owen wouldn't give her such a hard time coming here again.

"Looks like those two are going to get along."

"Oh yeah. Cole is great with kids." Sammy shrugged. "He loves teaching at the middle school and working with the teens in the after-school and summer program."

A pang of something akin to envy shot through Caitlyn. "I'm glad, Sammy. Again, thank you for taking Owen today. It means a lot."

"No worries there." Then Sammy's smile dimmed, and she wrapped her arm around Caitlyn's shoulder, her touch filled with concern. "You said Silas was staying at your place? You can't be okay with it."

"Silas... we agreed..." Caitlyn tried to gulp down her own fear. Sleep had become a luxury she could barely afford. Every creak of the floorboards, every unfamiliar sound from outside sent her heart racing, forcing her to check on Owen, his peaceful slumber a stark contrast to the turmoil within her.

Nightmares gnawed at her. Nightmares of Silas snatching Owen, of Pops vanishing into the night, leaving no trace behind. Every ring of the phone at work threatened to shatter her precarious hold on reality. Would it be another threat from Silas? Or worse, a report of her child missing or Pops?

Late at night, in the quiet solitude after tucking Owen in, she'd composed a desperate text to Antonio. Each time she'd delete the message before hitting send. Finally, she settled on a short, cryptic text.

Silas is back. He's staying above the garage.

Throughout the night, she stared at her brother's number, desperate for him to answer. She couldn't tell him any more than that. Only what she shared with Sammy. Even now, she feared she may have blurted too much.

Silas expected her compliance. She'd thought they were safe. He'd had years to serve before she should worry. No matter how hard she prayed, nothing went in her favor. She chose her next words wisely. "I told Owen to stay away from the garage."

"Is it wise to let him stay on your property?" Sammy asked cautiously.

What choice did she have? Same old Silas. Same old Pops. She should have known he would fall right back into Silas's plans. She prayed her father would come to his senses. Getting stripped of his cut and removed from his position with the Ghost Riders didn't keep him from seeing Silas's manipulation. What did she know? According to her father and brother, females needed to let the men handle the business. Caitlyn lost her business, and soon, she'd lose so much more if she couldn't get Silas to leave.

"It's not like I have a choice. He's got Pops back under his influence again, and he's warned me about keeping Owen away from him."

"What does he want?" Sam reached for her arm and squeezed it. "I keep thinking back when…"

Guilt churned in Caitlyn's stomach. The knowledge about Silas's interest in Sammy's brother kept her lips sealed. How much was someone willing to pay Silas to find Sebastian Daniels? Why? What had the man done? Sammy's brother was a cop. Caitlyn tried to take a breath to ease the tightness against her ex-husband, making people disappear for a price.

"I'm… uncertain," Caitlyn finally managed. It was the truth, technically, but a truth born from a tangled web of secrets. "He's out of prison, so he needs a place to crash, and he still considers me his wife," Caitlyn finally said.

Cole walked past them again and winked at Sammy. She giggled and then gave him a stern face that made him grin. It sent flutters in Caitlyn's belly, seeing the two of them so in love. She never had that with Silas. All she'd ever been was his property.

She bit back the bile rising in her throat. He'd take Owen. He'd hurt her father. Or worse. He'd kill him. Or her. She took a shaky breath, pushing down the panic.

Sam's eyes softened. She licked her lips. A nervous habit Caitlyn noticed over the years they'd known each other. The sound of clunking against the back wall of the barn reminded her she didn't have much time until work started. A horse rattled a water bucket, the heaviness of it bumping against the planks of the stall.

"Are you okay?"

Why did people keep asking her that? Daniel asked her that, too.

Caitlyn took her hand and squeezed it. "I'm okay. I'm just... I'm scared he might hurt someone."

She expected a dismissive scoff or maybe a comforting hug, but Sammy's grip on her arm tightened, her blue eyes widening. "There's something you're not telling me, isn't there?"

Caitlyn looked down at her feet, the weight of it all pressing down on her. "I can't. Please don't ask again."

"Caitlyn." Sammy pulled her into that hug. "We've always confided in each other."

"I know." But the fear of putting Sammy's brother in danger was stronger.

Sammy pulled back from the hug. "What is God telling you to do?"

The unexpected question sent a jolt through Caitlyn. When was the last time she'd spent enough time with God to find out? Caitlyn remained silent.

"You'll get through this. You're strong. And you're not alone."

"I know." Caitlyn blinked away the blur of moisture in her eyes.

"Your siblings still aren't coming around?"

Caitlyn bit the inside of her lip to distract her from the tears threatening to build and spill over and shook her head. Crying again was the last thing she planned to do while dropping off Owen.

"What about the lawyer?"

"It's not an option right now." Caitlyn had asked Regina to pick up more hours at La Rosa's. The hourly lawyer fees took a day or more's wage to cover.

"Well, you have me and Cole." Sammy shouted down the aisle. "Isn't that right, Cole?"

"You name it, babe." He stuck his head around the corner of the barn and waved.

"He has no clue what you said," Caitlyn deadpanned.

"Nope, but when my parents return, I'll have my mom contact Seb. He's bound to have some connections to ensure Silas goes back to jail. Or at the very least, you and Owen are safe," Sammy said.

"Seb? As in Sebastian?" Her heart skipped a beat.

"That would be him." A hint of pride crept into Sammy's voice.

"Don't do that," Caitlyn blurted.

Sam tilted her head. "Cat, I want you to be safe. I know Seb's in a different county, but he might have a way to find out about Silas's parole or contact the parole officer. You can trust Seb. He's a good cop. He's one of their best undercover guys."

No… No… She didn't want to hear this…

"Then we shouldn't get him involved." She tried to reason with Sammy as much as herself. "He's probably undercover, and you don't want to distract him from his current case, right? It might take a long time to contact him or for him to respond."

"Maybe," Sammy said, unsure.

"Please don't involve your brother." Caitlyn hoped she didn't sound too desperate.

Sammy's lips twitched in thought. This wasn't a math quiz. It was her life. Caitlyn's. And Sammy's twin brother. Caitlyn's expression must have been enough to sway her because she said, "Okay, I'll wait until Mom and Dad get back. Mom will be eager to send him photos and stuff from the trip. Once she hears from him, then I'll check in with him. In the meantime, though, maybe we could contact that detective who was on Silas's case."

Caitlyn helped save the detective's life, but he disappeared after Silas's trial. A frustrated sigh escaped her lips. With no way of contacting the detective and no ties with the local law, she said, "I don't know."

"I pray for him. What happened changed his life. Changed everyone's life, you know."

She did know. Silas almost killed the detective. God had crossed their paths for a reason. Almost as if they were meant to meet, but then the trial happened, and the detective chose a path away from her. Maybe it wouldn't have worked, anyway. If not for God's intervention, the Ghosts would give him more reason to flee. Still, a flicker of longing sparked in her chest. He'd been kind and attentive, his concern for her safety tinged with something more. Like the stronger "something" building between her and Daniel. It was dangerous. She was a danger. No man would ever be safe in a relationship with her. The detective was right to leave.

"I'll figure it out," Caitlyn reassured her, putting on a smile. A nervous smile to keep from blurting why Sebastian couldn't help her. Bringing up the detective reminded her of what Silas was capable of, given the chance. There was an answer. Surely, there was a way out. One that kept her family safe and Sammy's. Which yanked at her heart. She cared. Oh, how she tried not to care about that man.

"God will help you. Lay it at his feet, Cat. Pray and wait. Don't do anything rash. Promise me?"

The detective offered for her to run. He wanted her to start a new life with him. It hadn't felt right. Something made her stay. Her son. Her father.

Maybe God hadn't been listening when she asked to keep Pops sober and Owen away from motorcycles. That was why she closed the shop. If not for needing to keep the lights on, she might have stopped doing custom paint jobs altogether. People would have come around, but the memories tasted bitter. They rose like bile, making her ill as they all came rushing up at once. Her entire body trembled. Her chest tightened, and her breathing got painful.

"Cat." Sam sat her coffee on a nearby saddle hanging on the wall. It tilted and spilled over like Caitlyn's emotions. Sam wrapped Caitlyn in her arms while the sobs broke out. "I've got you, Cat. You're not alone. Dear lord," Sam prayed over

Caitlyn's sobs. Caitlyn cried harder, gulping for air and clinging to Samantha Daniels and her soulful prayers. Even though she heard none of the words, she felt the intentions and silently pleaded with God. *Someday, please let Sammy forgive me for not telling her everything.*

The sounds of a vehicle approaching caused Caitlyn to pull back. She swiped at her tears. "I should go. I need to get to work for my shift." She glanced around. Several horses grazed out in the field, while around the side of the barn, Cole led two horses. Owen followed. A horse trailing behind them. All three horses wore saddles, ready for the upcoming tour ride across the battlefields.

"Cole can handle this group. Owen and I will take the next. Don't worry. Owen's going to get along fine here with the horses." Sammy switched their topic of conversation.

"He talks of driving a motorcycle."

"Like his momma. Come on, *chica.* You don't want to be late for your shift."

Caitlyn laughed at Sammy's attempt at slang. After their talk, her eyes appeared watery, and her face pale.

Caitlyn's chest refused to ease. If something happened to Sammy's brother because she kept silent... She stifled back another choked sob. Sammy rubbed her back as they walked. She didn't deserve a friend like Sammy.

12

The porch light cast a warm glow as Sebastian strapped on his helmet. Yeats sat perched on his Harley, a hulking black machine with a glint of chrome in the light. He tossed a jacket toward Sebastian. The familiar weight of the leather grounded him.

"Where did you get this?" Sebastian's thumbs brushed against the logo of the club Yeats ran with, much like the one Sebastian missed back in Johnstown. The Soldiers of Christ was another chapter of the Christian Motorcycle Association.

"Don't get your panties in a wad. It's a loaner." Yeats lifted his chin. "Heard you tangled with some biker crew down south," Yeats said with a mischievous grin.

A wry smile tugged at Sebastian's lips. "South, huh?"

Yeats ran a hand through his hair, the movement revealing the scar behind his ear. "I looked at a map. Was I wrong?"

Sebastian zipped up his worn leather jacket, the familiar coolness a grounding sensation after a long day in the sun. "Alright, alright," he said, a playful jab barely masking the deeper memory it stirred. "Just promise you're not trying to recruit me again. Told you, clubs are a closed chapter for me."

Yeats gaze lingered on Sebastian for a beat, the lack of his friend's usual affable grin reaching his eyes. Sebastian knew the haunted look in those eyes all too well.

"Listen," Yeats said, forward on the seat of his Harley, "where we are headed, that patch might actually be useful. Wear it, don't wear it, it doesn't matter. But don't say I didn't warn you."

Sebastian wrestled with the tug of exhaustion battling within him. "Where are we going?" he asked, picturing the comfort of the couch in Yeats' living room instead of a night out.

"Ghost Rider Tavern," Yeats announced, a hint of a smirk tugging at his beard. "Guy I know said an old friend returned to town."

Sebastian raised an eyebrow. "And this old friend wouldn't be me, would it?"

Yeats chuckled. "Don't get ahead of yourself, Seb."

Sebastian narrowed his eyes. "Your intel source is a Ghost Rider and has information related to Caitlyn, doesn't he?"

"That's why you should come." Yeats turned the key, and the Harley rumbled to life.

Apprehension cinched around Sebastian's gut. "A biker bar?" he muttered, the image of flashing lights and sirens pulling at the edges of his memory. The choked cry of a woman echoed in his head—Audra. He'd been undercover, infiltrated a similar club, and brought down their whole chop shop operation. But it went sideways, and Audra ended up caught in the crossfire.

Sebastian's leather boots crunched on the gravel as he walked to his bike. He cautiously swung his leg over the seat.

"Tavern," Yeats corrected him with a roll of his eyes. "Besides, wings are half-price tonight."

"It's not my scene anymore." Sebastian couldn't help thinking of the biker woman with the green hair, watching from the sidelines as Caitlyn took the safety course at the range. Despite the looks she got from some, there was not a single complaint. A wave of nausea washed over him—the image of Caitlyn waiting patiently, forever loyal, like the woman with green hair. Like Audra, until Pike tried to harm her and dispose of her newborn in a dumpster where one of Sebastian's Thunder Valley brothers found the baby alive.

He took a deep breath and started his Rebel while the memory of her pleading for help etched into his soul. But instead of Audra's face envisioned in his mind, Caitlyn visualized there instead.

For the first time in a week, they wouldn't have another slice of cardboard-like pizza from the Italian place where Caitlyn and Yeats' new girlfriend worked. He'd been living off takeout for the past few weeks, all because Yeats was too lazy to stock the kitchen. Whenever Sebastian went grocery shopping, Yeats would complain about the "pointless" endeavor. It was like living with a teenager on summer break as they spent their days playing video games. Caitlyn's son had a real knack for it. He constantly kicked Sebastian's butt in Mad Dash 12.

Being an undercover cop didn't lend itself to having a family of his own, and seeing how hard Caitlyn was trying to take care of her son and father only reinforced that decision. She'd made it clear she didn't want him coming around her house. The last two weekends, Sebastian stepped off the range to allow Caitlyn to teach when they had fewer students than needed for two coaches. But he stayed to ensure no one gave her a hard time on the range. Other than the guy who talked way too much for Sebastian's liking, the courses ran smoothly.

"I told you I'm done with this kind of life," Sebastian shouted over the revving of Yeats' motorcycle.

"Sure, you are," Yeats scoffed. "The big bad Beast still has his motorcycle and his cut."

"Don't call me that!" Sebastian growled, kicking his motorcycle stand up and preparing to ride after Yeats.

The arrogant ex-ranger's lips quirked into a half-smile, and his eyes betrayed a hint of amusement despite the tension that hung in the air. He gave a nonchalant shrug and called, "So, have you tried Zelda's parmesan garlic wings? They're to die for."

"Are you seriously trying to change the subject?"

"I need your help on this one," Yeats said. Another deep rumble filled the air from Yeats' Harley. "You haven't been off your couch all week playing those video games like a preadolescent kid."

Ignoring Yeats' jab, Sebastian fired up his own machine and gave into curiosity about what lay beyond the double doors of the tavern. "It depends on the game," he countered, gunning the engine louder than Yeats'.

"Come on, I could go for some wings, at least get something from it even if we don't get any info. And besides, I figured you'd want to meet Cat's brother Casper."

"Casper?"

Without another word, Yeats revved up his motorcycle and drove off. As they arrived at the entrance of the Ghost Riders' Tavern, Sebastian swore under his breath. It was a massive two-story building with a wraparound porch and stairs curving up to the second-story balcony overlooking the bar and dance floor. An ominous headless-horseman figure hung above the door, and the porch, painted in faded blue and white, had Harleys scattered around it. Thumping music echoed through the night air from within its walls.

They parked off to the side of the building with other lines of motorcycles.

"You said something about Cat's brother." Sebastian shoved his motorcycle key in his pocket.

"Antonio, but his road name is Casper. He's Caitlyn's brother. She has an older sister who got married after their mother passed."

Sebastian forced a smile, the information swirling in his mind. Cat's brother was a Ghost Rider. She never mentioned it. Why wasn't he surprised by it?

Yeats' playful jab barely registered. "Good to know," Sebastian finally said, his voice gruff. His mind raced to piece together the fragments he knew about Caitlyn.

"You can't tell me you weren't just a little curious."

"I thought you warned me not to get involved." Sebastian glanced around, not sure coming here was a good idea.

"Attached. Rumor has it her old man might be back. That's why we need to go see the Ghost Riders."

"Instead of asking Caitlyn?" What if she found out about them making inquiries, and it spooked her more? The first time he had gone undercover was partly because of the thrill of protecting people and keeping justice alive. Sharing information without permission might get him in serious trouble with Caitlyn. If Caitlyn felt like Sebastian and Yeats were prying into her personal business and didn't respect her boundaries, it could make it difficult for her to trust him in the future. Not that he deserved her trust, since he couldn't offer his own.

"Keep your cool and follow my lead, yeah?" Yeats nudged Sebastian through the saloon doors, a low murmur rippling through the bar as they entered. The air hung thick with the smell of sizzling burgers, stale beer, and a faint undercurrent of something sharp and metallic—a scent bringing unwelcome recognition through Sebastian.

The dim interior was a kaleidoscope of worn leather and chrome. Patrons, a mix of weathered faces and young bucks, crowded around battered wooden tables, their backs adorned with colors that spoke of loyalty and brotherhood. The occasional flash of ink peeked from beneath their t-shirts. It was a scene ripped straight out of his life with the Sharks he tried to keep buried.

A knot of tension tightened in Sebastian's stomach as he scanned the room. Every rumble of conversation felt like a scrutinizing gaze, every glance a potential threat. In the back corner, a lone pool table held court. A gaggle of men gathered around it, their laughter punctuated by the sharp crack of breaking cues. But Sebastian's focus snagged on two figures at the bar.

Yeats squeezed his shoulder reassuringly. "Easy there, brother. We're neutral, and they respect that here. Nobody's looking for trouble." He steered Sebastian toward the bar, but Sebastian couldn't tear his eyes away from the men Yeats approached. A wave of fury washed over Sebastian. These were the men who harassed Caitlyn on the range that first day he worked with her. Blue, with a red-and-blue bandana tied around his head. Grover, his eyes hard and calculating, a constant twitch at the corner of his mouth.

"Blue, Grover," Yeats greeted them, clapping each on the back. "You remember Daniel, Cat's partner on the range?"

Blue's gaze on Sebastian hardened at Yeats, mentioning Sebastian's name. "Dan, the man," he said, shaking a finger at him. "You're that 'training wheels' guy working with Cat teaching folks how to ride motorcycles."

Grover elbowed Blue in the ribs and nodded toward Sebastian. "Better watch your step, though," he said darkly. "Cat's old man doesn't take kindly to anyone chasing after his kitty cat."

Sebastian squared his shoulders, preparing to say something, when Yeats muttered, "Silas is back? I thought he was in for a time." A hint of disbelief lay under his breath.

Blue stiffened and stepped back, his eyes flicking to the front entrance. "You want me to take you to him?" he offered.

"He's here?" Yeats asked, sounding non-committal.

Sebastian clenched his jaw. What information was Blue offering, and at what cost?

As if on cue, a figure appeared from the shadows at the far end of the bar. A ruddy-faced man with broad shoulders, short dark hair, and a face with the lines of life lived hardened and weathered lumbered into view. He moved with a slow, steady purpose, stopping a few feet away when they were all within clear view.

"Stop bothering my patrons, Blue," he rumbled, demanding respect. The bandana-wearing man visibly shrunk under the man's gaze. A nervous cough escaped his lips as the clinking of glasses and the low hum of music seemed to fade into the background.

"Silas won't like this. These people don't belong here," Grover said, giving his cut one last yank for emphasis.

Butch, as Sebastian recognized the man who came to the range that first time with the woman with green hair, tilted his head toward Blue. He fixed the bandana-wearing biker with a hard look. "And what kind is that?"

Before Blue could reply, Yeats cut in, his voice booming with a forced joviality. "Any friend of mine is welcome here. We're good." The declaration effectively shut down any further hostility, but a heavy silence descended upon the group. All eyes turned toward them, and Sebastian cupped the back of his neck. He never went anywhere without his gun tucked out of sight and a knife out of habit. Sweat gathered between his shoulder blades.

Yeats rapped on the bar and ordered them both drinks to break the unnerving silence. A man at a nearby table lifted his chin toward Sebastian. "You're the one who made Blue wear a helmet." The man smirked. "We could use someone like you."

Sebastian tilted his head toward Yeats, searching for a cue to respond. Yeats met his gaze with a neutral expression. "He's with me."

A man behind the bar slid glasses with ice and two cans of soda in their direction.

Grover's fist slammed against the bar, calling for a drink, but the sound echoed in Sebastian's ears like a gunshot. His heart hammered against his ribs as Butch leaned forward, looming like a threat. The casual banter around them replaced by a suffocating stillness.

"Don't you two got somewhere you need to exist?" Butch asked.

Relief washed over Sebastian as Blue and Grover grumbled their way toward the pool tables. Butch's gaze, sharp and assessing, landed on Sebastian. "Where do I know you from?"

"The motorcycle range." Sebastian popped the tab on the soda and inhaled the carbonated drink to ease the coil in his stomach. One wrong word, one misstep, and everything he'd been doing these past several weeks to protect his family and stay alive, would force him to leave again and find another way to protect them. He wanted a life away from his old life, a new life, and leaving Caitlyn and Owen bothered him. Why did he ever think he could come this close to home, and no one ever recognize him?

Yeats leaned closer to Butch, his words meant only for the Ghost Rider President.

"Is Casper around? I needed to talk with him."

Sebastian used the opportunity to scan the room, looking for an escape route if needed. On the counter, the glass with ice condensed on the surface of the bar. Sebastian returned his gaze to Butch, waiting for the inevitable moment the man shattered his facade.

"What is it you need to say to Casper?" Butch raised an eyebrow, his gaze flickering from Sebastian to Yeats, before sweeping across the room to take in the position of Blue and Grover at the pool table.

"Silas is back," Yeats said loud enough for Butch to hear over the hum of conversation and clatter of glasses further down the bar.

"You don't think Casper knows that already?"

"Maybe." Yeats furrowed his brows, the lines on his forehead deepening. "The real question is why and how he's back."

A humorless scoff escaped Butch's lips. "And you think Casper can give you the answers?" He didn't bother to hide the amusement curling the corners of his mouth. "Casper's my right-hand man, though not necessarily by choice."

Butch turned away from them to take a drink order from a woman clad in combat boots and tight leather shorts who sauntered up to the bar. Yeats seized the moment to lean toward the kitchen and call out to the waitress for two orders of wings to go.

Butch meticulously placed the drinks on the tray. The woman came around to deliver them to the patrons. Yeats took a long swig of his drink, then argued, "I can't just stand by when one of my rider coaches is affected."

"We take care of our own." Butch gazed beyond Yeats to the door. A chill snaked down Sebastian's spine as the door creaked open, admitting a man with a buzz cut and thick black tattoos that snaked up his arms like predatory vines.

Yeats turned, leaning his elbows back on the bar. Blue and Grover shouted greetings, while others went back to their meals and games of pool, but a few eyes lingered on them. Yeats lifted his chin. "Casper."

"What's up?" Casper's eyes held a glint of steel as he approached. Butch moved on, but not before exchanging a brief look with Casper.

"I thought I agreed to send some men to help with parking for bike week," Casper said.

"It's not that. I figured I'd check on the family," Yeats said, turning as Casper joined them at the bar.

"If Cat needs something, she'll call." In other words, the guy avoided going there. Sebastian took another sip of his drink to calm his irritation.

"This the new guy?" Casper eyed Sebastian, sweeping his gaze over him. Normally, Sebastian would offer to extend his hand to the biker, but under these circumstances, that would make him look like a fool, so he just nodded and replied, "Dan."

"Dan?" Casper asked, his eyes narrowing as he scratched the side of his nose. His gaze flickered between Yeats and Sebastian with a hint of skepticism. "That's it? Just Dan?"

"Daniel has been helping me on the range and at the landscaping business. He's new in town. I'm introducing him to the area." Yeats said, gesturing to Sebastian before nodding toward Butch behind the bar.

Butch was in conversation with another customer, but occasionally, the Ghost Rider President glanced in their direction. Sebastian itched to get out of there. The few couples and the party of five who occupied tables around them did little to ease the tightness cramping his back muscles.

"We came for the wings," Sebastian said, not wanting to draw any more attention by staying too long. "I heard they're the best."

Casper nodded approvingly at Butch before turning back to them. "Anything Zelda makes is the best."

Sebastian turned away from Casper and Yeats, feeling the attention of several people upon him as Blue and Grover observed from a pool table in the opposite corner of the bar. A green-haired woman approached and eyed them suspiciously when she saw the bag of containers beside them. Yeats tapped him on the shoulder, and Sebastian followed him toward the door. Once outside, the tension in his muscles relaxed slightly. A sensation ran across his hip, and Sebastian pulled out his other phone. It vibrated in his pocket to alert him to the same strange number calling it again.

"You, okay?"

"I suppose it's time I check in with the missus."

———

Caitlyn gazed across the driveway, lingering on the gleaming motorcycles lined up in front of the garage. Each chrome curve and powerful engine made her nauseous.

"Silas," she muttered under her breath. A wave of paranoia, cold and relentless, washed over her, making even the most basic tasks seem daunting.

Over the past week, her world shrank to the suffocating confines of Silas in her space. Silas, with his manipulative charm and veiled threats, weaseled his way back into controlling Pops once more. What threats had he used on her father to get Pops to open the restoration shop against Caitlyn's objection? Where would she paint and work on motorcycles and have her space? It infuriated her how Pops allowed Silas to take over his life again. And what choice did she have? It wasn't like Silas would obey any kinds of legal action she took to keep him away.

Even the motorcycles seemed to mock her with their freedom. Once they lined up for restoration and custom services. The ones parked now made her want to heave. She knew those motorcycles and having them on her property tainted everything she tried to avoid all these years with Silas gone.

Whether or not Pops gave his permission, Silas moved into their old apartment above the garage. Though Caitlyn refused to let him closer than that, his looming presence came as a reminder of the constant danger they were in until Silas got what he wanted. But would he stop there? What if, once he found Sam's brother, he didn't move on? What if he stayed? Her heart raced, and she jumped at the sound of the Jeep door echoing in the driveway.

Owen stepped out of the Jeep, his eyes scanning the property, first with curiosity and then confusion. She quietly uttered a prayer in Spanish and kept her gaze averted from the windows of the garage apartment because they were being watched. Taking a deep breath, she softened her tone.

"Help me bring in the groceries," she said, trying to keep

an air of authority, despite her weariness. "And don't even think about going over there. Got it?"

Owen huffed as if offended, but he knew better than to challenge her.

"Can't I at least look?" he pleaded, pointing toward the motorcycles parked near the garage.

"No," Caitlyn said sternly, grabbing two bags from the back of the Jeep before making her way up the porch stairs. Owen followed reluctantly, glancing longingly at the bikes before turning away.

"You'll get to ride one soon enough," she said over her shoulder, sensing his eagerness to drive a motorcycle. Grumbling, Owen carried the groceries into the house with his arms, and Caitlyn, who had a few more bags in her hands, greeted him.

He followed her outside to an old Chevy near the bottom of the stairs that led up to the apartment. Inside, they could hear gruff voices and angry shouts. Caitlyn paused at the base of the stairs, the sound tightening the knot of worry in her stomach. Glancing up at the building, she saw no sign of Pops. A wave of apprehension washed over her. Was Silas yelling? Was something wrong?

"I can't see Pops?" His eyes pleaded for her to let him.

Caitlyn forced a smile for Owen. "Looks like Pops isn't available right now, *mijo*," she said softly, ruffling his hair and resting a hand on his shoulder. "He has other things on his agenda." Internally, she debated her next move. Like Owen, curiosity tugged at her to seek the commotion above the garage, but what if Silas saw her and misinterpreted it as her spying on him?

Owen stared at the building, brooding silently before finally turning back to Caitlyn. "It's because of that man, the one who is my father."

Caitlyn hesitated, knowing lying to her son would only cause them problems later. She took a deep breath and exhaled slowly before finally speaking. "It's complicated, *mijo*."

"I don't understand."

"It's best you don't," she said sadly, not wanting to hurt Owen, but this was for the best. For them both.

But Owen wasn't ready to give up so easily and stepped closer to her with a determined expression, declaring what little independence he still had. "What if Pops needs me?"

Caitlyn's heart ached for him. She hated keeping secrets, but she couldn't bear the thought of him anywhere near Silas and hugged her son closely. Engine grease stained the back of his t-shirt, and the air smelled of gasoline. She looked into his big brown eyes, determined not to show him her worry.

"Then I'm sure he'll come looking for you."

Owen contemplated what she said, "But what about the man, Silas?"

"What of him?" Caitlyn asked, softly.

"He's my father."

"*Sí, mijo,*" she said firmly, "but he's no *padre*. It is best to keep your distance from him. He won't be staying for long, so don't get attached."

Her son's gaze skittered away, and he shifted uncomfortably, shrugging his shoulders to hide his emotions. Owen's voice was quiet but determined when he spoke, a sign that his grandfather had been at work, instilling the warped belief that men should avoid showing their feelings.

"Pops said I should clean up the garage some more." Owen followed her through the door into the kitchen, where he dumped the groceries on the counter. "He needs me. How else can he get the shop on its feet again? That's cool, right?"

"The shop is fine the way it is."

"But Pops said you'd get to paint more. You love to paint bikes," Owen argued.

Caitlyn paused, placing her bags next to Owen's on the counter, when she heard Owen call his father by his proper name, a slight gesture of defiance that Pops had allowed. At least they hadn't gotten close enough for Owen to call Silas Papa or Dad like most kids.

She had to find a way out of this mess with no one getting hurt. Leave it to Silas to try to pull her back into his shady business deals. She didn't want to be involved and didn't need him or Pops to continue doing custom paint jobs for customers. She enjoyed having the option of choosing what jobs she accepted. Fear tightened around her heart as she thought of what had happened before. She couldn't bear to endure it again.

Rather than argue, Caitlyn changed the subject. Owen's bottom lip trembled as he looked down at his feet, but he nodded somberly when Caitlyn suggested they see Sam at the farm later. She adjusted her grip on the plastic grocery bags and smiled reassuringly at him. She should have told Owen more about his father. What kind of mother would she be to not protect her child? But how could she wipe away the dream of a father in Owen's mind by drowning it in the reality of all the bad things Silas did, which ended up landing him in jail? Or that it was Caitlyn who made sure he went there in the first place?

He looked so much like his father, with that same defiant chin tilt.

With a gentle hand, she brushed an errant strand of hair from his face and forced her voice to remain steady. "Owen, I know you want to help Pops and hang with Silas. It's best we leave them to settle things in the garage first." And conclude Silas's business here. What made him think he could reopen their business and then go causing trouble with her friend's family? Did he not think he'd go back to jail again?

One other option lingered in the back of her mind. She considered it long ago, and Sam tried to talk her into doing it. With Silas back, Caitlyn might not have a choice.

Looking at Owen, she said, "For now, you'll go stay with

Sam. I know she appreciates all the help of having you there."
And she needed to make plans, regretting, once more, having
to involve Sam.

Owen scowled and wrinkled his nose in disgust. She
smiled sadly, unable to explain why he had to go, or why his
grandfather might be in trouble. One day he'd understand, if
not from her, then from experience.

"I promise it won't be every shift," she said, reaching to
brush some stray hairs from his forehead. Owen ducked
before she could touch him. "If you stick to the farm and help
Sam out, I can get you that new video game you've been
talking nonstop about."

Owen gave her a sidelong glance. "You mean the one Dan
already bought me?"

"Dan? Did he tell you to call him that?" Her stomach fluttered. She tried to play it cool by pretending not to know who
he was.

"His name is Daniel, so I called him Dan. He said it was
cool."

Caitlyn's stomach twisted into a knot as she loaded
groceries onto the kitchen counter. Silas' menacing words
haunted her with each item she placed in the cupboard.

She glanced up to see Owen put a can of beans away in
the pantry, his brow knitted. She couldn't help but remember
how quickly things had changed since she first met Daniel and
the feeling that he could be someone she'd eventually rely on
even though they had just met.

Despite all her doubts about his intentions toward them, it
was clear he was trying to get to know them—but could
Daniel protect them from Silas? Her ex was a powerful man
who often got what he wanted through any means necessary.

The thought of taking Owen away and leaving Pops here
sent daggers through Caitlyn's chest—but she would do whatever it took to ensure her son's safety, no matter the cost. No
matter how much pain it may cause her or anyone else.

13

Sebastian rode out of town, the sun setting in a glorious array of oranges and pinks. He left the town behind and ventured toward the empty field that stretched before him. Driving his Rebel farther into the countryside, he reached the deserted grounds of a long-forgotten battlefield. He left his motorcycle and walked along the tree line. The wind picked up and rustled his clothing as he took in the scene before him.

The sky was now a deep navy blue, and the stars were coming out, twinkling in the night sky. Sebastian approached a tall cannon in the middle of the field. He pulled out his cell phone and hit re-dial. It was dangerous to dial an unknown number, but he hadn't heard from Haden. They'd agreed to use the burner phone for an emergency. If anyone caught Sebastian, he didn't want them tracing his calls back to his friend. Luckily, it was probably a scam call, and he tensed when a voice came on the line.

"Hello?"

Not a scammer. "Hello."

"B?" came the voice on the other end.

"Yeah. It's me."

"We thought something happened to you. I've been calling for the past few days."

"I didn't recognize the number." He sighed with relief. "I took your advice. This way, it's not traced back to my main number." And he wouldn't have had any way to tell him until now. Sebastian glanced around the shadows, watching for movement as low-laying fog drifted across the land in the distance, resulting from the humidity and the rain coming at night. Farther out, a flicker of light breached the darkness from a car's headlights, illuminating a portion of the field as it descended the road. The light did not stretch far enough to reach him.

Sebastian took a few steps farther back into the dark. "How's Holly?"

"Stressed."

"Anything I can do to help?"

"Come back to us? Bring a wedding venue with you." Haden barked a short laugh.

"If only," Sebastian muttered.

"Sorry. I didn't mean to joke."

Sebastian sat alongside the cannon, looking off into the horizon. "Wedding plan trouble?" He didn't want to address the fact he might never return to Johnstown.

Haden let out a humorless chuckle. "You have no idea."

"That bad?"

"Hols' mother objects to every venue. I don't see why it should matter. We're paying for this shindig."

"This is what? The second time you've postponed?"

"Third, actually."

"Listen, you need a place. I know someone."

"Yeah, I'm getting ready to elope. Charlie thought it was a good idea, too."

For a minute or two, Sebastian lost track of the reason for the call. It was as if he wasn't in hiding or avoiding his brothers from back in Johnstown. The struggles Haden and

Holly faced with her mother made Sebastian wish he could see them get married. The wedding talk reminded him of Holly's father, Charlie Brooks. After an accident that nearly took Charlie's life, Sebastian worried about the old timer.

"How is good ole' Charlie?"

The first mistake the Sharks MC made was going after Charlie. The man ran Brooks' Motorcycle Shop. He led the Thunder Valley MC as president until his accident last year. Holly returned home to help care for him. She and Haden worked out their long-standing differences, but then the Sharks tried to kidnap her. Sebastian helped her escape. At least he'd done that one thing right.

"Rehab is treating him well. He won't ever be out of the chair, but he seems to have accepted his new role." Charlie Brooks was wheelchair bound for the rest of his life because of the accident.

"Good to hear." But Sebastian had been lingering here for too long now, and despite wanting to talk to Haden longer, he needed to get back and check on his surveillance videos at Grace Meadows. The eerie quietness of this place sent prickles against his skin.

"You've been trying to reach me. I doubt it was about family." Sebastian hated he needed to be so abrupt. He hated it more that he wouldn't be there to stand beside his best friend when he got married.

"You need to lie low. I called to tell you not to come back here."

Closing his eyes, he figured Haden was contacting him because something had happened. He prayed for good news —not this time.

"B?"

"Yeah, I'm here," Sebastian said, opening his eyes and staring out the darkness blanketing the sky. Faint twinkles of stars glittered in the black.

"There's been someone asking about you."

Sebastian scratched his jaw. "I'm listening."

"Chris. Said you and him were tight." Chris, aka Chum, was nothing more than a tadpole to the Sharks when they were both prospects. A guppy in Pike's eyes. Several times, Sebastian noticed Pike let things slide with Chum. Things other men would have gotten punished far worse than the young man alongside him. He chalked it up to Chum's connection to the club. Chum was the son of one of the members, and for reasons Sebastian had yet to discover, Pike let Chum slide. Except Pike was dead. And the Sharks disbanded. Most, if not all, sat in the state pen. It seemed Chum got exempt from it, too.

"He had a thing for Audra." Just saying her name splintered a piece of him. An image of her dying in his arms flashed through his memory. He closed his eyes against the recollection. He should have been there to keep her safe. Her son would never meet her.

"He's been asking questions. About you." Haden's voice drew him out of the past.

Maybe he lost his way without a club. "How long ago?"

"Joined a few weeks ago."

"And he's been asking about me?" He needed to know more before deciding how to handle the situation.

"At first, it was comments. He claimed he wanted to change his ways. He's been attending church with Larry and Marge. They've sort of taken him under their wing. Some others are convinced he has hero worship, but I don't know. There's just something about the way he showed up and joined. A few days ago, he came to the shop and asked about your old ride."

"What about it?" Sebastian held his breath.

"I got the new frame. I've been rebuilding it."

"I told you not to bother."

"What kind of brother would I be?"

"What does he want with my old ride?" Sebastian gulped

in a breath. "Everyone knows your place burnt and Charlie's bike collection with it. Only you knew my ride was in that collection."

"That's my point."

Sebastian gazed at the path back to his motorcycle. A dark shadow lingered around it. He watched, but nothing stirred. Rising back to his feet, the ancient battlefield creeped him out, and he wasn't easily one to get spooked.

"Tell Holly to call Samantha Daniels at Grace Meadows. Tell her you're a friend of mine. You've always wanted a destination barn wedding, right?" It was hard to imagine Haden getting married while Sebastian would have to remain in hiding. This wasn't the way Haden wanted it when he asked Sebastian to be his best man. If they came to Grace Meadows, Sebastian wasn't sure he could resist the temptation of spying on their wedding. An eerie feeling of being watched, a pricking sensation at the back of his neck, caused him to turn around. His gaze swept across the deserted battlefield.

"Riiiight," Haden said, slowly.

"Thanks for the info. I'm glad Chris showed up with you all. I don't think he's dangerous. Just lost." For now. "Stay safe."

"Same."

Sebastian ended the call. Scrolling through his phone, he saw the notification and sucked in a breath. He had an email from his sister, Sam. Glancing around, he hit the app and opened the message. Scanning through the lines quickly, his hand tightened on the phone.

I know you're busy keeping the bad guys from hurting other people. I know you won't respond to this message, and that's okay. I am not giving up on you. I miss you. I hate to ask, but if you have a minute, I have a friend who is in trouble. Sadly, you've never met her because you never come home. Long story short, her ex is out of prison. It's too soon. Can you find out why? Please, Seb. It's important. I love this person like a sister. Her ex's name is Silas Varela. He's a past associate of the Ghost Riders.

Stay safe.

Sam

Sebastian drove his motorcycle to La Rosa's and parked it beside Yeats' big black hog. The smell of freshly baked pizza was in the air when he opened the door. He spotted Yeats in a booth flirting with a waitress, Alison, and sipping on a Coke. He held up a hand when he saw Sebastian and motioned for him to join him.

"You check in with the missus," Yeats said, nodding at the pizza counter and winking at Alison as she turned to go. "Grab us another Coke, would you?"

"Whatever you say, Yeats." Alison gave them a rosy-cheeked smile.

Sebastian slid into the booth. The message from Sam was hot in his pocket. He pulled out his phone, flipped to the email, and slid it toward Yeats.

Yeats spun the phone around to read the message. His face remained neutral.

"Why is Sam asking about Silas Varela?" Sebastian kept an eye on Alison getting his drink. Watching to see if Caitlyn came.

"Sheesh. Don't say his name. It's as bad as saying *Voldemort* around here."

"You're gonna compare a dude to a villain in a kid's book?"

Yeats took a sip of his Coke before answering. "Sam's probably worried about Caitlyn. She's been leaving Owen out there while she's here working. Caitlyn and Sam are good friends. They both dated that troublemaker, Alex, back in high school."

Sebastian pulled the phone back. "Why didn't I know this? I never met her in high school."

"She came late in the year. She's a few years younger. You were gone by the time Cat and Sam started hanging out together."

He turned off the screen and leaned back into the booth as he shoved the phone back in his pocket. His sister's painful expression, the tears rolling down her face from that night, knocked the wind out of him. He promised God he would spend the rest of his life seeking justice and protecting girls like his sister. Then Audra's dying face appeared in his mind. Right until the end, Audra protected her son and others by passing on the information needed to bring down the Sharks for their illegal activities. He should have been the one protecting her. He should have followed and kept a closer eye on his sister. No gun or badge could put an invisible shield of security around them. Sebastian let himself believe if he did as he promised, God would do the rest. He almost laughed at the foolishness of it. Yet, he'd kept his promise. Sebastian did what he told God he would do. So why, then, did those he tried to protect get hurt? What made him think it would be different with Caitlyn?

Yeats glanced over his shoulder at Alison. The short blond spoke with a customer at the counter. Sebastian could see his drink by her arm. He needed it now. The scents of garlic and yeast turned his once-growling stomach sour as the seconds ticked.

Yeats warned him about the Ghost Riders' creed—about Caitlyn. He liked the woman and cared about her kid. Okay, maybe it wasn't the right word. He liked Audra, too, and cared about her like a sister. Caitlyn wasn't anything near the sister vibe. The woman caused him to do things, nice things, like mow yards, buy ice cream, and play car racing games with her son. He needed to get out while he still held part of himself together.

Caitlyn wasn't a free woman. The Ghost Riders still considered her one of them. Now her old man was back. Had she gone to Sam? Is that why his sister was asking? He swiped his hair off his forehead in annoyance. Did Sam know he was close by? Too many questions swirled in his mind.

"You should find someone else to work at the motorcycle range."

"You're leaving." Yeats, with his dark curly hair and black beard, shook his head. "Are you going back? Are you taking back your badge?"

"No." He didn't add a few choice words because the family was having dinner nearby. What once became a forced way to converse to fit in with the Sharks, now was too easy to slip into, and now that he no longer had to pretend, he wanted to be one of them. Would he ever be Sebastian Daniels again? Most likely not. Sebastian Daniels disappeared the day Audra died.

Yeats leaned on his elbows on the table. "I didn't take you for the type to let a bunch of bikers run you out of town."

"I'm not running." Yes, no, okay, maybe. He was one for three, and the odds were still stacked against him.

"Then what are you doing?"

On the other side of the counter, Sebastian caught sight of Caitlyn, her black hair pulled up in a messy bun and those faded blue jeans skintight. She had flour on the front of her shirt. The woman could have worn a burlap sack and been just as gorgeous.

Yeats followed his gaze and grinned. "You care about her and the kid."

Sebastian scowled, a reflex more than anything. He wasn't ready to admit the truth, even to Yeats. Yeats took a long drink of his soda and lowered the glass, his gaze steady on the waitress a few tables over.

"Never pegged you for a blonde type." Sebastian lifted his

chin as the waitress returned with his drink and another for Yeats.

"Alison and I go way back. Her brother Chase is a member of the Soldiers of Christ, like us."

"Like you. I'm still affiliated with the Thunder Valley Chapter. Once a brother, always a brother."

Yeats' gaze followed Alison again. They both went silent as she approached.

"What can I get you two brothers tonight?" Alison pulled out her pad. "Pepperoni or pineapple and ham?" Fluttering her lashes at him, Yeats stared so hard that Sebastian feared his friend would drool on the table.

"I think you should bring him both." Put the poor guy out of his misery.

Sebastian grinned as Alison jotted down the order. "Medium or large?"

"He likes 'em large." Sebastian took a large gulp of soda to prevent her from seeing his mischievous grin.

Alison rolled her eyes and turned to leave. Yeats reached over, took her hand, and let her fingers slip through his as she left them. Then he turned and growled, making Sebastian laugh.

"Alison, is that the one you've been seeing? You've been holding out on me."

"Stick around, and you might find out a few things," Yeats said.

"I can't."

"What did the missus say?" Yeats asked.

Missus was Yeats' code word for the mysterious person on the other end of the burner phone. Sebastian filled Yeats in on what Haden told him.

"He thinks this guy hanging out with them is bad news." Yeats' voice lowered to a whisper as he glanced around the restaurant.

"Yeah, I got that impression."

"You think the guy's dangerous?" Yeats asked.

"No." Chris had trouble fitting in, but Sebastian hadn't expected him to try tracking him down. Maybe finding Thunder Valley would help the younger man get back on the right track again. "I think you have bigger problems here."

"You mean Silas?"

Yeats filled Sebastian in about Silas, who had been involved in robberies, assaults, and even murder charges. A chill ran down Sebastian's spine as he listened.

"He shot a detective investigating him, tossed him in the outskirts of town for dead. Caitlyn hid the guy to protect him. Then she testified against Silas. Later, she discovered Silas and a few others were using the shop to launder cash."

"And her father, Welder?"

"He didn't have a clue. By then, the man had drunk his days away and trusted Silas with running the business. Casper tried stepping into Welder's place to smooth things out at the club, but Welder and Casper had some kind of disagreement, and Welder gave the power to Silas. It caused a rift in the family and almost divided the club."

A jolt of concern shot through Sebastian as he watched Caitlyn reach up to shove a pizza into the oven. Her movement was awkward, and she flinched back with a startled cry as she bumped into another worker. Heat flared in his chest—a mix of protectiveness and something more.

"You change your mind?" Yeats said from across from him.

"I'm not getting involved." The flimsy excuse tasted like ash in his mouth. Getting involved meant potentially facing Caitlyn's old man. He didn't have the luxury of another complication, especially one that could endanger keeping Caitlyn and Owen safe.

Caitlyn's ex wasn't the only complication. There was Caitlyn herself. What if she discovered his identity? He couldn't let that happen.

Yeats scratched his beard. "You have a funny way of avoiding women."

"You have terrible taste in pizza toppings for an ex-ranger," Sebastian muttered, downing the rest of his soda in one gulp.

"A little pineapple never harmed anyone." Yeats lifted his gaze, watching for their food to arrive.

Sebastian spun his empty plastic cup in his hands, the ice rattling. "I'm still not getting involved... it's a bad idea." Losing Caitlyn's trust and seeing the spark of betrayal in her eyes gnawed at his conscience.

Yeats leaned back, crossing his arms. "That bad, huh?"

Sebastian held up the glass as Alison returned with their order. She placed it on the table and took Sebastian's empty glass to refill. He tapped a rhythm on the table, waiting for her to depart from their table. She winked at Yeats as she headed away.

Yeats crossed his arms on the table and waited.

"You don't know what happened." Hot, searing heat, a phantom echo of a bullet tearing through flesh, seared into his shoulder. His vision swam, and he fought the urge to gasp for air. But the moment passed as quickly as it came, leaving him shaky and pale.

"Someone died on your watch," Yeats said, reaching for a slice of pizza. "I get that. You put bad guys away. All's good in the world, right?" Yeats' sarcasm hinted with understanding.

Sebastian scoffed.

"It's about the woman. Something bad went down, and you lost her and now you blame yourself. Did you love her?"

Sebastian considered the question. His gaze drifted to Caitlyn. She'd disappeared into the kitchen somewhere. Did he love Audra? Maybe he did. Maybe he cared about her a little more than he wanted to admit, if he were being honest with himself. They both carried complications, but that wasn't what Yeats was asking.

"Like a sister. She was eighteen, maybe nineteen. I'm sure the mother had something to do with getting her mixed up with Pike and his crew. She would graduate in another year from college. I don't even remember what degree. Pike went after her. She helped a woman escape, and I helped her. All I could think of was, 'What if she'd been Sam?' I holed her up in a motel and warned her to avoid contact with others. Of course, she didn't listen. I couldn't protect her. I—" Never one to cry, the admission choked him up.

"Seb, It's okay."

"Daniel."

"Daniel." Yeats repeated, then took a bite of his pizza.

Sebastian scrubbed a hand over his face, the gesture rough. The last thing he needed was Caitlyn to see him unravel. He prayed she never questioned his past.

He downed the rest of his soda in a single gulp, and a memory of Audra and her baby rose to the surface. Her son would never meet her. He failed to protect her.

"You need to let go. It wasn't your fault."

"How do you know?"

"Because I know you," Yeats said firmly, meeting Sebastian's gaze. "You blamed yourself for what happened to Sam, and you're doing the same thing with that woman. You did what you had to do." He paused, then added, "Sometimes, things fall apart even when we do everything right. But that doesn't mean there's no hope."

"Hope," Sebastian muttered.

Yeats reached for a napkin, wiping a smudge of grease from his hand. "The hope that comes from knowing you're not alone in this burden. Have you considered…giving it to God?"

Sebastian's lips thinned. "There's nothing to give." He slouched into the booth.

"There's always something to give. God is big enough for our worries. He wants us to share them."

"I did." Sebastian hissed out a breath. "He did nothing about them."

"The answers are not always the ones we want. Remember when your father told you not to mess with the John Deere, and we both thought we could get it out and surprise him?"

Sebastian winced. "Yeah. Don't remind me." That summer, his father made him till his mother's garden by hand. He also rebuilt the entire south pasture's fence. Yeats' father took away his driving privileges for a couple of months.

"Didn't work out the way we thought it would. Had we listened to your dad, we wouldn't have worsened the situation."

"It doesn't get any worse than this."

"How do you know? What's God telling you to do?"

"I don't know." He stopped asking, or maybe he'd stopped listening. Seeing Audra lowered into the ground sealed a part of him so deep the pain nearly ran him through.

"You got to talk to him. Pray." Yeats leaned back and put his arm up in the back of the booth. "Now, what are we going to do about Samantha's email?"

Yeats might think prayer was the answer, but Sebastian knew better. He needed a more strategic approach to navigate this situation without revealing his true identity to Caitlyn.

"Nothing. I need to talk to Caitlyn first." Sebastian slipped off his jacket and got comfortable watching Caitlyn in the distance. Considering the trust they'd built, having Caitlyn discover he was related to Sam might sever their relationship. In her anger, she might keep him from hanging out with Owen. He needed to ensure they were both safe, even if it meant facing her wrath one day.

Alison headed in their direction with his refill.

"And this Chris guy?"

"He's the least of my worries."

14

Caitlyn, her hair damp with sweat that clung to her temples in tendrils, struggled to balance an orange cone precariously on the stack. A bead of sweat rolled down her cheek, leaving a cool trail contrasting with the warmth spreading through her chest. It wasn't just the exertion of teaching motorcycle safety all day. It was the man standing beside her.

Daniel's gaze was unwavering. There was a hint of amusement in his eyes, a playful glint that mirrored the butterflies erupting in Caitlyn's stomach. Caitlyn forced a smile as she grabbed the remaining cones. Turning toward the storage shed, a strong hand brushed against hers as Daniel reached out. His fingers skimmed along hers, sending a spark against her skin.

Caitlyn flustered, quickly pulled back, shoving the cones into his waiting arms.

"Hey," he said, his voice laced with a casual ease that sent a tremor through her. "Let me take those."

Caitlyn hesitated but allowed him to take the cones from her. "You did great with the guy who missed the turn twice. I wouldn't have gotten him to follow directions without your patience."

"I've had some practice over the years dealing with troublesome people," he said.

"Really?" Caitlyn's curiosity peaked. "What did you do before coming here?"

"Security," Daniel said, lifting the cones with ease. "Let me take you and Owen away from this for a bit." Caitlyn mulled it over for a minute. It was such a bad idea, but... "Owen would love that," she admitted. "I work tonight, and Owen will be at Grace Meadows with Sammy."

"You're a good mom, Caitlyn," Daniel said, his gaze softening. Her smile faltered. She hadn't expected the compliment. The reminder of Owen, why she couldn't get close to someone like Daniel, hung heavy in the air. "Monday?"

But before she could respond, Daniel reached out, his thumb brushing away a stray strand of hair that had escaped her ponytail and tickled her cheek. The sensation of his touch lingered on her skin, like a spark igniting a bonfire within her.

Caitlyn held her breath. Her attraction to Daniel, this yearning for life without fear, threatened to consume her. The weight of Silas's demands, the potential consequences for her and Owen, threatened to suffocate her.

"You seem...tense," Daniel murmured, his voice a husky whisper. His eyes, the color of the sky on a clear sunny day, so blue and vivid, searched her face. "I promise to make it fun."

Suddenly, a glint of chrome caught her eye from the far end of the deserted parking lot. A black motorcycle with blue flames across the tank approached the church's parking lot. Panic flooded her veins. It was Pops' Harley. It couldn't be a coincidence. The man astride the bike wasn't her father. His build didn't match.

Caitlyn couldn't tear her eyes away from the approaching motorcycle. Her gaze darted around the practice range, searching for a hiding place, any place that wouldn't give them away. Daniel stood beside her, his presence a comfort even as it amplified her terror.

"Is everything alright?" he asked, his voice laced with concern as he leaned closer.

"It's nothing," she said as the unmistakable roar of Pops' motorcycle engine filled the air. Caitlyn wrapped her arms around her waist. *Seriously, Pops? You let Silas take your motorcycle?* How did he know where she'd hidden the key?

The engine roar grew closer, each rumble a hammer blow to her already fragile composure. "I...I think I left something back at the shed," she stammered, her voice barely a whisper.

"Go on," Daniel said, seemingly oblivious to the urgency in her voice. "I'll finish up here and bring these to the shed."

The calmness in his voice spiked her growing panic. "No," Caitlyn blurted, the word escaping her lips before she could stop it.

His smile faltered, replaced by a flicker of confusion. This wasn't the time to explain.

"I don't want to hold you up," she said, forcing a lightness that felt hollow. "I can finish here."

Daniel's smile faltered slightly, replaced by a hint of confusion. "Hey, we're partners, right? I am not about to leave you with all this."

Caitlyn wanted to scream. With every second passing, the motorcycle roar got closer. She needed to get Daniel to leave. Why did he have to be one of those guys who always wanted to help and think of others before himself?

"I, uh..." She kept her focus on the motorcycle, turning into the parking lot.

Daniel followed her gaze. "Maybe you should be the one to let me handle this."

Caitlyn's heart swelled. Daniel played video games online with Owen for the past week. He didn't have to do that, nor did he have to stay and face Silas. Caitlyn shook her head.

"No. Go. Please." Caitlyn chewed on her lip the closer the motorcycle drove toward them. "I can handle this."

"Caitlyn, I'm not leaving you alone."

Her gaze went back to the motorcycle. "It's better if you do."

Daniel gave a long look toward the approaching motorcycle. He brushed his fingers against hers, a lingering touch that quickened her heartbeat. "If that's what you want, but I'm holding you to it."

Spending time with Daniel outside the confines of working on the range was exhilarating, but terrifying. Right now, she needed him to leave if that were ever to happen.

"Take the back way out of the parking lot," she pleaded. *What was Silas doing here? A few Ghost Riders showed up for the morning session. What did they tell him?*

Daniel's eyes narrowed, and he pressed his lips together. A muscle in his jaw jumped. "I can stay."

"I can take care of myself. Please. Leave. I don't need more trouble, okay?"

"Did I say I didn't like this?"

"Yes." She chewed on her lip, glancing between the approaching motorcycle and Daniel.

"I'll be across the street at the ice cream place if you need me." He strode to his motorcycle, and Caitlyn turned her back, watching as Silas approached. A few moments later, she heard Daniel pull away on his Rebel.

God, why did her life have to keep getting more complicated?

As Caitlyn reached the shed, relief washed over her, mixed with a sliver of guilt and excitement for the unexpected date. But the sight of Silas riding on Pops' motorcycle quickly overshadowed the excitement. Silas finding out about her seeing Daniel outside of work sent a jolt of fear through her. What was she thinking, giving Daniel hope of something more when she'd put a target on his back for Silas's wrath?

Peeking out the shed door, she watched Daniel pull out of the church parking lot. The relief was short-lived. Silas drove toward her and stopped close to the shed. Stepping out and leaning against it, the tingles of excitement from earlier vanished, replaced by the heavy dread settling in the pit of her stomach. "What are you doing here, Silas?"

"Are you going to spread those cones for me, Kitty Cat?" Silas snickered.

Her eyelids fluttered with annoyance. Two more motorcycles pulled into the parking lot. Blue and Grover drove in figure eight formation around the parking lines on the asphalt.

Ignoring them, she finished locking up and moved toward her motorcycle with practiced calm.

Silas dismounted his motorcycle, rolling back his shoulders and blocking her path. "It was a good move taking the kid to your friend's place. You find out anything?"

"You could have asked me that at the house," Caitlyn said, wanting to put distance between them. He knew where Owen was. Of course, Owen would tell Pops. Her father no longer had a spine, and Silas's threats kept her from voicing any concerns to her father.

Silas shrugged, his eyes glinting with a predatory gleam. "What can I say? I wanted to meet the new guy my woman works with and check out where she works."

"You just missed him," Caitlyn stepped around him, her jeans pockets feeling too tight as she tried to fish her key out.

Silas tilted his head and watched her. "What do you say we go have some ice cream? It doesn't look like he went far."

"Leave him be, Silas," Caitlyn said, refusing to look in the ice cream shop's direction. "We work together. Nothing more." She grabbed her helmet and pulled her ponytail down low to accommodate it.

"That's right, Kitty Cat. Nothing more. Because you're mine, and you'll get me that information."

"I'm working on it."

Silas grabbed her by the jacket. Despite the heat, she'd been wearing it all day for demonstrations. "Work harder. Maybe you should focus on hanging out with that friend of yours instead of playing teacher. Time is ticking. You don't want to keep me waiting much longer."

He yanked her closer, and the visor of Caitlyn's helmet fell. His gaze fell to her lips. "I think I'll get me some ice cream after all."

A chill swept over Caitlyn. "You don't have to do that. I'll get you what you want." Her voice wavered, despite her effort to put up a strong front.

"That's my girl. Protect the innocent no matter the cost. I know you'll get me that information because if I come across it from another source... the deal is off, and you'll be next on my list, sweetheart."

———

A relentless buzz ripped through Caitlyn's sleep like a buzz saw. Disoriented, she blinked at the unfamiliar shaft of sunlight slicing through the blinds. A quick glance confirmed it. She'd slept way past a decent hour. Shame washed over her, laced with guilt. She promised to take Owen to the video game store and to get a new pair of boots to work at Grace Meadows with Sammy.

Last night, after getting home from La Rosa's, she cleaned the pile of dishes in the sink and moved on to the rest of the kitchen. By the time she finished, it was well past three a.m.

The whirring sound continued to drift through the window. It wasn't the usual morning symphony of birdsong. It was mechanical, rhythmic, and...in her backyard?

Frowning, Caitlyn stumbled to the window and peeked out. Her breath hitched. There in her backyard, pushing a lawnmower, stood Daniel wearing an old ball cap. He was bathed in the soft light of the rising sun, the white T-shirt clinging to his broad frame, emphasizing the easy power of his movements.

What was he doing here? She couldn't remember them

setting a time. They'd come too close the other day when Silas and his old pals came to the range.

The sound of the mower ceased, and he looked toward the house. He waved in her direction. Heat flooded her cheeks. She should probably call down to him, but she watched his biceps flex with each push of the mower.

Caitlyn grabbed the old cotton robe hanging from the open drawer of her dresser. She rushed down the stairs, fumbling to tie the belt. The cool air nipped at her bare legs, but she didn't care.

Daniel came around the side of the house, pushing the mower. His movements sent a subtle ripple across his biceps.

"Daniel?" she called out, her voice husky with sleep. "What are you doing here?"

He shut off the mower, and the look of surprise faded when he grinned back. "Good morning, sleepyhead."

"You really don't have to do that," she mumbled, glancing around toward the garage apartment nestled discreetly behind the house. There was no sign of Pops' motorcycle or any of the Ghost Riders near the garage, but worry gnawed at her.

"I know. I want to," he said, pushing the mower closer to the porch. "Besides, a beautiful morning like this deserves to be spent outdoors. Not cooped up inside."

He stopped in front of her. The scent of freshly cut grass and something faintly citrusy mingled in the air.

"Actually," she began, searching for the right words. "About the other day…"

Daniel lifted his ball cap, wiping sweat from his brow with his arm, then settled his cap back on his head. For a split second, she caught a lighter tone of his hair near the roots and attested it to the sun, catching the strands at the right angle. She imagined his hair lighter with the intensity of his blue eyes, so different from her Hispanic inheritance.

"Don't worry about it," Daniel waved it off, but Caitlyn

saw the flash of disappointment cross his features. "I'm glad you're safe."

Her stomach sank. "Would you like a drink? I might have some sweet tea."

"I've got water in the truck, but thanks."

She noticed Yeats' landscaping truck for the first time. "Did you mow my entire lawn?"

"You must be a deep sleeper, or you worked late last night." Daniel leaned against the porch. "I'm sorry I woke you all up. I almost brought you coffee, but didn't know if you were a drink it black, cream, sugar, or fancy coffee type."

"You don't need to bring me coffee or mow my grass. We work together, Daniel, and I don't want to spoil our friendship."

"Ouch..." He placed a hand against his heart. "She pulled the friend card."

"It wouldn't be wise for me to lead you on," she said, unsure if she believed herself. A thousand what ifs ran through her mind, and none of them led to a place that changed the here and now.

Daniel rounded the porch and placed his foot on the first stair. "I'm asking you to go out for a fun afternoon, and you can bring Owen. Or we can meet for coffee and get to know each other. If you want to be friends, I'm okay starting there."

Before she could respond, the door creaked open, and Owen piped up. "Finally. You're awake. Are we going to the store? You promised."

"We're going. Give me a few minutes."

"Hey, Dan! Are you coming, too?"

Caitlyn's heart melted at Owen's inclusion of Daniel. Her son was spending more time with Daniel online, and a part of her worried. What if Daniel decided their life was too complicated or dangerous for him? Owen was attached to Daniel, and losing him as a part of their lives would crush her son.

"Sorry, bud. I've got three more stops today before I'm free to play."

Owen's face fell.

"Daniel and I were just discussing going on a tour of the battlefields," Caitlyn said, trying to distract Owen.

"Been there. Did that. On horseback," Owen huffed.

"There's a place close to here, less than an hour's drive, where we can race go-karts if you're down with that?" Daniel asked, offering an alternative.

Owen's face brightened. "H—Yeah!"

"Hey!" Caitlyn whirled around toward Owen. "We don't talk that way in this house."

"Pops and Papa…Silas do," Owen challenged her.

"Whatever your mom says goes, else we can't hang more if she doesn't approve," Daniel said, a look of confusion on his face.

"What I don't approve of his language." She pointed at Owen and realized she'd been speaking in Spanish. No wonder Daniel was confused, but he followed enough to know she wasn't happy with her son.

"I'm sorry." Owen glared at her, a deep scowl on his face. "Can we still go with Dan to drive the go-karts?"

"I'll think about it while you change out of your PJs and get ready to go to the store."

As Owen turned and went back inside the house, Caitlyn sighed. "Alright. Text me when you're done for the day, and Owen and I will meet you at La Rosa's. We can go from there on this adventure you've proposed." Hopefully, it was somewhere out of town where Silas or his buddies wouldn't be able to spy on them.

Daniel's gaze lingered on her for a beat too long. With warmth in his eyes, he said, "Deal." Before she could savor the feeling, a sharp crack from the garage ripped the air.

"That's my cue to get out of here." He winked and went to retrieve his lawnmower. She stood on the porch, her heart caught in her throat as Silas sauntered out of the garage. He paused, glancing at her, then at Daniel, who kept his head down and loaded his lawnmower on the back of the trailer attached to Yeats' truck.

Silas headed in her direction. Her lungs froze as he neared. "You can cancel the lawn boy. I take care of what's mine."

Daniel got in the truck, tilting his head away from them so as not to see his face.

"This isn't your lawn." Caitlyn's heart hammered against her ribs. Relief washed over her as Daniel pulled away in Yeats' truck and trailer. He made it away without encountering Silas. That was something, but the respite was short-lived.

Silas grabbed her by the chin. "I get done taking care of business here, and we'll be moving to a place of our own. You find out where Daniels is?"

Caitlyn's stomach churned. Moving? With Silas?

She didn't want to anger him. "Sammy hasn't heard from her brother in a couple of years." Caitlyn avoided looking at him, not wanting him to see the lie. She hadn't asked Sammy anything more about her brother.

"A man doesn't leave his family and not stay in contact. Sooner than later, he'll turn up, and you better hope your friend tells you where."

"Ready!" Owen burst out the door on the porch and slowed at the sight of Silas.

"What's the hurry?" Silas asked.

"Mom's taking me shopping. I'm getting new boots and trading some of my old games for a new one."

Silas ran his gaze over her. Caitlyn pulled her robe closer together, the thin fabric offering little comfort against the sudden chill that had settled over her.

"Is that so?"

"Give me a minute to change," Caitlyn said, her gaze

darting between Owen and Silas. "Owen, you need to go inside and make sure your room is clean before we leave."

"What?" Owen glared at her.

"Let the boy be, woman." Silas reached in his front pocket and pulled out a wad of cash. He pulled a few bills loose and handed them to Owen. "Keep your old games. You play them?"

Owen nodded, his eyes wide.

Caitlyn's skin crawled as she watched the exchange.

"This should be enough to get a new one and those boots."

Caitlyn opened her mouth to protest, but Owen took the money and looked at her expectantly. She rushed up the stairs to change, knowing better than to ask where Silas had come across that kind of money. Arguing with Silas in front of Owen could only escalate the situation and cause Owen to have questions she wasn't sure how to answer. Giving Owen a nudge into the house ahead of her, she vowed to keep her son from falling into the same life as his father. As she changed, a small voice of doubt whispered in her ear. Was she making a mistake by letting Daniel get involved in her life?

She had to be careful to walk the tightrope between protecting her son and keeping them all safe. But for now, she had to focus on getting them out of there, away from Silas's watchful eyes.

15

The late morning sun glinted off the mirror of Caitlyn's SUV as Daniel pulled his truck up beside her.

"He's here!" Owen exclaimed, pointing at the truck.

Caitlyn forced a smile, her stomach twisting into a knot. She spent the morning wrestling with her conscience, torn between the fear of Silas and the hope of spending time with Daniel. Ultimately, she decided to see where things might lead with Daniel. It was easier to explain the change in plans to Owen than Daniel's role in their lives.

Daniel stepped out of the truck, a slanted grin on his face. She rolled down her window and Daniel gripped the seal and bent to peer in at them. "Ready to go, bud?"

Owen nodded eagerly, a large curl of his dark hair falling between his eyes. "Wait until you see the new game I got. It's so cool!"

"You can tell me all about it on the way. You riding with me?"

Owen looked at Caitlyn, and she nodded. She'd hoped he would offer. If anyone passed by, they'd think she was at work. "I need to be back by four."

"Four. Got it." He walked around and opened her door.

Stunned by his gesture, she stared at him until the other door slammed from Owen getting out. She rolled the windows up and got out of the SUV. The vehicle door between them, he leaned in, breathing in deep. "You showered."

"You expected me to show up smelling of sweat and gas from the lawnmower?" One of his brows rose.

She almost leaned farther, enjoying the scent of his woodsy cologne. "Is this new?"

"The smell?"

"Well, it's not grass or lawnmower," she said, her cheeks getting a little hot.

"Oh, yeah. I borrowed Yeats' shampoo." Then he pressed his finger to his lips. "Shh… Don't tell him."

"Come on. Let's go!" Owen tilted his head back and groaned. "We don't got all day."

Daniel chuckled and Caitlyn stepped out of the way, sweeping his arm for her to step away from the door. She didn't bother correcting her son's bad English.

"Best we get this show on the road," Daniel said.

Owen wasted no time. He wrenched open the truck door and clambered into the back seat. Caitlyn hesitated for a moment, having second thoughts. She worried if Silas or one of his friends caught them what implications it would bring. *You better be worth it, Jones.*

The drive to the go-kart track was filled with Owen's chatter about his new game. Daniel listened and asked questions, and if she didn't know better, she'd say Daniel was as excited as Owen about the new game. Caitlyn tried to keep up with their video game talk, but her mind kept drifting back to La Rosa's.

When they arrived at the go-kart track, the air buzzed with the roar of engines and the excited chatter of several other families with kids around Owen's age. Owen practically leaped out of the truck, his eyes wide with anticipation.

Daniel held open the door for Caitlyn to get out of the truck.

A warmth spread through her at the gesture. She chewed on her lip as Owen ran ahead. Daniel reached out, his fingers brushing lightly against hers as he offered a hand to follow. Caitlyn hesitated for a split second, a part of her wanting this connection and the other part cautious, protective, holding her back. Owen, oblivious to what was behind him, shouted for them to hurry. Caitlyn laced her fingers through Daniel's. He gave her hand a squeeze, sending a thrill through her. She glanced over at Daniel, and he grinned. "Why don't we grab some hot dogs and a drink before we hit the track? There's mini golf, too."

Owen turned, walking backward. "Mini golf?"

"I thought your mom might want to play," Daniel said.

Owen snorted. "Mom's gonna beat you on the track. After me, of course."

He smacked his chest, and Caitlyn laughed. "*Mijo*, this is not a competition."

"Says who?" Daniel asked, his eyes twinkling. "I fully intend to burn some rubber on that track. If you don't want to race, I won't hold it against you."

Caitlyn let go of his hand, wishing for a moment she still held it. Losing his touch made her want to grip it again, but her cheeks heated, too embarrassed to reach out and take the man's hand. This wasn't a date, and her son was watching. "I'll leave you both eating my dust."

"I don't know, Owen. Sounds like a challenge to me," Daniel said.

Owen shouted ahead of them, "I'm gonna win!"

"Hot dogs first," Caitlyn said. "Race second."

"Aw, Mom!"

"Your mom's right. We need sustenance if we're going to race."

Caitlyn nodded, her surprise outweighing her apprehension. Daniel caught up with Owen, and they headed toward the concession stand. As they waited for their food, Caitlyn thanked God for a normal day, away from the Ghosts, as a brief respite from her life.

The hotdogs were greasy, the fries crispy, and the drinks cold. "A little racing fuel."

Caitlyn unwrapped her hotdog, and there was a dollop of ketchup and mayo already mixed on the bun.

"Mayo and ketchup together?" Daniel asked with mock horror, snatching a fry from her basket. "I almost didn't put it on. I thought Owen was joking."

"Well, the joke is on you," Caitlyn declared, taking a bite. Once she swallowed, she patted her lips with a napkin and said, "It's a delicacy."

Owen laughed, following Daniel's lead and stealing another one of her fries.

"More like an abomination." Daniel attempted to take another, and she pulled her fries closer to protect them. "What do you have on yours?"

"Mustard."

"Keep it away from my fries." Caitlyn grabbed a fry and dipped it in her ketchup and mayo from her hotdog.

"Mine, too." Owen gave Daniel a look that made Caitlyn laugh.

"Don't tell me it's two on one here?" Daniel threw up his hands. "I thought you were with me, Owen?"

Owen unwrapped his hotdog and took a huge bite. While chewing his food, he shook his head. "K... up" he said around, trying to chew.

"Mouth closed while you chew. We don't need to see your food, and we're not in a hurry," Caitlyn said.

"Says who?" Daniel asked.

"Are we having a food eating contest?" Owen asked, taking another big bite.

"No," Caitlyn said the same time as Daniel. They both locked gazes for a long moment.

"We'll save that for on the racetrack," Daniel said, grabbing a few fries from his basket.

"Just wait until you see my driving skills." She took a bite of her fry

Owen's eyes sparkled with excitement. "I'm gonna beat you both."

"Then you better eat up." Daniel lifted his brows and reached for another fry, this time from Owen's basket. "Going to burn a lot of fuel when we race."

Caitlyn reached for one of Daniel's fries as he reached for hers. They both paused, mid-reach, and Caitlyn grinned. She snatched a fry. Then took two, dipping them in ketchup and mayo.

"Hey!" Daniel exclaimed, mock outrage in his voice. "Two fries? That's a declaration of war. What say you, Owen?"

Mouth full of hotdog, her son wholehertly agreed. Two against one.

Daniel winked and slid his fries closer.

After they finished, Daniel tossed away their trash. "Alright, racers," Daniel said, wiping his hands free of the trash. "Time to put your skills to the test."

Owen and Caitlyn exchanged a determined look. She held in her laugh and grinned at him. They followed Daniel. "Mom, don't be too sad when I win."

Caitlyn brushed her hand over his head. "I'll do my best."

Daniel glanced over his shoulder at her, and Caitlyn chewed on her lip. He put on a pair of sunglasses and gave her a lopsided grin that sent a flutter in her chest. If she wasn't careful, she might like Daniel... too much.

The go-kart track was a blur of color and speed. Owen, fueled by hot dogs and excitement, took the lead. Caitlyn, determined not to let her son show her up, pushed her kart to its limits. Daniel, however, seemed to hold back, letting Owen maintain his lead. What was that man doing?

"Come on, slowpoke!" Owen yelled over the roar of his

kart as he neared her. Caitlyn gritted her teeth and pushed harder, but Owen was a natural. He weaved through the bend with ease, his kart a blur of red. As they neared the final lap, Daniel finally picked up the pace and came up alongside her. Both Owen and Daniel passed her. He pulled alongside Owen, their karts bumping slightly.

"Hey, no funny business!" Owen shouted.

Daniel's kart swerved away, and Owen surged ahead, crossing the finish line just a hair's breadth before Daniel. Once they came to a stop and exited the go karts, Caitlyn threw her hands up in mock defeat. "Alright, alright, you both got ahead of me. But next time..."

Daniel laughed, pulling off his racing helmet. "Next time, I won't go easy on you." He pointed. "Either of you."

Owen's grin widened. "See, Mom? I told you I'd win."

"You did, *mijo*. You did." Caitlyn helped him take off his helmet. She gave Daniel a sidelong glance, and he shrugged. Her eyes narrowed on him.

"Again?" Owen asked after their third race, trying to keep her from taking off his helmet.

"You got us that time," Daniel said. "We'll have to save the rematch for another day. Your mom said she needed to be back by four, and we haven't hit the golf course yet."

Owen shoved the helmet at Caitlyn, a pout on his lips.

"You're too old to pout," she told him. "If this is how you act, then Daniel won't bring us again."

They played a game of mini golf, where Owen and Daniel turned it into another challenge. Caitlyn finished last and was almost reluctant to hit her ball through the clown's mouth to signal the end of the course, but she couldn't remember the last time she'd had this much fun in one afternoon.

As they walked back to Daniel's truck, Caitlyn wrapped her arm around Owen's shoulders. "We'll come back soon."

"Before school starts?"

"When is that?" Daniel asked with interest.

"We've got a month and a half yet," Caitlyn answered.

"Plenty of time for a rematch," Daniel said, approaching the truck and holding the door open for them. Owen hopped up in first and slid to the middle. Caitlyn brushed against Daniel, her heart lighter for once. Like Owen, she wished they had more time.

Before she got in, Caitlyn turned and looked at Daniel. His eyes remained hidden behind his sunglasses, but her gaze fell to his lips. Chewing on her bottom lip again, she tore her gaze away and hopped up into the truck. Slowly, Daniel shut the door, pausing momentarily. She looked up from buckling her seat belt. He tapped on the truck's hood and went to the other side.

On the drive home, Owen leaned against her. His eyes drooped from the long day of shopping and racing. Forty minutes later, they arrived back at La Rosa's. Neither spoke, with Owen napping against her for most of the ride back.

"It's almost four. I'm sorry. I should have tried getting away sooner, so we had more time. What are you going to do with Owen?" Daniel asked, pulling in beside her SUV.

She pulled out her phone and winced. "Could you take Owen to Grace Meadows for me? Sammy will expect him. I can call her and let her know you're dropping him off." The ease with which the request tumbled out surprised her. Just this morning, the idea of anyone watching Owen beside Sammy would have filled her with anxiety. But seeing Daniel interact with Owen chipped away that apprehension.

"Or he could come hang with me for most of the night. He's got the new game he hasn't played yet," Daniel proposed. The side of his mouth ticked up. Owen sat up, rubbing his eyes, and Caitlyn leaned away as her son stretched his arms.

Torn between Owen going to Grace Meadows and the unexpected warmth of Daniel's offer, she sighed. Not ready to explain what was happening between them, Caitlyn couldn't bear to keep much more from Sammy. And Caitlyn needed more time to figure *this* out. "I'd really like him to stay with Sammy tonight. No offense, but she's expecting him."

Daniel scratched the side of his face. "Yeah. I can do that."

A wave of gratitude washed over her. "You don't know how much I appreciate it." She turned to Owen and kissed him atop the head. "Daniel will take you to Sammy, and I'll see you after work. Be good, *sí?*" Daniel hurried from the truck and made his way around to grab the door for her.

Daniel took off his sunglasses. He leaned close, his voice a seductive murmur. "I'm here for you. Anytime. And, hey," he added, a playful glint in his blue eyes, "maybe we can find some time for a game of mini golf, or go out for a bite to eat, just the two of us."

Caitlyn's heart skipped a beat. "Maybe," she said, biting her lip and tilting her head up a fraction. Daniel's gaze lingered on her face, a slow smile spreading across his lips. He reached out, his fingers brushing a strand of hair from her cheek. His thumb grazed her lower lip. Their eyes locked, and Caitlyn held her breath, her gaze flickering to his lips and back to his eyes, a desperate hope blooming in her chest.

Daniel's gaze followed hers a moment. A flicker of something intense passed between them. Caitlyn's heart hammered in her chest, but instead of finding his lips on hers, a chaste kiss landed on her forehead. The unexpected tenderness sent a jolt of electricity through her. It sparked something sweet and confusing. Disappointment battled with a surge of affection as he pulled back, his eyes hooded from view for her to see if his emotions mirrored the swirl of those awakening inside her.

"See you soon?" he asked, his voice barely a whisper.

Caitlyn nodded, watching him walk back to the other side of his truck. As he drove away with her son, her hand lingered on the spot where his lips had touched her.

16

Sebastian's heart pounded in his chest as he pulled into Yeats' driveway. He had to think fast. "Just need to make a quick stop. You good, bud?" He glanced at Owen, who was happily engrossed in a game on Sebastian's phone. Thank you, Jesus, for the distraction.

"Stay here," Daniel told him and got out of the truck.

Opening the front door, Daniel stayed on the porch to keep an eye on Owen. "Hey, Yeats," Daniel called. "You in there, man?" A beat of silence stretched. Daniel wished he hadn't given Owen his phone, but both Yeats' motorcycle and another one of the company trucks was parked near the house. "Yeats!"

Just when worry built, Yeats lumbered out into the living room. "What's wrong?"

Daniel breathed a sigh of relief that whooshed past him like a summer breeze. "I need a favor."

Yeats approached him, his hair damp and wearing a pair of long shorts. "What kind of favor?"

"I need you to take Owen to Grace Meadows." Seeing Sam would blow his cover, and he couldn't afford for his sister to know he was this close by right now. Plus, he hadn't spoken to her in years. The fact he read her emails and never responded to them sat heavy in his conscience. He'd chosen silence as a shield to protect them both. But the bigger terror was Owen.

He glanced back at Owen, who looked up and gave him a thumbs up. He waved at the kid. If Owen discovered the truth about his identity, it would shatter everything. The trust they'd built, the life he carved out for himself. It would vanish in a puff of smoke. He couldn't let that happen. Not for Owen. Not for Sam or Caitlyn or even himself.

"Can you take him out to Sam?" Sebastian asked.

Yeats stared at him in disbelief.

"I'll owe you one," Daniel pressed. "You know why I can't go there."

"I know." Yeats placed his hands on his hips, looking more amused than anything. "I'm wondering how you got yourself in this predicament."

"I took Caitlyn and Owen to Chambersburg to that go-kart place. We ran late, and Caitlyn was going to be late for work if she took Owen there herself."

Yeats nodded, his mouth twitching to hold back the smile. Sebastian wanted to wipe it from his face as soon as he let it appear. "Listen," he said, trying to ignore the amusement dancing in Yeats' eyes. "This is important. You can check on Sam for me. Make sure she's okay, alright? But under no circumstances can you acknowledge you know I'm here or that you know about the email she sent."

Yeats' amusement vanished, replaced by a solemn under-standing. He met Sebastian's gaze, the weight of the impor-tance settling between them. Yeats rolled back his shoulders. "Sure, I'll do it. I don't mind checking on Sam. You'll have to explain to Caitlyn why Owen rode with me instead of you."

"I'll tell her it was the French fries."

"I'm not even going to ask," Yeats said. "Give me a minute to change. I'll take your truck so he doesn't have to get out."

"Change?" It was Daniel's turn to give Yeats a hard time.

"Like I'd go see Sam looking like this," Yeats snorted, heading back the hallway.

Daniel headed back outside. Steeling himself, he opened the truck door. Owen kept his head bent and playing a game on his phone. "Hey, bud. I'm going to need my phone back in a minute. Yeats is going to take you out to Grace Meadows."

Owen looked up, and his face fell. "I thought you were taking me. Mom said."

Those big brown eyes, a shade darker than his mother's, almost gutted Sebastian. "Something has come up, but tomorrow after work, we'll play that new game of yours."

"You don't have it," Owen said.

Daniel wiped his hands on his jeans. Since when did a kid make him nervous? "Yet. I'll get it to play. Can't be without my game partner."

Owen handed back the phone. "Cool. Tomorrow, right?"

"Tomorrow." Sebastian fist-bumped the kid, stepping back as Yeats jogged toward them. He changed into jeans and a short-sleeved shirt. Daniel tossed him the truck key. "Be good."

Owen pffted.

Yeats slid in the truck and lifted his chin toward Sebastian. "The little man and I got this. You do what you need to do."

"See ya, Dan."

"You owe me," Yeats said, starting the truck and closing the door.

Sebastian watched them pull out of the driveway and walk back into the house. Inside, he sat on the couch, pushing his fingers through his hair. He was off the hook. But how much longer could he keep this up? He couldn't keep avoiding Sam forever, not when she and Caitlyn were friends. He needed time to figure out how to handle keeping them all safe without screwing things up with Caitlyn.

Sebastian's fingers flew across the controller, the video game's rhythmic clicks and beeps filling the living room's silence. He was deep in concentration, battling a challenging boss, when the rumble of Yeats' truck pulling into the driveway broke his focus.

He paused the game and set the controller down, walking toward the window to watch as Yeats climbed out and headed towards the house. Opening the door for Yeats to step inside, Sebastian asked, "Got Owen settled in?"

"Yep. Sammy was happy to see him. Me too." Yeats grinned. "Shame you had to stay here. That a new game? Owen said Silas got him that."

Sebastian glanced behind him at the television. "Huh, Silas bought it for him."

"And then you bought it while I was out. Afraid the kid was going to kick your butt in this game, too?" Yeats tossed the truck keys at Sebastian, and he caught them.

"Demo. No harm in checking out what the kid is playing," he added quickly.

Yeats caught his eye with a knowing look. "Right," he said. "Just checking out the competition, huh?"

Sebastian forced a smile. He wasn't sure if he was annoyed at Silas for buying the game, or himself for allowing the other man's actions to make his defenses rise. Silas was the boy's father. No matter the type of man he was, who was Sebastian to rebuke the man for wanting to give his son a gift?

Yeats changed the subject. "Figured you were watching me on surveillance in the barn."

"I checked the cameras earlier, and there wasn't any motion triggering the camera alarms."

"That's good. You got ones in the house?" Yeats fell back into his favorite recliner and hit the button for his feet to recline.

"I couldn't risk setting off the house security system. I'm good, but not that good." Sebastian leaned back against the wall, looking forward to playing the video game. He had a few more hours until Caitlyn's shift ended for the night. "What took you so long?"

"Sammy invited me to stay for dinner," Yeats said, leaning his head back and patting his stomach. "Couldn't say no to smoky barbecue ribs. She used your mom's recipe." A satisfied smile spread across Yeats' face.

"You didn't bring me back any?" Sebastian forced a playful jab, but envy filled him. The image of the warm family dinner, laughter echoing through the house, sent a familiar wave of loneliness crashing over him. Years of keeping his distance from his family had carved a silent chasm between them, and it ached with a hollowness he couldn't fill.

"And have her ask questions? She had Cole, Owen, and another teenager there to feed, too," Yeats said without looking at him.

"Sounds like you had a good time." Sebastian glanced at the clock on the wall. Caitlyn's shift ended in a couple of hours. Yeats had taken his time dropping off Owen and lingering for dinner. He knew Caitlyn would be okay getting off after ten, but the thought of her alone caused a prickle of unease to crawl up his neck.

"I think I'll head over to La Rosa's soon to wait for Caitlyn to finish work."

Yeats opened his eyes and sat up. "Why?"

"She might get stuck being the last one out," he said, vaguely. "I figured I'd grab coffee and keep her company until she finishes locking up the place."

Yeats raised a brow. "Caitlyn's a grown woman. She's been taking care of herself long before you came along."

"I know," Sebastian said, his voice tight. "It's just... with Silas back in town, it doesn't hurt to be around." He wouldn't let her face her ex-husband alone again. The man scared

Owen, and while Caitlyn hadn't admitted it, she was clearly afraid, too. She needed someone to be there for her, even if she only allowed him into her life as friends.

But tonight, with Owen safely at Grace Meadows, Sebastian harbored a secret hope. There had been a shift in Caitlyn's demeanor all day. The way her hand held his when they spoke, the lingering glances she seemed to steal his way, and the way her eyes softened when they met. Maybe, just maybe, after tonight, when Owen was safe, he could finally act on the growing urge to kiss her, for real, not just a friendly brush on the forehead.

But a knot tightened in his gut. Silas loomed in the background, putting more strain on Caitlyn. Yet, the thought of her caught alone with her ex filled him with a protective urge. What if the next time Owen got scared, Sebastian couldn't get there in time?

"I'll go with." Yeats put his feet down and motioned to get up.

"Nah, man," Sebastian said quickly, the idea of a third wheel shattering his plans. "We've got an early morning tomorrow, and we've got those trees to plant at the park in Biglerville."

"It might not be a good idea to take the truck. Logo and all," Yeats said, his brows furrowing. "I can contact Jax and see if he and a few others from the Soldiers of Christ can drive by and keep an eye out. I was thinking of bringing it up at our next meeting this Saturday, anyway."

He should have known Yeats would be one step ahead. The man could have gone up in the ranks in the Army if not for the incident that had sent him home and haunted him at night. Sebastian woke many a night to Yeats' night terrors.

"Thanks." Sebastian grabbed his jacket and keys. "I'll take the Rebel this time. Don't wait up." She needed to know he had her back. *Lord, please don't let me fail again.*

17

Sebastian waited outside the diner in the parking lot for over an hour. After monitoring the security cameras at Grace Meadows and playing several levels of a word game app on his phone, Sebastian was getting impatient. The ice in the coffee was halfway melted. It was already past ten, but Caitlyn still hadn't come out. Bored with the game and nothing happening on the security feed, Sam's email came to mind. Using his burner phone, Sebastian sent a quick message to his old police chief, Razek. He might not be able to do anything to answer Sam's email, but Razek could on his behalf. Razek might give him grief for it later, but Sebastian was willing to deal with it if it meant getting Silas away from Caitlyn and Owen.

He pocketed his phone and walked around the corner, a spark of anticipation igniting in his chest. The place was empty, save for Caitlyn, who was cleaning under the warm glow of the overhead lights. Her hands moved efficiently as she wiped down the counter. Even in the distance, he caught the way the light glinted off her black hair, the soft curve of her cheek as she tilted her head. A wave of longing washed over him, a bittersweet pang for the life he wanted with her, shouldn't want with her. Not yet. Not while it wasn't safe for them to be together.

He probably looked like an idiot walking around the front by the large windows. He stood there with a sweating iced coffee in his hand as Caitlyn finished her work. Stalker much? The self-deprecating thought soured the sweetness of seeing her. About to tap on the glass, Caitlyn turned and headed to the back. Sebastian abandoned his post and walked the length of the building on the parking lot side. After all, lingering in the shadows made him appear more guilty of spying on her. As he walked, a car engine rumbled. He tensed, his gaze snapping toward the sound. A large black sedan pulled up to the curb. A man got out, his movements measured and confident.

From his shadowed position, Sebastian couldn't make out the man's face. He was tall and broad shouldered. Dark hair with a wave or maybe a natural curl. He started walking toward the diner, and Sebastian stepped back against the brick of the building. The man stopped just short of the entrance and looked around. Silas? His head turned, standing under the lamplight. The man gazed at Caitlyn's SUV first, then Sebastian's motorcycle. They were the only two vehicles left in the lot. Then the man smiled coldly. Calculating.

A sudden surge of rage rose within him. His hand instinctively reached for the familiar weight of the holstered gun strapped to his ankle. But he forced himself still. The man approached the diner's entrance. Sebastian squinted, looking for any signs the man was packing heat. His throat tightened as he remained quiet.

The man pounded on the door, his voice echoing in the silent night. "Cat!"

Seconds stretched into an eternity. Caitlyn wouldn't answer. The diner was closed. Frustration etched on his face, the man stalked back to the SUV. Sebastian stayed hidden, his gaze glued to the taillights of the retreating car, memorizing the license plate as it disappeared into the darkness. Only then did he allow himself to exhale, the tension draining from his body, leaving behind a cold sweat.

Somehow, he needed to find a way to ensure her safety without jeopardizing his own cover or exposing her to the truth of his past. That was where Razek came in. His old police chief told him to call him if he ever needed anything. Sebastian prayed he made the right choice. He couldn't stay here forever pretending to be someone else.

The back door swung shut behind Caitlyn. His heart hammered against his ribs. Laughter and adrenaline filled the day, creating an almost family-like atmosphere. But now, with it winding down, she looked tired and worn. Caitlyn wasn't wearing the same shirt as when he dropped her off.

"Caitlyn," he said, stepping out of the shadows and walking toward her. The other man was still fresh in his mind. Disappointment flickered in his chest. He wanted to question her about the man and, at the very least, warn her of his presence, but he didn't want to scare her.

Caitlyn stopped short, surprise crossing her features in the glow of the outside lights. The streetlights cast a golden glow on her face, highlighting the soft curve of her cheek and the sparkle in her eyes. "What are you doing here?"

"Would you believe I was out taking a walk?"

"It's almost eleven o'clock at night."

"Sleepwalking."

"Have you been here long?" she asked.

"Long enough." He fell in step beside her and held out the iced coffee. She paused, then took the offering.

"Mmmmm," she hummed, taking a long sip of it and twirling the straw, the plastic bending slightly in her grip. "So, you saw the guy at the door?"

"Yep."

"You stalking me?" she asked directly, her eyes narrowing.

He held her gaze for a long beat, searching her face for

any signs the man upset her. "That obvious, huh?" He winked, hoping to lighten the mood.

As they walked, her posture shifted, her shoulders eased, and her grip on the straw loosened. He'd taken a chance, a good one, according to the smirk on her face. They walked in silence for a few minutes until they reached her Jeep. Caitlyn turned to him. "You waited all this time to bring me an iced coffee?" she said, her voice tight with emotion.

"I wanted to make sure you were all right." He tucked his hands in his pockets before succumbing to the temptation to brush the stray hairs from her cheek.

"Because racing go-karts is tough on a girl," Caitlyn responded, twirling the straw between her fingers once again. Despite the teasing, vulnerability crept into her voice.

"How did you know I needed this?" She sighed and took another long sip.

Sebastian played it safe. "Long day, and I admit I wanted to spend a few minutes alone with you without Owen." He chose his words carefully, hoping it would spark a flicker of something more in her eyes. A hint that maybe, just maybe, this pull toward her wasn't all one sided.

"We do that on the range on the weekends." She tilted her head, sipping her ice coffee.

"That's work." But before he could continue, Caitlyn spoke, a hint of apprehension. "I suppose you're wondering who the guy was, trying to get in." She twirled the straw so the ice cubes inside her cup spun. "I wouldn't have let him in."

"Who was it?" Sebastian pressed gently.

"We've had one date. Don't go all possessive on me," she said. "Or I'll have to dump you, and I would get awkward working together. Let's not get awkward."

"You considered today a date?" A satisfied smirk tugged at his lips. Sebastian tilted back on his heels. The call to Razek nagged in the back of his mind as he tried to contain the playful grin.

Caitlyn hesitated, then nodded slowly. "Yeah, didn't you?"

"If that's what you want to call it." He leaned closer to her. "But next time, *I* plan to take you out," he emphasized. "Just the two of us, the traditional way."

The lightness in the air dissipated, and Caitlyn's shoulders slumped. "I'm not sure it's a good idea anymore." She motioned between them. "You and me outside of work, that is."

"Because of the guy at the door? Was that your ex?" Sebastian asked, softening his voice to gauge her comfort level. Part of him wanted to brush aside Silas as a mere inconvenience, but the call to Razek weighed heavily on him. Could he handle dealing with Caitlyn's ex while protecting his family?

"Yeah. That was Silas. But I know my ex. He won't stick around once he gets what he wants. It's just a matter of time." Caitlyn's admission about Silas sticking around for what he wanted sparked a protective urge in Sebastian. Razek couldn't answer his call fast enough.

"Then it's a good thing I've got time. I'm here for you," he said, taking his hand out of his pocket and running his fingers across her cheek. Her lips parted, and she stepped back, letting his hand drop. He glanced around the darkness. It wasn't safe for them to linger out in an empty parking lot in the dark.

"Thanks for walking me to my car and the iced coffee." They stood there for a moment. The air crackled with a tension that both exhilarated him and terrified him.

"I have to pick up Owen. I'm late as it is. Everything went well when you dropped him off?" Caitlyn asked, digging in her pocket.

Sebastian cupped the back of his neck. The night flew by, and he wished they had more time, but the ever-present reality of his hidden past slammed the brakes on it.

"Sure," he replied, his voice gruffer than intended.

"Well…," she said, a flicker of something unreadable in her eyes. Was it apprehension, or perhaps a hint she regretted leaving too? "Good night."

"Good night," he said, his voice softening. "I can't promise I won't show up after you get off work to walk you to your car." The words tumbled out, a mix of concern and a desperate attempt to extend their time together for a mere minute. "I want you safe."

"You think Silas would hurt me?" She pulled out her keys. He prayed Razek followed through with his text request and helped Sam, who could pass it to Caitlyn to end this Silas business.

"I think you're a strong, independent woman who can take care of herself."

"But you came to check on me, anyway?" She unlocked the Jeep and held open the door.

"I came to steal a few minutes with you and bring you iced coffee," he said, his voice coming out gruff, hoarse almost.

"You shouldn't have," she whispered, but her eyes said the opposite. And that smile in the dim light inside her vehicle made it worth it. She bent her finger and motioned for him to come closer. He swallowed hard. The look in her eyes, the invitation of her lips, crumbled his resolve. He took a step closer, his heart lodged against his ribs. Each inch that narrowed the distance between them sent a jolt of electricity through him. This wasn't part of the plan. But her eyelashes fluttered. Her lips parted slightly. As if drawn by an invisible force, Sebastian's lips brushed hers in a tentative kiss, a whisper-soft exploration that sent a wave of forgotten tenderness crashing inside him. A soft sigh escaped Caitlyn as she leaned to embrace him. His fingers found purchase on her jaw, tracing the curve with a newfound reverence. A deep sense of finding a missing piece he hadn't even known he lost, like coming home, resonated on a level far deeper than he thought possible. When their kiss deepened, a key turned in a long-locked door. He wanted to lose himself in this moment, forget the shadows looming over their lives and soak in the warmth of her presence. When their breathing became ragged, a nagging voice in the back of his mind whispered a warning that had him break away from her.

Their breaths mingled in the cool night air. Caitlyn's eyes glazed and her lips parted, taking in shallow breaths. Sebastian leaned his forehead against hers.

"Goodnight, Caitlyn," he whispered, pulling back. His voice was thick and ragged.

"You should be careful going out in the dark by yourself," she replied, her voice a mere whisper.

"I'll keep that in mind." He leaned in again, this time for a quick, chaste kiss on her forehead.

"You can't follow me," she said, getting into her Jeep as he held the door and shut it once she got settled inside.

Caitlyn rolled down the window. Worry etched across those amber eyes. "Promise me."

His emotions and his mind went to war with each other. He wanted to protect her and her son, but a cold sweat broke out against his skin. "I want to see you again before Saturday."

"You can always bring me an iced coffee." Caitlyn glanced inside her Jeep and frowned at the time on the dashboard. "I need to go."

Reluctantly, Sebastian backed up and watched her drive away. Shaking his head, Sebastian reminded himself that she had a son to care for, and he needed to take this new relationship slow. Kissing her this soon might have been a bad move. Would she regret it tomorrow?

He watched her Jeep disappear down the road. He would give her a few minutes of a head start before following up to make sure she got home safe.

In the distance, he heard a car door shut; a set of headlights turned on, shining in his face. Sebastian held up his arm to block the light. A second later, the sound of a gun firing broke through the night.

————

Caitlyn drove down the street, reaching for the radio to chase away the lingering silence, and a wave of guilt washed over her. Sam. The two pizzas and order of wings she promised her for keeping Owen still sat on the diner counter. Silas' unexpected visit threw her off completely, and Sebastian's surprise iced coffee and that kiss. Oh, that kiss had derailed her.

Turning back around, she returned before the guilt morphed into a low-grade worry. This might also be a good way to test if Sebastian followed her. A black SUV sped past her in the opposite lane. She wrestled with the steering wheel, narrowly avoiding a collision with a car that drifted across the center line. Shaken, Caitlyn muttered, "Someone needs to retake their driver's test."

She took a deep breath, thinking it was a bunch of teens hurrying to get home before curfew, and pulled into the parking lot and spotted the motorcycle parked at the end. Why hadn't Daniel left yet? She half expected him to follow her home.

A knot of unease tightened in her stomach. Leaving the car door hanging open, she rushed toward the bike. A dark stain spread like a malevolent shadow, its edges catching the harsh glare of the streetlamp. She rounded the corner of the bike. There, sprawled on his back, lay Daniel.

"Daniel?"

There was a shallow moan, a ragged gasp that sent relief, sharp and unexpected, battling with an icy wave of fear. Caitlyn's knees buckled beneath her, the gravel biting into her exposed skin as she collapsed beside him.

"No... No..." she choked out, the terror taking over. This

wasn't supposed to be happening. Not like this. Not Daniel. Reaching out, her hand hovered above him, trembling. She found his pulse. He was warm and groaned at her touch. But a dark stain bloomed on his shirt, centered on his chest.

This was her fault. *This was her fault.* Grabbing her phone, she turned on the light. She found the hole where the bullet went in. Pressing down on it with one hand, she heard him grunt and try to twist away.

"Lie still. I'm calling 911."

"No... ambulance..." His words came out in ragged gasps, barely audible.

All the air sucked into Caitlyn's lungs wouldn't release. "You're shot."

Despite the pain etched on his face, a flicker of recognition ignited in his eyes. "Caitlyn..." His lips moved slightly, forming a single word.

Her name, uttered with a rasp, stopped the universe around her. "You need an ambulance, or you're going to die."

"Not bad." He coughed and rasped. "Give me a minute. Okay?"

A minute? Caitlyn rocked back on her heels. She kept her phone tilted, using it as a flashlight. "I need to call 911."

"No. Don't." He coughed, then groaned.

"I'm so sorry," she said, fear sliding down her spine. "I should have known this would happen. I was careless, and I didn't think..." A sob caught in her throat.

"Not. Your. Fault. Drive by. Shot." Daniels groaned. He rolled to his side.

"They saw us," she muttered, followed by a few choice words in Spanish. She should have warned him. Her eyes filled with tears. *Keep it together. You can't help him if you're falling apart.*

"Don't get up. I'm calling for help." If anything happened to him... She bit her lip to distract from the tremble in her chin. *Silas.* Of course, someone saw them together. The guy who came after hours? Or earlier today?

"No cops. No hospital." Daniel groaned again, trying to sit up straight.

"You're *bleeding!*" Caitlyn helped him, spewing out more of her native tongue, expressing her exasperation with the man. Fear gripped her as she pressed on his wound. "You need an ambulance. I have to call the cops. I have to call *someone.*"

"No cops," Daniel said firmly, though weakly.

"Why not?" Caitlyn demanded, her question hinged with desperation. An ambulance and a hospital would save him quickly, but the pleading in his eyes wounded her. The raw fear flickered within their depths and held her back.

A horrible suspicion formed in the pit of her stomach. The thought of cops arriving, of prying questions and unwanted scrutiny, sent an icy shiver down her spine. But what other options were there? Was Daniel *loco?* She couldn't leave him here to bleed to death. And that's what would happen if she didn't get him medical attention soon.

"No cops," he whispered, grimacing.

Already, someone could have heard the shot and reported it. She listened for sirens. Hoping someone else would take this decision out of her hands.

Blood seeped from his wound between her fingers. Since the cops or a hospital was out of the question, he left her with only one other option.

"Fine. No cops. But I'm not letting you lie here and die, *sí?*" *Oh Lord, what had she done?* The black SUV barreling down the street couldn't have been a conscience. Did Silas do this, or had he sent someone else? Daniel just had to come to La Rosa's. An iced coffee was not worth his life.

She maneuvered her phone with one hand, not letting go of him. Ignoring the grunts, she kept pressure on his wound. The phone rang and went to voicemail. Tonight, he made her break all protocol and revert to Spanish. Better, for he wouldn't understand her prayers and her venting at herself. What was she thinking, giving Daniel hope of something more when she'd put a target on his back for Silas's wrath?

She kept a blanket in the back of her Jeep. She grabbed his hand and placed it on his wound. "Press and don't move." Caitlyn sprinted for her vehicle. The sounds of sirens came from the distance. Took them long enough. Thankfully, the bulb in her Jeep needed to be replaced for weeks and didn't light up inside when she popped the back hatch. Searching in the darkness, her hand landed on the blanket she kept there. Snatching it, she slammed the hatch, startled herself, and ran back to him.

She pressed the blanket to his chest. "Hug this. Press it against the wound."

He moaned, falling back, and she caught him. "*Eres un hombre tonto,*" she hissed.

"I like it. When you. Talk. To me, that. Way." He'd tried to make a joke or perhaps was using sarcasm because he couldn't be flirting with her at a time like this.

Daniel gestured with a thumb toward the motorbike parked nearby, its chrome gleaming in the moonlight. "Call Yeats. He'll know. What to do—."

"You have a bullet in your chest. You need more than that," Caitlyn said, thinking about the best course of action given the situation at hand. The sirens grew louder. If she didn't act soon, he would lie there and bleed to death. But if she called an ambulance, there could be more trouble than necessary... And the police...

Making an exasperated sound in her throat, she grabbed him by the arm on his good side. "Come on. Can you walk? We need to get you in my car. I'll call Thomas on the way."

"Yeah. Might need a pull off this pavement." Daniel said with a rasp in his voice. She bit her lip harder, knowing this would hurt him more than her as she took that good arm and yanked. He got his feet under him, and she caught and supported his weight as he stood. Daniel swayed and her knees almost buckled. This wasn't a good idea. What if he died in her car?

"You better not die on me," she grunted, adrenaline giving her strength.

Lights appeared in the distance. Seconds felt like minutes, and they had to go. Not if he didn't want the cops involved. "Let's go."

She opened the passenger side of her Jeep, helped him inside, and slammed the door. Racing to the driver's side, she got in. She must have left it running the whole time. Not bothering with his seat belt, she put it in reverse and got them out of the parking lot just as the lights of a police car crested the high slope of the road coming toward them. Her breath held in her lungs as she put her foot on the gas.

"Hey," Daniel laid his hand on her arm. "You don't want to give them a reason to chase you for speeding."

Swallowing down the hysteria, she nodded. She'd dropped her phone on her lap, and he scooted back as he grabbed the device that slid between her legs. "Phone," he said, as if to reassure her he wasn't after something else.

"Take me to the monument on the battlefield south of here. I'll have Yeats meet us there in case someone is still watching. I don't want anyone else following us."

"You'll be dead," she said, feeling another fit of wetness as more tears flowed. "You worry about staying alive. I'll worry about telling Thomas where you are later."

His head rolled to the side. His fingers moved in the darkness. The front of her phone lit up. "What's your password?" His voice sounded slurred. The phone slipped from his hand, falling with a thud onto the floorboard. "Daniel." She looked over at him. His other hand slipped from the blanket.

"Daniel!" she shouted, watching the road in front of her,

looking back behind her. "Don't die. Please. Please. I will get you help. We are almost there. Don't die," she repeated over and over until it became a whispered mantra the entire way.

18

Thomas stood in the clinic's waiting room, his back pressed against the wall. Caitlyn sat in the chair across from him. Her fingers flew over the letters on her phone's screen.

"What did you say to Sam?" Thomas asked, his voice a low rumble.

Shame, a cold, metallic taste in her mouth, tainted the fleeting reprieve of finding Daniel alive. She lied to Sammy, another thread woven into the tapestry of deceit that was quickly strangling her life.

"Emergency at work," she mumbled, the words like ash in her mouth. It wasn't a complete lie, but the tangled mess of the truth might cause Sammy to question her decision against her better judgment to call the police.

"How long will this emergency last?" Thomas raised an eyebrow. They both knew Sammy wasn't easily fooled. She had a sixth sense for the truth. As her best friend, Sammy deserved the truth, but to do so might put her in as much danger as Sammy's brother. In all the years they'd known each other, Caitlyn hadn't once met Sammy's twin, and if she'd seen a photo of him, she didn't remember. She imagined he would look much like his sister.

"I asked her to keep Owen for the night. I wasn't sure how long it was going to take before I could get there."

"Did you get Alison involved in this elaborate lie?"

Taking a deep breath, Caitlyn hit send on another message to Sammy, expressing her gratitude again for helping her. The weight of everything over the past several weeks threatened to suffocate her. "No."

"Good. The fewer people involved, the better," Thomas said.

Her voice was hoarse as she finally spoke. "It's my fault this happened." Yet, here she was, trapped in a web of deceit, her world unraveling thread by thread.

Thomas's voice, usually a steady rumble, held a hint of surprise. "You didn't cause this," he said, his words firm but soothing a tiny part of the storm raging inside her.

Caitlyn squeezed her eyes shut, tears leaking past her lashes and tracing hot tracks down her cheeks. "I did, Thomas," she confessed. "I kissed him." Helplessness burned a fiery path through her gut as she lifted her head, met his gaze. "Silas did this. I know it was him. Someone must have seen us, and it's my fault. I'm so *stupid*."

Pushing off from the wall, he went over in front of her. Without a word, he reached out, his hand warm against her cold skin. Her head tilted as he gripped her wrists gently, tugging her to her feet. Drawing her into his enormous chest, she sank against Thomas. He wasn't the kind of comfort she usually sought, but right now, she needed this lifeline. As he wrapped his arms around her and leaned his head against hers, the scent of his cologne and steady rhythm of his heartbeat against her ear offered a sliver of solace. His embrace was like a solid barrier against the world falling apart around her.

"He's going to be okay," Thomas murmured. "Stop blaming yourself."

Caitlyn buried her face against his chest, the fabric

absorbing the fresh wave of tears welling up on her lashes. A choked sob escaped her lips. "What if I hadn't returned?" She sniffled against his shirt.

"No what-ifs," he stated firmly but with a gentleness that soothed the raw edges of her fear. Thomas prayed aloud while he rubbed her back in slow circles, mimicking how one soothed a babe. More tears spilled over her lashes. As the tension ebbed from her shoulders, a fragile sense of calm settled in its place.

Finished with the prayer, he reassured her. "It's a good thing you forgot something and turned back."

A flicker of hope ignited in the darkness of her lingering fear. "Is he going to be mad I brought him here?"

Thomas chuckled, a low rumble that vibrated against her ear. "Yeah," he admitted, "but he'll get over it."

Shortly after, she brought Daniel to the clinic near Hanover and called Thomas. It was past two in the morning, and the doctor hadn't returned yet with a report. They wanted to ship him to the hospital in Carlisle, but Thomas took the doctor aside and spoke with him to change his mind. Thomas must have known why Daniel wanted to avoid the cops because the nurse on duty wanted to call the cops too. Thomas assured them the proper authorities were on their way. By law, the doctor had to report someone with a gunshot wound, but she brought Daniel here because Antonio's wife, Daralyn, worked the night shift as a nurse for the clinic. Daralyn helped members of the Ghost Riders in the past, but Daniel's wound was beyond Daralyn's skills. He left her little choice, and she wanted to keep him alive.

Thomas stepped in to handle the doctor and the police.

"Why doesn't Daniel want the police involved?" Caitlyn demanded, backing away from Thomas. "You said he wasn't a charity case. Is he a criminal?"

"That's not my story to tell." Thomas let her go and scratched his beard. "Pops at the house? If Silas did this, maybe you should stay with Sammy tonight. Or what about Casper's place? I'll text you when he wakes up."

"It's already too late for me to go home, and I can't leave. If anyone asks, I'll tell them I slept over with Sam."

"Yeah, that's probably best."

They fell into a prolonged silence. Thomas was keeping something from her. She needed to wait to hear it from Daniel. Whatever it was, she hoped it explained why Daniel didn't want her to call the police. Why did she listen to him and not wait for an ambulance?

Where was the doctor? Why was it taking so long?!

She needed to clean the blood out of her car. Was Silas at the house waiting for her? Sam assured her Owen was fine, and Cole stayed later than usual. Caitlyn paced in the waiting room.

"Pray with me?" Thomas asked, holding out his hand for Caitlyn to take.

"Of course." Her grip on Thomas tightened. Would God hear her after what she'd done? Having the man she was falling for almost die because of her actions was a suffocating weight to carry. As Thomas bowed his head in prayer, a silent plea for Daniel's recovery, Caitlyn repeated the sentiment with a fervent plea of her own. He asked God to protect them, Cat, Owen, Pops, and the Daniels family. When he finished, Caitlyn pulled away, her eyes wide. "What about Sammy and her family?"

"She has Owen with her," Thomas said, and Caitlyn sank back down into her vacant chair. On the wall, a television ran infomercials with no sound and captions at the bottom of the screen.

"Silas knows he's there when he's not with Pops," Caitlyn said, her chest tightening and making breathing hard. "Owen knows better than to go with him."

"I'm sure he's safe. Isn't Cole there with Sammy?"

Caitlyn wrung her hands and nodded.

"It's not Owen and Sammy I'm worried about." Thomas leveled his gaze. "If Silas did this, he'll hide out for a while until he thinks the air is clear."

But the clinic was on the edge of town, tucked away in a less-than-desirable neighborhood. Caitlyn could almost feel the threat of danger on the horizon. Silas wasn't one to accept failure. If he intended to kill Daniel, he'd see the deed done. And what of Sammy's brother? She grew almost nauseous enough to become ill.

"Did you notice if anyone followed you?"

"No. I made sure not to come here on a direct path. If someone followed me, hopefully, I lost them. You're avoiding my question."

Thomas peered over at the young woman sitting behind the reception desk, a magazine in her hands. The clinic was empty apart from the two of them. Thomas walked toward the reception desk, his eyes flicking around the room. He scanned the walls, the floor, and the ceiling as if searching for something. Caitlyn followed his gaze and looked back at him. What was Daniel hiding? Why would Thomas protect him like this? Why had she?

Even if Silas followed them here, this place had cameras. Security cameras. That was what Thomas was seeking. Did he think it made it safer from Silas and to protect them if they stayed in the areas with cameras?

This whole thing was a mess. Because of her, Daniel was fighting for his life on an operating table. Maybe she should have let the doctor ship him off to the hospital.

The woman behind the desk looked up, her eyes widening slightly when she saw Thomas approach. She opened her mouth as if to say something, then quickly shut it again.

"Any updates on Daniel?" Thomas asked, his voice firm but gentle.

The woman picked up her phone and made a call. A minute later, she hung up and gestured toward the hallway.

"He's in the last room on the right," she said. "They just put him there a few minutes ago. I'm sure the doctor is on his way to speak with you shortly."

Caitlyn returned to the waiting area, away from the window. Staring at the floor, she avoided eye contact with Thomas and hugged herself tightly.

As if on cue, the doctor appeared. He wasn't old like most doctors Caitlyn saw, or maybe it was because her doctor was nearing retirement age that Caitlyn had this assumption of doctors being aged with white hair. He wasn't the same doctor she saw Thomas speaking with upon his arrival. This man might have been an intern. His white medical coat said Sanyal. "Your friend is well. The bullet missed the heart by a few inches. It appears he has scarring from a prior gunshot wound."

A wave of confusion overcame her, and she asked, "Was it bad? When he was shot before?"

Thomas lowered his chin, listening as Caitlyn neared. The doctor continued, but neither man answered her question.

"He'll need to be transferred to another facility. Normally, we'd have sent him to a hospital, but I understand your circumstances. You don't wish for this," Dr. Sanyal said, his Indian accent making Caitlyn focus on understanding his English. At first, Caitlyn assumed the man was an intern, judging that he might not be older than his late twenties. It would be too impolite to ask him about his age and accreditations after saving Daniel's life.

"Can't he stay here for a few days until he's well?" Caitlyn asked, stepping up beside Thomas. She didn't mind when he put his hand on her back.

Dr. Sanyal frowned at her. "We have patients who come in that are in trouble. I help. I do what I can. I can't go against the law. If your friend is in trouble."

"I told you. He's a cop," Thomas said.

Caitlyn froze, the icy truth holding her still. Cop? The

image of Daniel in a crisp uniform shattered the image of the man she brought into the clinic hours ago.

Thomas's phone rang, shattering the stunned silence. He held up his finger, a silent apology, and stepped away from the doctor to answer. "Yeah?"

Caitlyn tried to listen, the shock overridden by a need to understand.

"Yeah. Someone shot him. I thought you'd want to know." Thomas kept his voice lowered, most likely to avoid it echoing down the sterile hallway.

"Depends on who's asking," Yeats said and listened before replying. "Yeah. Just checking. He's alive, but I've got him at a clinic. We need to keep them from transporting him to a hospital or alerting the local authorities. The person I suspect who did this most likely has eyes and ears everywhere in the county."

After a brief silence, Thomas turned, his gaze locking with Caitlyn's. "More than his own family. Which isn't as much as I can say about you. I don't know you. How can I trust you?"

Caitlyn chewed on her lip as she stood, torn between going to see Daniel or hearing the rest of Thomas's phone call. "If you mean sending him a new identification and expecting him to hide, he won't." Thomas frowned. Walking over to the doctor, he held out the phone and said, "You'll want to take this call."

Caitlyn approached the nurse at the station. "What room number did you say he was in?"

The young woman looked up and glanced between Caitlyn and the doctor. "Are you his wife?"

Caitlyn nodded, leaving it to this moment for her to choke up on a lie. What was one more if it got her in to see Daniel? They both had a lot to answer already.

"Down the hall, room 313."

Trembling, Caitlyn pushed past Thomas, ignoring his furrowing brow. Each step down the hallway echoed the hollowness in her chest. Hot and scolding, it scorched her. Had he used her, their connection, Sam, to get to Silas or the Ghost Riders? But why not join them? Why the secrecy? Tears welled in her eyes. A cop would want the police involved after getting shot, wouldn't they? Unless... a horrifying thought slithered into her mind. Was Daniel a dirty cop?

Hot tears streamed down her chilled skin. Reaching the room, she paused, the urge to storm in strong, but fear slowed her down. Did she want to see him? Yes. But what would she see? A man she thought she knew, or a stranger playing a dangerous game?

Daniel slept. His face was pale, and the hospital gown slipped down from where the wires ran up, and the bandages peeked out. Pulling up a chair near his bed, she sat and wiped away the remains of her tears from her cheeks. Determined to wait until he was awake, she laid her hand over his.

"If you're okay, then I'm okay."

This time, she was lying to herself.

———

The sterile white of the ceiling swam into focus, accompanied by a dull throbbing behind his eyes. The rhythmic beeping of the heart monitor mimicked the frantic drum solo his nerves were playing.

A low moan escaped his lips as a fresh wave of pain rolled down his side. Sebastian tried to shift, but a sharp tug near his shoulder sent a jolt through him. There, a bandage peeked out from under the thin hospital gown.

"Audra." He swallowed, his throat dry, his voice hoarse.

A cup of water pressed against his lips. "Sip."

Then he saw her. Caitlyn. Realization hit him like a freight train. Waiting for her in the parking lot. Shots fired—the burning sensation in his shoulder.

Curled up on a chair beside the bed, her face etched with

worry as she slept. Relief washed over him, warm and sweet, pushing away the pain for a fleeting moment.

"She's been here since she brought you in. She refused to leave your side until you woke." Thomas sat the cup on the tray near Sebastian on the opposite side away from Caitlyn.

"Daniel?" Caitlyn whispered, scrambling to her feet. "You're awake."

"I'm a hard man to kill."

Her smile faltered. She looked pale, her eyes shadowed with exhaustion, but relief flickered across her face. "I'm so sorry. This is my fault," she said, her voice thick with emotion. Sebastian turned his head to look at Yeats.

"I've got it under control. Razek is on his way. I'm sorry, man. I didn't know who else to call. Figured you didn't want me contacting the missus."

"No. You did the right thing," Sebastian said, grateful to live another day.

"Missus? You are married?" Caitlyn withdrew from him.

His stomach clenched. She deserved the truth. Sebastian lifted his hand, captured hers, and tried to get her to stay. "No."

"Sorry," Yeats huffed. "I'm making a mess of this. I need some coffee. I'll let you two talk while I fetch us some caffeine."

"Daniel, what is going on?" The fear and hint of betrayal laced in her voice struck him worse than the bullet. Closing his eyes, he took a deep, shaky breath, fighting the wave of dizziness washing over him. "Caitlyn," he said, tugging her closer, his voice a harsh whisper of hoarseness. "Let me explain."

"Explain? You could have died. Kissing me is not worth your life."

A smile twitched on his lips. "You're right. I can't kiss you if I'm dead, but your kisses aren't what got me shot."

Her cheeks turned dark pink, and she held onto his hand.

"Does this have anything to do with why you're hiding and refused to wait for the cops or an ambulance?"

Guilt gnawed at him, but he couldn't allow Caitlyn to think any of this was her doing. Closing his eyes, he fought the pain medication dripping in his IV, making him drowsy. "Did Yeats tell you?"

Caitlyn released his hand and rolled her eyes. She walked over and grabbed the cup of water. Pressing it to his lips, she waited for him to ease the dryness in his throat.

"I heard Thomas on the phone. Who is 'the missus' if you're not married? And I know this is my fault. I got careless, and one of Silas's men must have seen us in the parking lot."

His skin became clammy against the cool sheets. "My name isn't Daniel Jones. It's Sebastian Daniels. 'Missus' is a code word. I used to be a cop."

Silence descended upon the room. The sterile scent of disinfectant became stronger. Sebastian peered at Caitlyn, his heart monitor beeping with the skip of the beats in his chest. Caitlyn stared at him, her face a mask of shock and disbelief. Mascara smudged under her eyes, making them appear darker. "Sebastian. Sebastian Daniels," she murmured, as if testing the name on her tongue. "You're Sammy's brother."

Sebastian forced himself to meet her gaze. Her brown eyes widened with hurt at the depth of betrayal. His throat constricted, making simple words a struggle. "Yeah," he finally managed, the single syllable a world away from the explanation he wanted to offer. He could see the wheels turning in her mind, piecing together the fragments of his past actions. His secrecy.

Her connection with his sister, Samantha, made their relationship more complicated, and now it was out in the open. The cold drip of the medication in his IV was nothing compared to the chill spreading through his chest.

"Does Sammy know?"

Would she believe his motives weren't malicious, that he'd

never meant to deceive her? "No. I needed to remain anonymous to protect my family. I never meant to lie to you, Caitlyn," he said, his voice strained.

Her cheeks turned a dark pink. "I never intended to put you in danger." Panic rose in his chest, the monitor beeping faster. "I care about you and Owen. I don't care about Silas. We'll deal with him. Together."

Tears welled in her eyes, mirroring the dark storm of emotions brewing in the reflection of her eyes. Anger, confusion, hurt—they all swirled in her gaze. "You're Sammy's brother," she whispered, the words sounding hollow in the sterile room. "She doesn't know."

He took a shaky breath. "There are bad men after me," he confessed. The gravity of his situation finally laid bare. "I needed to stay close to ensure they didn't come after my family." His gaze darted to the window. "They wouldn't hesitate to hurt anyone to get to me, especially..." He trailed off, his voice choked with emotion.

"You're an undercover cop." She covered her mouth with her hand.

He tried to reach for her, but that arm was heavy, and pain shot through his shoulder. "I'm not a cop. Not anymore." He needed her to believe him.

Her hand dropped from her mouth, and her eyes narrowed. "Sammy said you were good at your job. You'd do anything..."

"I'd do anything to keep the people I care about safe," he interjected.

"Did you know Silas was getting out of prison? Is that why you came here? Why did you take the job with Thomas? You befriended my son."

Her words cut through him like a knife. Everything he'd done, the lies he'd had to live... "Thomas offering me the job has nothing to do with you or Silas, Caitlyn. Listen to me."

Caitlyn shook her head and backed up. The judgment in

her eyes was more painful than the pain from his bullet wound. He hoped a flicker of trust remained beneath the confusion and anger.

"I'm sorry, Daniel. Sebastian. Whatever your name is…" Caitlyn gnawed on her lip until it bled. "Silas is on a manhunt, and he's been looking for you. I didn't recognize you because your family is so private, but he'll find you, and I can't stop him."

19

Caitlyn pulled up alongside another vehicle at Grace Meadows. She left as soon as Thomas returned with coffee. Daniel's pleas to hear him out and explain sent a jolt of anxiety coursing through her. After what she said, she couldn't stay another minute. The aftertaste of her confession lingered on her tongue and stung.

Besides, he needed to rest, and she needed space. At least she told herself as much on the drive.

She cast a hesitant glance at the house. Seeing Sammy's truck parked out front complicated things further. Spotting Owen inside the barn, Caitlyn stepped out of the Jeep. A wave of tenderness loosened some knots twisting inside her. He disappeared then came back a minute later, a broad smile on his face at the sight of her, oblivious to the dangerous web Silas tangled around them.

"Hey there, *mijo.*" She forced a smile, the guilt souring in the pit of her stomach. He raced towards her, enveloping her in a big hug.

"Ready to go?" She brushed her hand across Owen's dark curls, so much like Silas's hair, before he started cutting his

curls off. They were the one thing that made Silas approach-
able when he joined the Ghost Riders. Her heart twisted.

"Where did you go last night?" he asked as they walked
back to her Jeep.

"Nowhere." Her smile became strained. "I thought you
liked it at Grace Meadows."

"You scared me," Owen said, looking at her with bangs
falling across his eyes. "I thought something happened."

Something had happened all right. Sebastian Daniels
happened, and she feared there was no going back.

"Yo, Owen!"

Caitlyn turned as Cole came jogging up. "You forgot your
hat."

Owen reached for it, but Cole was faster. He landed the
ball cap down on Owen's head. It had Grace Meadow's logo
across the front. "Be careful getting home. There's a storm
coming from the south."

"Thank you. Please tell Sammy I'm sorry I missed her."
Guilt and relief filled her. It wasn't her truth to tell. Her
stomach knotted. Caitlyn wouldn't be the one to tell Sammy
her brother got shot. Sammy came into Caitlyn's life when she
needed a friend the most. The Daniels family never treated
her differently, even when she needed a place to hide an
injured police officer until she could get help. Sammy was the
only one she trusted. And what would Sammy think of her
knowing what Caitlyn knew? Keeping information from her
would appear like a betrayal.

"She rode out to the back forty to check on the horses
before the storm. I'm heading out to join her. I don't like her
out there alone, but Owen and I had to fix a stall door. I guess
it was good we stayed behind." Cole grinned.

"I appreciate you being here for Sammy and helping to
look out for Owen."

"Everything okay? Sammy said something about an emergency?" Cole asked, looking genuinely concerned.

"Fine. Closing took longer last night, and then a friend of mine was involved in an accident." Caitlyn avoided Cole's gaze, unable to meet his sincere concern with her fabricated story.

"It wasn't Dan, was it?" Owen gripped her arm.

"D-Dan's fine," she stammered, tears threatening to well up in her eyes. "We should go. Cole needs to help Sammy, and it doesn't look like it will be long before the storm catches us." Caitlyn wished she could swallow back her earlier words. She blamed it on the lack of sleep, caffeine, and her brain trying to process the truth about the man she came to care about. Her chest burned with the knowledge.

"Stay safe," Cole said, pulling out his phone. He seemed distracted, and Caitlyn could relate. She was holding him up from riding out to help Sammy.

"Thanks, you too," Caitlyn murmured.

Leave it to God to put her in another mess. She shouldn't have gotten involved. Yet, she couldn't help herself. Sebastian Daniels nudged at a dormant part of her as she locked away the day she locked Silas away.

Owen slid into his seat inside the Jeep and slumped the entire ride home. As soon as she parked in the driveway, Owen raced off toward the garage. She saw men gathered there, and Pops standing by his old Harley. "Owen, wait!"

"I want to help Pops," he whined.

"Let the boy be," Pops shouted. "Come now, we've got a ride to fix."

Owen bounced between them. Caitlyn swallowed hard. If Pops' motorcycle was here, did that mean Silas was nearby? She walked over enough to peer inside the garage. Pete, one of her brother's friends, emerged with a wrench in hand.

"Okay, but don't go anywhere with anyone." Caitlyn glared at her son. "Understand?"

Owen took off toward Pops.

Needing a shower and a few hours of sleep, Caitlyn

relented. Normally, she didn't start until late afternoon, but Regina asked her to cover for Alison, who claimed to have asked to have the day off weeks ago. It didn't escape Caitlyn's eye the way Alison waited on Thomas. The girl had a crush on the Soldiers of Christ Christian Motorcycle Club's Treasurer and Regional Director of the Motorcycle Safety Program. It's a good thing Thomas did both, or Caitlyn might not have the extra income she needed working the weekends coaching on the range.

Inside the house, she climbed the stairs, determined to take a shower. A dark shadow greeted her in the hall. Leaning against her bedroom door, her breath caught in the throat. "Silas."

"Kitty Cat." He uncrossed his arms and stepped closer. She stumbled back, her heart racing at the sound of his voice. Deep shadows curved under his eyes, and the unkempt, disheveled hair sent alarms in her head. She took a deep breath, appalled by his spicy body wash and a metallic scent that made her nose scrunch.

"What are you doing here?" she hissed sharply. "You have no business in this house."

He lowered his chin, the light from a hallway window casting his shadow longer past her bedroom doorway. His gaze was intense and steady, boring into her like he could glimpse inside her soul and read its secrets.

"I just wanted to see you," he said, each word coming out slowly as if it were too heavy for him to speak to them all at once. "You didn't come home last night."

She shut her eyes to close out the pain that rose within her chest, but it was no use. It still burned with every breath she took.

"Don't pretend you don't know why," she tried to keep the quiver from her voice. "I want you to leave now."

Silas smirked. "You forgot whose house this is."

"It belongs to my father."

"Who paid the place off?" With money from his illegal parts smuggling operation.

She shook her head. Pops kept them in debt. Without a treasurer, the Ghost Riders would have run in the red under her father's leadership.

"You did what you set out to do," she said, her voice shaking more with fury than fear. "Leave us be, like you said, and don't come back."

"Oh, I know you don't want me here, babe." Silas sauntered toward her. Caitlyn locked her legs, unable to move. His knuckles brushed across her cheek. His thumb pressed against her lips, pulling down on the bottom one. "I came to tell you that you did good, *muñeca*. I was starting to doubt you would, but then I knew you would do whatever you needed for the good of our family."

He patted her cheek and walked away.

"What d-do you mean?" Her voice pitched. Of course, he came to brag. She played along, hoping Silas hadn't discovered his hit attempt failed—a headache formed in her temples. Last night, she slept a little on the chair in Daniel's room at the clinic.

Silas pressed his fingers to her lips. "Did you cry for him? Is that why you didn't bring our son and come home last night?"

"What I do is none of your business," she said, leaning back away from him. "You said you would leave Pops and Owen alone. You need to leave."

Slowly, he smiled. "You're right, babe. When I get back, we'll renegotiate." He leaned in, sniffed her, and she jerked back from him.

"What do you mean?"

"I promise nothing will happen to my son or your father. You and I? We're not over." He turned and strolled down the stairs.

"Silas!" she hissed, and he chuckled, a dark rumble in his

chest. Caitlyn followed him down the steps, her pulse quickening with each step. Before she could protest further, his large hand clamped down on her upper arm, stopping her in her tracks.

"Don't worry, *mi amor,*" he breathed, his voice barely above a whisper. "You proved yourself. Now, you be a good momma to our son. I don't want you working at that place or on motorcycles anymore, understand? What you need, I will provide."

He released her, his dark eyes still locked with her gaze. She wanted to scream at him. Or laugh. Definitely laugh. It bubbled deep in her gut, but the sounds wouldn't escape. Daniel's life depended on it. She stood there in silence, watching as he opened the front door.

When he was gone, Caitlyn collapsed against the door and sighed a long sigh of relief. With shaky fingers, she fetched her phone from her pocket. Pressing her finger to the screen, she unlocked it. Scrolling through the contacts, she called Thomas.

"Pick up. Pick up," she muttered, listening to the phone ring. Afraid Silas might hear her, Caitlyn tried hard to leave a cryptic message in Thomas's voicemail. Half in tears, she cried into the phone. "Thomas, I'm sorry. Daniel didn't make it. Silas is here, and I think it's best we all grieve separately." She hoped he understood the warning. Daniel was gone, and in his place, a stranger lay in that hospital bed.

There was no telling what Silas would do if he discovered Daniel... Sebastian was alive.

She had to find a way out of this. Owen deserved a better life. Nor could she let her ex catch up with Sebastian Daniels to finish the job. *Not Daniel, please Lord, not her friend's brother. Not the one who bought her son ice cream and followed her home. Not the man...*

Not the man she loved.

She told him not to follow her. Did he even have a chance

there in the parking lot? Grabbing clothes, she locked herself in the bathroom for a quick shower. Keeping her cell phone on the top of the toilet, she hoped Thomas got her message. If she texted him, would Silas find out?

She couldn't take the chance he wouldn't take her phone and read her messages. Fear from the past reared its ugly head as she turned on the water to the shower.

Inside the shower, she shivered and scrubbed her body quickly. Silas wouldn't harm her. It wouldn't bode well with the Ghost Riders. She hadn't betrayed the club. Once a Ghost Rider, always a Ghost Rider. Under Butch's leadership, she was safe. Ever since Silas's dealings and her father's struggle with staying sober, Butch had kept the club on the good side of the law. An enforcer for the club, he challenged those loyal to Silas. Many left, except Blue and Grover. They always seemed to go with the flow. Had they been the ones to shoot at Daniels? Had they been keeping Silas up to date all this time?

The Ghost Riders no longer tolerated illegal activity within the club, but deep down, she knew it wasn't true. Had Butch let Silas return? Had her brother?

Silas may have wanted Daniels dead for the bounty, but someone else made the call.

A horrifying truth clawed its way to the surface. Questions flooded her mind: What happened to him? Why did someone want him dead? Regret wrung her inside out. She should have given him the chance to explain. But the revelation of his true identity left her reeling and unable to bear his presence a moment longer.

"You're a pain in my butt, Daniels, you know that?" she said to herself and no one at the same time. Scrubbing her hair with a bar of honey-and-cinnamon-scented soup, she said, "You better be worth it."

20

The sun had just set, and the night air was still heavy, like a warm blanket, as Chris pulled his motorcycle into the deserted parking lot off Route 15. He took a deep breath and glanced around to ensure no one was in sight. He was supposed to meet someone here, and their directions made it clear to come alone.

Chris stopped the bike and killed the engine, and the silence that followed seemed to stretch on forever. He rolled back his shoulders, stretching after the long ride. It cooled down enough from the hot day to blow wind in his hair. For the first time in a very long time, he felt good. So good. His brother would have been proud. So much for the young brother who got in the way. Oh, no. Chris proved his worth. He was smarter than his brother. Why bother getting blood on his hands when he could pay someone else? He learned that from Pike. Maybe his brother taught him something after all.

Time passed. Where was he? Chris shifted uneasily when suddenly he heard a low voice from the shadows. "You Chum?"

Chris's hand instinctively went to the gun tucked beneath his leather jacket. "Are you the one they call Shadow?"

He scanned the alleyway, trying to locate the source of the voice, when he noticed two figures emerge from around the abandoned gas station.

The two men were both tall, wearing long leather jackets, and one guy wore a rag tied around his head. They were both thickly built, and Chris watched as their dark figures stopped a distance away. Both men stood far away enough in the darkness he could make out their silhouettes, but not their faces.

The one who spoke stepped forward. His face came into the shadows of the lights of a vehicle going down the highway.

"I thought this was a one-on-one meeting," Chris said.

"For you," Shadow said. "You have my money?"

"You have my proof?" Chris asked.

The man beside Shadow stepped forward, pulled something from his pocket, and Chris clenched his fists. For a fleeting moment, he itched to go for his gun, but the man pulled out a phone. He clicked on the screen and held it up to play a video. It was dark in the video, too. Chris made out the sign of a restaurant called La Rosa's and listened to the squeal of tires, the loud bang of shots fired. Under the streetlight in the parking lot, a man fell.

"Pause it."

The man touched the screen.

"Zoom. I need to see him."

The head rag wearing guy complied.

Chris squinted. Beast changed the color of his hair. Even in the light spilling over the fallen body, he made out the brown instead of blond. The build matched, and the side of his face was unmistakable. Chris nodded, and the video resumed. Tires squealed and took off again. The video ended. The man with Shadow put the phone back in his pocket.

"Pay up."

"Not so fast." Chris kept his hands where both men could see them. Did they think he wouldn't know? It had been weeks since Shadow was released from prison. Chris expected him to contact him sooner to say the job was done. Weeks he waited for the news. He hung out with that old man Larry and his wife, hoping to get a lead on Beast's whereabouts. He searched the obituaries. Nothing.

Until Chris got the call. The muscle in his jaw jumped. "Where did you find him?"

"Gettysburg. You want me to pick off his family, too? That will cost you extra."

Family. It occurred to him to go after the family first, having Beast experience losing his family one by one.

"No." That would take too much time. He needed to clean this up before it got too messy.

"Then I guess we're done here. Just hand the rest of my cash over, and we'll go," Shadow said.

"I would, but Beast isn't dead," Chris said. "I came here hoping you'd prove my information wrong." A mixture of anger and disappointment churned through him. He paid a lot of money for this hit and pulled strings that, if traced back to him, would cost him more than his day job. All this, and he expected the assignment to be done. Maybe Pike was wrong. Maybe he had to handle this on his own to ensure it got completed.

Shadow and his companion exchanged a wary glance, but neither of them spoke.

"You shot him. Good job," Chris said, done wanting to get this over. "I wanted him dead. Now, he'll run again. I was told you were the best. I got you out of prison early for this."

"What other proof do you want?" the companion asked.

"Your video proves nothing." Chris trembled with fury. "I'll finish the job myself. You can pay me to fix your failure."

Shadow took another step toward Chris. He reached behind his back, then Shadow's companion pulled out a small handgun.

"Don't do it." He held out his hand.

"Give us the cash."

Chris growled, frustration keeping him frozen. They dared pull a gun on him. "I don't pay for incompetence."

The man with the gun looked over at Shadow.

"He means failure." Shadow curled his hands into fists. "I don't take a job I can't finish. And I will finish this one."

"You had your opportunity," Chris said. "I can't afford any more failure." He suspected his brother laughed at him from the grave. Two men came out of the darkness from behind Shadow and his companion, each with a gun pointed at Shadow. Another man walked out from the other side of the front to join Chris.

"What's this?" the companion asked.

"Insurance," Chris explained. "Meet my new friends from the Devil Demise. They've wanted to meet you for a long time. Apparently, you know them?"

"It's been a long time." Shadow looked at the man stepping up beside Chris.

Shadow's companion glanced around him. "What should we do? I didn't come here to die."

Shadow held his gaze with the enforcer from the Devil's Demise. The enforcer turned his gun sideways and stepped closer to Shadow. Chris stepped back. "I'll leave you all to catch up."

"What the—?" Shadow's companion yelled as Chris turned his back and got back on his motorcycle.

"You set me up!" Shadow yelled. "I'll see you dead for this!"

Chris turned the key and brought his motorcycle back to life. The rev of the motor beneath him gave him a sense of eerie peace. In the end, everyone got their due. He turned his motorcycle around and headed for the highway.

———

Sebastian shifted uneasily in the hospital bed, his chest throbbing dully. He looked up at Yeats, who sat in a chair nearby. The doctor threatened to call the cops if Sebastian got out of bed before his seventy-two hours of observation ended.

Staring up at the ceiling, Sebastian listened to Yeats, but he wasn't able to take his thoughts away from Caitlyn. Her pale face and dark, sad eyes nearly gutted him. And the revelation about Silas hunting him was like a kick in the face.

"There's more," Yeats said quietly. "The local guys found a slug in the brick behind you. I don't think they missed the first time."

Sebastian shuddered, remembering the sound of the gunshot close to him. "Did anyone hear the second shot?"

"No. You're lucky Cat followed her instincts and came back."

Sebastian sighed, relieved, but still worried about Caitlyn being put in danger because of him. "Maybe," he drawled, holding onto the ache in his arm. His gunshot wound might have missed his heart, but it flared up the old injury. "She shouldn't have done that. It wasn't safe."

"Why? You think someone could have been watching?" Yeats leaned back in his chair. He had to be uncomfortable sitting there most of the day.

"You're sounding like a cop."

Yeats steepled his fingers together as he thought silently for a few moments.

"Who did you call when Caitlyn brought me in?" Sebastian grunted, trying to shift his weight on the bed to turn toward Yeats. Instead, he made his head turn.

"Razek."

"Well, if it had to be anyone, I'm glad you called him instead of the locals." Sebastian went to raise his good arm, then let it drop. He felt like he got hit by a truck rather than a bullet.

Around them, the monitor beeped quietly above Sebastian's head, reminding them both that he was safe for now. For how long was anyone's guess

Caitlyn assured him she would not reveal his location, but how long before Silas found her? "I need you to send someone to watch Caitlyn. She's not safe. She should be halfway to Grace Meadows by now."

"I've already contacted Casper," he finally said. "He'll protect Cat, and the Ghosts needed to know what Silas is about. Someone must hate you bad to go out of their way to get you. Do you think they helped Silas get out of prison early?"

"No." Sebastian's voice rasped. "I've known for a while they would hunt me. Razek tried to get me to go into witness protection, but only because the feds got involved. Pike was dead, and half the members went to jail or split town. I should have listened to him and stayed if I wouldn't take on an alias. I wouldn't have brought the trouble here."

"That's my fault. I selfishly wanted you back. Maybe I was being cheap. I didn't want to hire someone with our business taking a leap this past year."

"It's all good. I wouldn't have come if I didn't want to, and part of me missed being home. I just don't want anyone else to get hurt." Sebastian closed his eyes. Caitlyn's worried face and Owen's bright smile faded to the memory of Audra's big, beautiful eyes staring at him with the light gone. He set up a fund for her son to go to college. They all did. Everyone in Thunder Valley pitched in to get it started. He at least owed Audra that. Her son deserved the college education she'd never gotten to finish. He saw the sacrifices Caitlyn made to provide for Owen, to take care of Pops, and vowed to keep them safe, no matter the cost.

"We need to find out who was behind this and get to them before they get to you."

Sebastian sighed heavily. "I don't care what the doctor

says." He reached for the wires, monitoring his heart rate. "Get me out of this bed and find my clothes."

Yeats put a hand up to stop him. "Relax. Breathe, Seb. Razek said to stay put while he does some digging. No one knows you're here. I have you registered under the name Michael Conrad."

Sebastian sagged back into the pillows, trying to ignore the pain in his chest and the fear that was taking root in his stomach. "I can't lay here waiting for someone to figure out I'm not dead and come to finish the job."

"Which makes it more important to figure out who tried to kill you. Drive-by shootings are not a thing in town. I told Razek about Cat's old man, and I mentioned Chris looking for you in Johnstown."

"I doubt Chris had anything to do with this. It might be no one involved with the Sharks, but since they killed Tiger, I can't rule it out."

"You're sounding like a cop." Yeats cracked his knuckles. "What do we do next?"

"First, we get me checked out of here. Then you can talk with that brunette from the pizza joint and see if she knows anything or worked that night beside Caitlyn."

"Then what?" Yeats raised a brow and smirked.

"I think we need to find a place for me to lie low for a while." Sebastian hated admitting he might need to stay off his feet longer than a couple of days. The first place anyone would start looking for him would be hospitals and clinics.

"Yeah, and I can think of one place that might be good."

Sebastian growled, knowing exactly where Yeats had in mind. "Don't say it."

Yeats opened his mouth to answer him when they were both interrupted by a knock at the door. A nurse peeked her head in and smiled when she saw them both awake and alert.

"Oh good, you're awake," she said cheerfully.

"I need to get out of here," Sebastian said.

"I'm Daralyn, and I'll be your nurse this shift," she said, nodding toward Yeats.

"You two know each other?" Was there one person in this county that Yeats didn't know? Sebastian frowned at the curvy, dark-haired nurse. Her bright pink scrubs were too bright in these drab accommodations.

"Daralyn is Casper's wife. It's good to see you, Dara." Yeats grinned.

"There is a police officer outside waiting to ask you some questions. The doctor wants to keep you overnight for observations for another day. You got shot," Daralyn said, as if he didn't know it.

Irritated by her tone, he said, "Great."

"What my friend is trying to say is he'll be happy to speak with the police, but he won't be staying the night. *Michael?*" Yeats stressed using the alias they set him up while in the clinic.

Sebastian gave Yeats a quick glance and jerked his head. "No. I said no police," he mouthed to Yeats.

"Razek." Yeats tilted his head toward the door. Wonderful. His old chief came the whole way here. For what? To give him a lecture? His father would do a fine job of that when he returned from that cruise with his mom. If he got it his way, they wouldn't even know he'd been here, let alone what happened. His eyes narrowed on Daralyn, then on Yeats.

Daralyn pressed her lips thinly as she checked Sebastian's vitals. Sebastian turned back to the nurse. "You need to unhook these wires unless you want me to do that myself."

"This really isn't wise," she protested.

"This isn't my first time getting shot. Remove the wires, then tell the cop to come in."

"Please," Yeats finished.

Daralyn shook her head at Sebastian. She glanced at Yeats as she took her rolling cart and left.

"I can see the wheels turning in your head. Why did you think

Caitlyn brought you here? You lost too much blood, and the bullet was still in you. Otherwise, Daralyn would have patched you up and got you out of here with no one the wiser," Yeats explained.

"How long do I have before anyone knows I'm still alive?" Sebastian grunted, his gut cramping.

"Caitlyn left me a message. You're dead, man. For now. Daralyn won't rat you out, and neither will Casper."

"You're certain?" Sebastian asked, the doubt battling his yearning for this to be over.

"100%. Casper might not be the best brother, but he'd never do anything that might involve Caitlyn or Owen getting in any further danger. It wouldn't surprise me if Casper sends men to keep an eye out if he doesn't himself."

A man wearing a dark suit and tie strolled in.

"Chief Razek," Sebastian greeted him.

"Conrad." Razek used Sebastian's alias. "I understand you are involved in a shooting that took place yesterday evening."

"Playing detective, now, are we?" Sebastian picked at the last piece of tape from the heart monitor. The machines made a beep, and the nurse rushed in, scowled at him, and shut them off.

"Someone must investigate. I understand you don't want the locals involved, but I've already spoken to them. Someone reported hearing two shots and saw an SUV speeding from the parking lot. Of course, they found nothing. La Rosa's security cameras didn't pick up that part of the parking lot."

"Figures," Yeats muttered.

"Caitlyn Cortés Valesa is the one who found you and brought you here. She works at La Rosa's."

"Are you asking? It sounds like you already know." Again, Sebastian glared at Yeats.

"You said you trusted him." Yeats moved away from Sebastian's bed, close to the closet filled with blankets and supplies.

"What didn't Yeats tell you?" Sebastian asked.

"It seems like there may be a gang connection to this. You hook up with another club? I saw you left your motorcycle at the scene. Your girlfriend claimed she told you to leave it there and took you home that night. You haven't been back to pick it up," Razek said.

Girlfriend? Caitlyn. Relief, mingled with a touch of unexpected gratitude, bubbled up. Maybe they still had a chance. She wouldn't let him get hurt, despite her feelings.

"She covered for me," Sebastian confirmed, a soft smile tugging at the corner of his lips regardless of the tightness in his throat. She might not have liked him keeping the truth from her, but she didn't want him dead. Despite her initial anger, she'd put herself at risk. A fierce need to protect her and Owen radiated within him, laced with a surprising tenderness and peace he hadn't known in a long time. She did that. She brought him peace. He wouldn't let Silas get near her or Owen.

"And my bike?"

"Don't worry, man, it's parked back at my place now. I asked a few members of the Soldiers to help. They're the Christian Motorcycle Club in this area," Yeats said for Razek's benefit.

"You have clubs in this area?" Razek asked.

"Two. The one I mentioned and the Ghost Riders. Hasn't been any trouble in a while."

"And you haven't gotten involved with any of them?" Razek asked, grilling him for facts. Reminding him of too much of his father. Sebastian knew his former boss had come because he wanted to help. Yeats was right. If Sebastian trusted anyone, it was Razek.

"No," Sebastian clarified. "I'm a motorcycle safety coach. I ride, but I'm not affiliated with any motorcycle clubs in the area."

"Caitlyn said it's her old man, Silas. He wanted Cat to go talk to Sam about finding Michael here."

"Silas Valesa, road name Shadow. He was to serve a sentence of twenty-five years with the possibility of parole after five. They denied him for six years, but recently, his parole was granted." Razek picked up the wire Sebastian disconnected. He twirled it with his fingers. "There is no connection to the Sharks."

"You know all this, how?"

"Not a time to get sarcastic," Razek told him. "I'm here because I need you alive. I don't leave my town or my county for anyone."

Razek's words grated. Sebastian ignored the draft at his back. A flicker of anger sparked at being reminded that none of them would be here if Sebastian hadn't failed in the first place.

"I'm sorry, I'm not at my best." His anger dissolved.

"Listen to the doctor. I've talked to the local authorities. They're digging up some information and keeping this on a need-to-know basis. I'm working on arranging somewhere for you to go where you'll be safe."

"I know a place," Yeats said. "It's the last place anyone would think to look."

"Or the first." Sebastian decided not to argue after the look Razek gave him. He respected the man, but every moment he stayed in his bed gave Silas time to go after his sister. Casper might have the Ghosts watch out for Caitlyn, but if there were Silas supporters in the club, Caitlyn, too, was in danger. He didn't trust anyone to keep her safe. Not even God. He'd trusted God to keep Audra safe. How could he trust God to do the same for Caitlyn? For Owen? For his family? "I'm not willing to take that risk."

"They hid slaves under the old farmhouse during the Civil War, and it kept those people safe. It will keep you safe," Yeats argued.

"How many people know about this place?" Razek asked.

"I'm not going home," Sebastian said, pinching the bridge of his nose and squeezing his eyes shut, tight. Taking deep breaths of air, tasting faintly of antiseptic and something like lemon, Sebastian tried to calm down.

"Only the family and me." Yeats smirked at Sebastian.

"Good." Razek reached into his pocket. He pulled out a phone. "Stay safe. I'll be in touch."

"There is no way we can sneak in there and stay under the house without Sam finding out," Sebastian protested.

"Who said anything about sneaking? You need to tell your sister you're here and alive before you never have the chance to see her again. Besides, you have no other choice. Caitlyn and Owen are at stake in this, too."

Sebastian leaned his head back farther into his pillows. Swallowing hard, he said, "Nothing can happen to Sam, Caitlyn, or Owen."

21

Caitlyn pulled up in front of the house. Leaving Sebastian at the clinic and pretending everything was normal during her shift proved harder than she expected. Owen spent the afternoon with Pops, but her nerves were on edge during her entire shift. Thomas called Alison during her break, and she put him on speaker while she ate. He sounded normal and promised to pick her up later that week. Of course he sounded normal. He knew all along who Daniel... Sebastian was, and the anger she carried was for both of them.

Poor Alison had it bad for the scruffy Motorcycle Safety Director, but Caitlyn hated to tell her that Thomas wasn't the long-term commitment type. She gave their relationship a few more months, tops.

How long would it have lasted with Sebastian? She wasn't sure she would ever get over his identity. But when Caitlyn thought of him and the kiss they shared... No one ever kissed her like that, like she was everything. Glancing over at her son, she smiled. His dark, wavy hair hung over his eyes. He smelled like horses, grass, and sweat. This last time, he brought his Xbox to Sam's for the night. Cole played with him, but Caitlyn could tell Daniel's absence from their game time bothered him. That kiss between them changed everything. The truth changed everything. It broke her heart, knowing soon her son's reality would shatter like hers had.

She was about to tell Owen, Daniel wouldn't be coming around anymore when she noticed the state police car parked in the driveway.

Owen's eyes widened as his body tensed. "Mom?" Her first thought went to her father. Old habits were hard to let go. Or had they come for Silas? Thomas's police contact moved fast to gather evidence, even though Thomas warned it would take a while to investigate. Despite the humidity in the air, Caitlyn got a chill. Taking a deep breath, she stepped out of the car and motioned for Owen to follow her. He hesitantly did so, staying close to her side as they entered the living room.

Pops sat in an old recliner, his eyes glassy and his neck reddening with increasing agitation. Since Silas returned, keeping Pops off the bottle became an impossible task. At any moment, she suspected Pops would show the cops his mean side. Two uniformed officers stood nearby, their presence looming heavily in the small room.

"Caitlyn," her father said, his voice strained. "They're looking for you. What did you do, girl?"

Her stomach churned as dread filled her.

"Are you Caitlyn Cortés Valesa?" one officer asked.

"Y-yes."

Owen moved closer to her side and crossed his arms. She knew he was trying to look tough and protective. Caitlyn suppressed a smile. Owen's attempt to be strong warmed her heart.

"Do you mind stepping outside and having a word with us?" the police officer asked, his gaze landing on Owen.

"What's this about?" she asked. Had someone seen her helping Sebastian into her Jeep? Did the doctor turn them in?

"We need to ask you a few questions about your husband, Silas Valesa."

"Ex-husband." Caitlyn felt herself freeze up and her legs wobble beneath her. "What about him?" she asked, barely able to find her voice.

"Mom?"

"Go play your games and put your headphones on," Caitlyn said.

Owen scowled.

"Go now, boy." Pops' voice boomed from his chair across the room.

Owen stomped away, but the sickening twist in her stomach kept her from commenting on his behavior.

Once Owen disappeared, headed toward his room, an officer—his tag read Hoffman—asked, "When was the last time you saw your husband?"

"Ex," Caitlyn corrected them again. Her voice held a tight edge, laced with a bitter truth she couldn't quite voice aloud. "And the day before yesterday. He left before I did when I took Owen to the sitter while I went to work."

"About what time would you say that was?" Hoffman asked.

"Around one o'clock."

"And you haven't seen him since?" the other officer asked.

"Why would I?" Caitlyn forced a nonchalant shrug, her gaze flickering away. "He knew he wasn't welcome here." A sliver of hope pierced through the rising tide of anger.

"This is the address he gave his parole officer for residence," Hoffman said.

If Silas discovered she ratted him out another time before Thomas's police contact from the hospital found proof to put him away again, she and Owen might not escape. But she was done with all the lies. "There's an apartment above the garage," Caitlyn added. "I didn't give him my permission to stay there."

"You can't kick a man out of his home. I own this place." Pops snapped at her. She bit her tongue from reminding him who paid the bills.

The other officer stepped forward, softer than his counterpart. "No one said you didn't," he said calmly, despite Pops' tirade. "But he was staying here?" Hoffman asked again, looking at Pops and back at Caitlyn.

Pops' words were gruff and sharp. "I told you he was," he said, gritting his teeth.

Caitlyn quietly said, "Pops," as she anxiously glanced from him at the two police officers.

Lopez, the second officer, asked, "I just want to confirm. Do you know where he was going? Maybe he was going to see someone?"

She gave them a few names, not sure what this was all about. "He left with Blue, I think. Pete and Grover have visited him since he returned. I'm not sure of their full names, but Pete used to rent the apartment over the garage until last year, when he moved across town."

"You don't know where they might have gone? What were they doing?" Hoffman asked.

"No. I don't want any part of anything my ex is involved in. He should never have gotten out of prison."

The officers shifted uncomfortably, and Pops asked, "What is this about?"

Lopez spoke up. "I'm sorry, Mrs. Valesa..."

"Cortés." There was no way she would let anyone associate her with Silas anymore.

"Cortés." Hoffman frowned. "I apologize for informing you that Silas Valesa is dead."

"Dead?" Had she heard him correctly? She glanced at Pops, and her father paled.

"His body was found by the river along Route 15 along with Earl Raynott."

"Earl Raynott?" Her mind raced to come up with a name.

At that very moment, Caitlyn's heart dropped into her stomach. Blue too?

Shock filled her body. Silas was dead. Daniels lived. Whoever put out the hit on Daniels must have known Silas had failed. They had no proof Silas did it, so who did Silas have contact with? She shot a glare at Pops, his mouth opening, then shutting.

Caitlyn's mind raced. Relief and sadness warred within her with every passing second. As Pops kept asking questions, she was suffocating, drowning in a sea of turbulent emotions. Caitlyn wrapped her arms around her waist and hugged herself.

The officers' questions were like needles piercing through her heart, reopening wounds that had never really healed. With each passing moment, Caitlyn became more torn inside. Part of her wanted to confess everything to the officers, but another part knew that doing so would only make things worse. Whoever put a hit on Daniels must have put a hit on Silas. And they'd only do that if they *knew Daniels was alive.*

At last, the silence was broken by the one officer's voice. "You drive a Suzuki C500?"

She nodded.

"Your motorcycle was found parked at an abandoned gas station along Route 15."

"What?" Caitlyn tried to process it. "I-I keep it in the garage."

"I gave him the key," Pops said, then commanded in Spanish for her to keep her mouth shut. Not to say another word. About what? What happened to her father's Harley?

Hoffman scribbled notes, and Lopez stood and listened until she finished. The officers thanked her for her time. As they left, Officer Hoffman spoke. "I'm sorry for your loss."

Caitlyn saw the officers out and turned to go to her room when she spotted Owen at the top of the stairs. "Oh, *mijo.*" She sighed, her heart sinking. How much did he overhear?

She rushed up the stairs, pulling her son in her arms, and sat beside him on the top stair.

Owen nestled into her embrace, his grip tightening on her back. "He told me I could call him Papa," Owen mumbled, his voice muffled against her shirt. "Is Silas... is my father dead?

"You heard." Tears streamed silently down her face. She choked out, pushing a stray curl from his eye, "You were to be playing your games."

"I was," Owen said, his voice small. "But then I thought Pops was in trouble, or Dan."

"Pops is fine," she reassured him. "And so is Dan. They wouldn't..." Her voice trailed off, unable to spill the ugly truth to her innocent son.

Down below, the door slammed, and she flinched. Owen looked at her with such despair it almost made her tumble forward on the stairs. "He wouldn't hurt Papa, right?"

"No, *mijo*, he wouldn't. Dan... He's a good man." Caitlyn took a deep breath and tried to focus on her son. She prayed over him, asking God to help them get through the following days, to give her strength for both of them, and to help Owen process the loss of a father who he barely knew. She allowed more tears to slip down her face, grieving along with her son.

———

The sterile scent of disinfectant assaulted Sebastian's nostrils the moment the door creaked open. He lifted his head from the scratchy white pillow. Finally. It felt like an eternity trapped in this sterile cage. "Yeats."

Yeats lumbered in, his usual swagger replaced by a deep furrow in his brow. A worn leather bag hung in his hand, a stark contrast to the pristine white bed sheets.

Sebastian's gaze darted toward the bag. "Food?"

Yeats tossed the bag onto the bed near Sebastian's feet.

"We're getting you out of here, partner." His voice held a gruff tenderness. "Those nurses look more scared of your gunshot wound than anything else. Seems bullet holes and blood aren't exactly their daily routine around here."

Sebastian reached for the bag, his stomach grumbling in protest. He shifted uncomfortably, the fabric of the hospital gown a constant irritant against his skin. A low growl escaped his lips as the pain flared again. "Starving."

"Got subs from La Rosa's waiting in the truck," Yeats replied, his voice softer now.

A knot of worry tightened in his gut. He pulled out the jeans, never happier to see a pair of faded blues in his hands.

"Caitlyn?" he blurted, not caring about the jeans nearly as much. Days had bled into each other since Caitlyn walked out of his room. Her shock and hurt burned into his memory. She hadn't returned. His calls went unanswered, his texts disappearing into a void. Yeats' brothers from Soldiers of Christ sent him reports, ensuring him Caitlyn and Owen remained safe.

Yeats scratched his beard. "No, Seb. Alison says she took a few days off." His voice paused, indecision in his eyes, then said, "Silas is dead. They found his body floating in the river along Route 15."

The news slammed into Sebastian, the breath catching in his throat. Dead? Caitlyn. Owen. "How long ago?"

"Two days," Yeats said, dropping his voice to a whisper and stepping closer. "Police are keeping it quiet. Seems the Ghosts are missing two other members. One found dead shortly after Silas, and the other vanished."

"Who was with him?" Sebastian pressed, his mind racing.

"Blue and Grover. Blue's dead, too. Figured you want to know, in case it changes your plans." Yeats glanced at the doorway, his eyes wary.

Sebastian threw the thin hospital blanket off his legs, the movement sending a fresh wave of pain through him. Gritting his teeth, he ignored it. "Pull the curtain. I need to get dressed and find Caitlyn."

"I'll find a nurse to unhook you, but first, let's talk about Sammy."

At the mention of his sister, a jolt of fear went through him. "What about Sam?"

He tried to reach for his phone and check the security cameras, but Yeats picked up the phone first.

"She misses you, Seb," Yeats said, holding the phone from reach. "She talks about you, tells everyone about how proud she is of her brother who's in law enforcement, but I see it in her eyes. The worry, the... something else."

Sebastian scoffed while trying to maneuver a leg into his pants. "She's got a life of her own. Showing up after all this time, without warning? No." Sebastian clenched his jaw, a tug of war raging inside him. Didn't Yeats think he ached to see his sister again? He watched her on the security cameras, but the fear of making her a target, of disrupting her life, kept him rooted.

"Look," Yeats pressed, frustration creeping into his voice. "Give Cat some time. She'll come around. And Sam... She's your sister. Don't you owe her the chance to see you again?"

"Not if it means putting her in danger." Sebastian huffed. He spent the last few days lying in this bed, having way too much time to think and worry. Caitlyn not answering him was nearly killing him. If not for Yeats sending men to keep an eye on her, he might have ripped out his monitor wires yesterday.

"What happened in Johnstown?" Yeats asked in a tone which said Sebastian wasn't leaving this room until he came clean.

Sebastian's grip tightened on the pants, his knuckles whitening. "A woman died. I failed to protect her. She had a child that's now being raised by a relative." Sebastian's voice grew rough, pieces in his chest tearing apart.

"You got the guy who did it, right? You took down the club, and they can't operate again," Yeats said.

Sebastian nodded, a lump forming in his throat.

"Then you didn't fail."

Memories of Audra ripped him in two. "She wanted a better life."

"What makes you think that baby doesn't have that? What makes you think she didn't want what was best for her child? Was she mad at you? Did she beg you to save her?"

Sebastian shook his head, blinking back the months upon months of sorrow and regret.

"Then you haven't failed," Yeats repeated, this time stronger. "The darkest night can lead to the brightest dawn. We don't always understand the path, and God always gives us the choice of turning around or choosing a different way, but there's always a plan, Seb. Stick with the plan."

Something dark and haunting flickered through Yeats' eyes. His friend never spoke of his time with the Rangers, but Yeats hadn't come home on his own, not like Sebastian. He chose to come home. To protect his family. Caitlyn. Owen.

No, Caitlyn wasn't going to drop her truth bomb, then avoid him.

Audra was brave, even in the last moments of her life. She protected her son, and without her, the evidence needed to put an end to the Sharks would never have surfaced. He understood Caitlyn needed to protect Owen. Without those past events, he wouldn't have found Caitlyn and Owen and the one thing he missed most—family.

He had a family to protect now—that is, if Caitlyn would forgive him, and they could start over. No more lies. No more hiding the truth.

Sebastian managed to put the other leg in his pants and slid off the bed to pull them up under his gown. The monitors behind him beeped unhappily with his movements. A sudden clatter from the hallway broke the tense silence and startled him. His heart hammering in his chest, he said, "Get me out of here."

"I'll find a nurse, but you got to swear to me, Seb, you'll see Sam before you go into hiding."

Dropping the gown and staring down at the wires stuck to his chest, Sebastian said, "Who says I'm hiding?"

22

Under different circumstances, Chris might have considered these people friends. Audra taught him about friendship. About trust. She bared her soul to him, even when his brother Pike stripped her of everything. Now someone else raised her son. It didn't matter if the little boy belonged to him or Pike. She should have told him what was going down before it happened. In a matter of days, he would have gotten her a new ID and made sure she was set up somewhere safe.

Would have...

But Audra was dead, and after spending time with Larry and the Thunder Valley Riders, a part of him became grateful for Charlie's help to keep Audra away from Pike. Another part of him remained bitter for the old man's help. He had a history of taking in strays, like Haden.

Audra wasn't a stray. She was lost, but Chris found her. Not Pike. But her mother had a drinking problem and sold Audra out to Pike. Anger boiled just under his skin. The woman spent enough time in the hospital. He hoped she learned her lesson. Audra deserved so much more. Yet Larry tried to explain to him that God would forgive the woman.

Maybe Audra would have, too. She was her mother and Emma's.

Chris never forgave his mother. She got what she deserved. His father made sure of it. No, Chris couldn't trust these people. They forgave people for the darkest sins.

And his were dark. So very dark.

Pike made him do it. His brother pushed him and pushed him, and Chris had finally thought he had outsmarted him. Pike intimidated those around him, using his leadership of the Sharks to get what he wanted, including Audra. Chris might have used his tech skills to gain him favors and amass his own wealth, but it failed to gain him competent contract work. No one would ever get the best of him again.

Chris stepped closer, drawn by the sound of Larry's voice. At the last meeting, they mentioned helping at an event this month. They were discussing their plans for the Gettysburg Biker Week. Some members took turns handing out tracts and water, with the other Christian motorcycle clubs attending. They discussed bike blessings. A concept Chris found intriguing. Did these people think if they prayed over a motorcycle, nothing bad would happen? He held back his snort with the thought and lingered close to the conversation. Many of the men planned to take their significant others with them. Some of the unattached men grinned.

"Captain!" A tall man with blonde hair held up his hand to Haden as he appeared inside the restaurant. Haden walked toward them with his Holly at his side. Every time he saw her, the woman kept a planner in one hand and held onto the club's Vice President.

"It's Vice, now, Dave," another man, in his mid-thirties to early forties, corrected.

"Hey, Axel, long time no see." Haden clasped the dark-haired man's hand and then Dave's. "Was wondering if something happened."

"Work." Axel rubbed a hand over his short beard.

"They've got me running stuff up to Canada now, and last week, I made three trips to Alabama."

Chris half listened to them talk, surmising Axel was a truck driver, and Dave, with the build of an Olympic wrestler, worked for a roofing company. Haden introduced them to Holly. She smiled with those peach-glossed lips of hers.

Today, she wore a long-sleeved t-shirt and a black leather vest with the club patch. Her jeans and boots looked faded and the opposite of her usual high heels and blouse he'd seen her in during previous meetings.

"Are you attending biker's week? Or are you too busy planning a wedding?" Axel asked.

"Oh, we're doing both," Holly assured them. Her arm stayed intertwined with Haden's. Chris tried to ignore the uncomfortable feeling gripping him. Never did he ever want a relationship with a woman where the woman could control him. By the look on Haden's sloppy grin, the man lost the battle long ago. Holly had him wrapped around her finger. Poor bastard.

"Biker's week first." Haden motioned to the waitress and pointed to the two vacant seats at the end of the nearest table. "Coffee, please."

"And there will be a wedding." Holly snuggled close to him.

"We're getting hitched in a barn," Haden said, ever so enthusiastic.

"In Gettysburg?" Larry's wife, Marge, asked. "Oh, what an answer to prayer. What did your mother think of the location? Will Charlie still be able to walk you down the aisle?"

Walk being the proverbial word. Everyone knew because of a motorcycle accident, Charlie Brooks would never walk again. Pike wanted to make sure Charlie understood not to get involved with his business. Trying to help Audra cost Charlie his legs. Chris tried to talk to Pike before having Charlie's bike altered. Not having the ability to walk wouldn't stop a man like Charlie Brooks. Chris wanted Audra safe from Pike, but he wanted to be the one who saved her. He wanted to be the one she came to for help, not Charlie.

They all thought him too weak, but he outsmarted them. What he did, he did for Audra.

Holly sighed, the look of a dream in her eyes. "It's perfect for us. Mother will attend because it's my wedding. We've worked out the details for Charlie to give me away."

Chris watched their exchange with curiosity. After being estranged from her father for years, she and Charlie reconnected. It was a God thing, according to Larry and their talks over the past couple of months.

Chris remained unconvinced.

If God only wanted the good for all, then why had Audra died? Why was her son being raised by her sister? Where was his and Audra's happily ever after?

"Congratulations," Chris said, entering the group conversation. "I hear those kinds of things are the trend. Non-traditional, I mean."

"It's not what we originally planned, but our dates kept getting booked and my mother kept vetoing every place until Haden remembered Beast's family has a stable in Gettysburg. We'd gotten to where I feared we'd have to elope and throw a party later."

Chris's smile didn't quite reach his eyes as Holly beamed about the wedding plans. "How... quaint."

"I did like the idea of an ice cream social," Rosco ribbed Haden, all in brotherly love. Chris hadn't noticed the trash man joining them until now. He glanced around, searching for Audra's sister and the baby.

His finger itched, and he wiped his hand down on his blue jeans. Soon. He promised the Devil Demise no more stalling.

"No wife or baby today?" Chris tried to sound casual. One thing he came to look forward to in these meetings was to see Audra's son. But today, Holly's news offered something even more hopeful than expected. Anticipation flowed through him. A wedding in a stable? Perfect. A smirk played on his lips as the others continued around him, oblivious as in his mind, he made plans.

"Isaac had a rough night, so I let him and Emma sleep in," Rosco said.

"Everything okay?" Chris asked, a palpitation of panic erupting in his chest.

"Teething."

"That can be brutal." Silver-haired Marge patted Rosco on the arm. "I'll pray for you throughout this time. Poor baby." She frowned and moved to the table to join Larry.

Rosco nodded in agreement. He moved for a cup of coffee, probably needing more than anyone else.

Holly flipped her hair from her shoulder and pulled out her planner. Chris glimpsed a small cross hanging around her neck. He both envied and pitied them all at the same time. To misplace one's trust in something... someone... whom they'd never met or seen. His own mother wore a cross like the one around Holly's neck. It did nothing to save her, either.

"We should all go to biker's week," the balding guy said from beside Larry. "It'll be a great way to get away from the day-to-day grind and reconnect with others."

"Yeah," another member chimed in, "and we can line up our motorcycles for Holly to walk down the aisle with Charlie for the big day."

Haden held out a chair for Holly, and they were the last to take their seats before the server arrived. "I like that idea. You're all invited."

"So, bikers' week?" Chris took a seat beside Larry, who insistence on sharing his faith everywhere they went. The older man made it his mission to get Chris to ask Jesus in his heart. At first, Chris found it admirable, then annoying. If Larry could see all the things in Chris's heart right this moment, he would stop trying to save Chris.

No matter how much God forgave, it wouldn't stop him from following through on the promise he made. It was do or die.

And the only one dying was Beast.

"It's like the one we have here in Johnstown," Larry explained. "Can we count you in?"

"Where do I sign up?"

23

The rhythmic drumming of fists against the door shattered the fragile peace Caitlyn had rebuilt within their home. Her heart lurched, cold dread slithering down her spine as her brother Antonio stormed inside the house. "It's good to see you, too," she muttered, closing the door.

"What the hell, Caitlyn?" her brother roared.

"Keep it down," she hissed. "What is your problem?"

"Owen is here?" His hardened gaze, as sharp as a shard of ice, zeroed in on Pops slumped on the couch. Pops, still half-asleep, lifted his head slightly, bleary-eyed and confused, his face etched with the lines of a life spent mostly at the bottom of a glass. He blinked at Antonio.

"He's with a friend." Caitlyn flinched as their father mumbled slurred words and waved his hand for Antonio to leave, the remnants of sleep clinging to his voice. Her father went on a bender right after the news of Silas's death. For the first time in days, peace and quiet filled the walls until Antonio came to disrupt it.

Antonio nodded. "Then I should be able to speak as I wish."

"And what is it you have to say?" she asked.

"Don't play dumb with me, Cat." He spat the words out, each one laced with venom. "Daralyn told me you brought that *la chota* to the clinic. You expected my old lady to put her job on the line for another one of your cop friends?" His voice dripped with contempt, the word *bolillo* stinging in her ears. "Another wounded savior trying to play hero for you? Did you not learn anything the first time?"

Caitlyn's already frayed nerves snapped. "What would you have done?" she shot back "He was bleeding out in the parking lot. He would have *died.*"

"I would have learned from the first time. What were you thinking? If I would have known this scheme of yours to bring another *poli* into our midst, I would have shot him myself."

"Is that what is bothering you? That you didn't know he was a cop?" Caitlyn laughed, a nervous tick that slipped from between her lips. "Well, neither did I. He fooled me, too. I didn't know who he was." And she should have. Deep down, all the signs were there in front of her face.

"You should have come to me and told me what was happening, then all this"—he threw up his hands—"could have been avoided."

"You say this as if I had a choice," Caitlyn said. "I am not like you, Toni. I don't let men to die because I'm too afraid to do what is right."

"No. You're right. I blame this one, *him,*" Antonio jerked his chin in Pops' direction. "You are a weak fool, old man. It wasn't enough to lose your position amongst the Ghosts, lose your honor. You had to take mine!"

"You lost your position?" Caitlyn gasped.

Their father grunted, the old man staring, his eyes troubled.

"*Sí,* sister. Grover told Butch that you let Silas come back, and Silas told them Pops invited him home."

"Lies," Caitlyn cried. "Grover is a wanted man, and Blue

is dead. He's trying to cover up his actions, which causes more trouble because Silas is dead."

"*Sí*, but I have been stripped of my cut and shamed because the past has tarnished my place in the club, and Butch warned against any trouble. If it wasn't for our *padre* inviting the devil amongst us, I would have been president of the club, not Butch!"

And Caitlyn might have lost the little freedom Butch gave her away from the club. Antonio held a strong code of loyalty to the club, more so than to their family, but his leadership would have fostered far worse results than their father.

"Bah! You are weak. You would never be the man Silas is. I married him to your sister to bring strength to this family," Pops declared.

Antonio's neck and face turned red with fury. Caitlyn jumped in front of him. "Silas threatened us. You see, Pops, he's not strong enough to defend us. If you would have been here, then maybe, but you disowned us." Caitlyn's chest tightened. "You brought this on yourself, brother."

Antonio raised his hand, and Caitlyn lifted her chin, daring him to follow through.

"Casper," Pops growled, "I am the man of this house. Leave. Get out!"

Antonio shook his head. "You're drunk, old man. Always drunk." His eyes glinted, and Caitlyn swallowed, bracing for the smack that didn't come. Antonio spit on the floor beside her.

"*¡Detener! ¿Te atreves a entrar a mi casa y amenazar a tu hermana?*" His gaze went to their father as Pops shouted in Spanish at Antonio.

Antonio's eyes widened, his body leaning away just as one of Caitlyn's mother's vases sailed through the air and shattered against the wall to the right of her. He stalked toward their father. Caitlyn grabbed him by the arm, and he tried to shake her off. He pointed his finger toward Pops.

"You're lucky he's dead. You have no honor. You would let him tear down this family again." Antonio stalked toward Pops, the old man not having enough time to react as the door flung open for a second time. Antonio reached for the sky, whirling around to face the *poli*.

———

Sebastian rapped on the front door. He held a small container of marigolds. Cat's Jeep sat in the driveway, and so did another motorcycle he didn't recognize. Raised voices came out muffled through the door. Something smashed against the wall with a shattering sound. Sebastian put down the flowers and reached for the gun in the back of his waistband. With one hand on the knob and the other holding his gun, Sebastian flung open the door and pointed the gun.

"Stop! Pol…" He stumbled over the last word. It slipped off his tongue, but no matter for Caitlyn's father, Pops looked shocked and stumbled back. Pops' hands froze in the air from throwing what looked like a vase. Casper, Caitlyn's brother, stood across from Pops and lifted his hands.

"I told you, old man, all you do is bring trouble to this family." Casper glared at Sebastian. He wore jeans with threads hanging from cut knees and a pair of black boots laced past the ankle. "He's got no business here. Get rid of him." Casper said to Caitlyn, standing close to the stairs where glass spread across the scratched wood floors near her feet. She looked pale, her eyes large, but instead of relief at the sight of Sebastian, those amber eyes turned darker with fury. She went off like a lit rocket, speaking rapidly in Spanish. He made a mental note to learn Spanish for the future. Casper answered her back, and Welder picked something else up, forgetting Sebastian held a gun on all of them.

"That's enough!" Sebastian yelled. Caitlyn stepped back as he stepped alongside her.

"Did you call him?" Casper asked, switching to English.

"No." Caitlyn shook her head.

"What are you going to do?" Casper nodded toward the gun. "You are not family. You have no right coming into this house."

Sebastian lowered his gun and placed his hand against Caitlyn's back. "The way I see it, neither do you."

Caitlyn stiffened under his touch. He leaned closer and whispered, "You okay?"

She glanced at him from the corner of her eye and nodded, her lips pressed thin. He knew she wanted to say something but held her tongue in check as Casper glared at them both.

"This is my son. And this is my house," Pops said, his hand shaking with what looked like the television remote in hand. Sebastian wouldn't tell the older man it would take more than a television remote to scare him away. He tucked his gun back where he kept it in his waistband.

"And I'm the man who intends to marry your daughter and raise her son like my own." It came tumbling out before he could think about what he said. Caitlyn gasped and turned her head to stare at him.

"Your kind isn't welcome here," Casper informed him, ignoring the mutterings of the older man beside him. Welder's hair was sticking out in tufts, and the old man sported several days' worth, if not a week's, of beard. The creases around the old biker's eyes had deepened since the last time Sebastian saw him.

"And what kind is that?" Sebastian asked as Caitlyn regained her composure, about to say something. Uncertain of her reaction to his next move, a touch of nervous energy filled his hands as he gave her back a rub. She relaxed under his touch.

"Because the way I look at it, family are the people who

look out for each other, take care of one another," Sebastian said.

"I take care of my family," Casper said, then turned to Welder, "I should have known you are nothing but a weak old fool. You let trouble right back into our lives. Did you think of that? Did you think of what it would cost us this time?"

Pops' eyes, rimmed with red and bloodshot, avoided looking at Casper. He muttered something low in Spanish. Caitlyn leaned against Sebastian, enough for him to feel the brush of her blouse against his arm. "Casper was cast out of the Ghost Riders. Grover told Butch that we let Silas come back, as if we invited him."

"He's back?" Sebastian asked, needing the man alive as a witness.

"He's in police custody, but you're the cop. You should know," Casper sneered.

Pops growled. "I did what I had to do for this family."

"You are no better than him. You didn't learn the first time!" Casper flung his arms and then strode past the old man.

As he tried to walk past Sebastian, he caught Casper by the arm. "You're one quick to judge." Sebastian looked at Pops. "I believe you."

"Says the man who is the target." Casper yanked his arm away.

"Coming from a man who understands what it's like to do things to protect others and fail." Sebastian looked Casper in the eyes. "Your father's drowning in a bottle, and what have you done to keep him from going under?"

"I'm not his keeper. Caitlyn wanted to stay here. She deals with the old man." Casper lifted his chin.

"Yeah, and she's done her best. More than anyone would be expected to do. Do you know how many days he was sober before his buddies came into town?" Sebastian's question caught Casper off guard. Casper frowned, looking at Caitlyn.

"One hundred and twelve," she said, meeting his gaze.

"It's not my problem."

"No," Caitlyn said, "He's mine because I chose to stay. You only come here because you need to blame someone. You're like him. Like father like son."

"Don't say that." Casper's nostrils flared, his hands turning into fists. Sebastian moved, putting himself between Casper and Caitlyn. Pops watched, his hands trembling, most likely from needing a drink. Sebastian would deal with him next.

"Why?" Sebastian knew he shouldn't taunt him. Caitlyn deserved better.

"I am nothing like *him*," Casper spat.

"Maybe. Maybe not," Sebastian said, trying to maintain his cool. "You said you take care of family. Where were you when the lawn was turning into a jungle? Are you going to wait until the porch falls off to help fix anything around here? Or do you just come to tell them what to do and delegate to a woman who's working two jobs, raising a kid, and taking care of her father?"

"You don't know what he has done," Casper nearly shouted.

"Does it matter?" Sebastian asked. "Since when do the sins of the father get held against the daughter? Or the son?" He thought of Owen. Where was the boy? Still keeping his gaze on Casper, he asked, "Where's Owen?"

"Sam's," she said.

Pops paced and glared at him. He shouted something in Spanish, and Casper shouted back. Caitlyn added a few words, and Sebastian held up his hand to stop the bickering. He dealt with enough domestic disputes before going undercover. He wanted to placate this and move on.

"Don't think you can come here and have a say in what we do because you got a thing for my sister."

"The only permission I need to date a woman is hers," Sebastian clarified.

Casper's eyes narrowed. His nostrils flared.

Sebastian turned to Caitlyn. "Are you okay?"

"Antonio is right. You should leave. I don't know why you came." Her eyes failed to meet his.

Yeats had warned him to give her more time. "We still have things we need to talk about."

"Maybe she doesn't want to talk to you," Casper said.

"And maybe this *chica* can talk for herself," Caitlyn retorted.

"Listen, I have a friend. If I ask, they might pull some strings to get Pops in a rehab in Philly."

Caitlyn's eyes narrowed. "Why would you do this?"

"Because if it's alright with you, I want us to be a family. You. Me. And Owen." Sebastian ignored the sound coming from Pops. Casper crossed his arms, his chin tilted down and his eyes boring into Sebastian's back.

"It's your decision. Tell me, and I'll make the call. Your father needs help. Let me help you help him."

"You're going to send him away to one of those rehab centers?" Casper grunted.

Pops ranted in Spanish as he headed down the hall away from them.

"Pops, wait!" Caitlyn went to go after him.

"Don't waste your breath," Casper told her. "It's a lost cause."

"You are a lost cause." Caitlyn jabbed her finger into her brother's chest. "You disowned us because you blamed Pops. Like Sebastian said, Silas would have killed Pops. And where were you to help us?"

Casper gritted his teeth, locking his jaw together. Sebastian waited as Casper lifted his fist, about to say something, then turned on his heel and strode away. Down the hall. Toward where their father went.

Caitlyn's eyes widened. She pressed a hand to his chest, just below his bandage. Instinctively, Sebastian's hand covered hers. He flinched, afraid her touch might aggravate the wound. The dark swirls of amber in her eyes seemed to deepen as her features etched in worry. The nurse, Daralyn, tried to talk him into staying longer at the clinic, recovering, but he needed to see Caitlyn.

More shouts came from down the hall. None of which Sebastian could understand. "I'm sorry. I'll do whatever you want to make it up to you. I never meant to hurt you."

His hand hovered hesitantly in the space between them, then landed softly atop hers on his chest. It was his eyes, however, that implored her. Caitlyn's shoulders slumped. "You will call your friend?"

"Done." He pulled out his phone, kept his eyes locked on hers, and waited for the person on the other end to pick up. It took less than ten minutes to make the arrangements, but her gaze kept locked with his the entire time. "They've got a bed. Can we get him there today?"

"Then we go. This is good. We can talk on the ride back."

"What about work? Owen?" he asked, waiting for the catch.

"Family first," she whispered, and the adamant look in her eyes made him reach for her. "Owen is staying the night with Sam, and I'm off work for another two days."

Sebastian wrapped his good arm around Caitlyn. "I'm not leaving you." He breathed in her scent to ease the anxiety building in him since he got in Yeats' truck to make the drive over here.

"I know." She gave him a tender squeeze, leaning into his chest, but not enough to press against his healing wound.

Sebastian's phone vibrated. "Do you think Casper will help?"

His phone went off again. Sebastian pulled it out of his pocket.

"I don't know. You saw how upset my brother was. Give me the address and the information. I don't think he'll help you here. You need to go and rest. Tomorrow, we'll figure things out." She wrapped her arms around him. Sebastian inhaled her warm and inviting scent, like walking into a kitchen after baking bread. He tightened his hold on her. Kissed her on the side of her head. Caitlyn turned her head, met his lips, briefly. "Go. I can handle it from here. You've already done enough."

Sebastian's phone vibrated again, a continuous buzzing that seemed to carry through his bones. He touched his phone, the security camera app opened, and any arguments he died upon his lips.

"I need to go," he said, his voice gruff.

Caitlyn pulled back, alarm flashing in her eyes. "Sebastian. What is it?"

"Something has triggered the alarms at Grace Meadows."

"Then I'm coming with you," Caitlyn said, her voice urgent.

"Let me handle this. It might not be safe."

"Owen is at Grace Meadows. If something was happening there, he could be in danger." She shouted in Spanish, and Antonio gave a muffled response from the other room. Sebastian headed for Yeats' truck and held open the door for Caitlyn. *Lord, don't let me fail.*

24

Chris stepped into the barn. The setting sun sent a stream of light through the top windows, casting a golden glow across the gleaming wood and meticulously swept aisle. The air hummed around him. Horses snorted rhythmically, contently munching in their stalls, and hooves thudded gently on soft bedding.

His eyes narrowed in calculating focus, scanning the stable. This wasn't the dusty barn he envisioned. A pang of doubt flickered through him, but a chilly reserve held him here. Gleaming brass nameplates on stalls and horses with braided manes made his lip curl. A silent message flashed across his phone screen. Good. He triggered the alarm.

He crept forward, retreating deeper into the stable. The horses swiveled their heads, their large, intelligent eyes filled with a question Chris couldn't answer.

Finally, he would have his chance to avenge his brother's death and fulfill his promise to the Devil's Demise, if he joined them. That old man Larry put ideas in his head. Maybe after this, Chris would find a new woman and make a fresh start. He might even stay with the Thunder Valley gang. Watch over Audra's boy. Wouldn't that be something? They accepted him.

"No matter what you've done," Larry told him. "Be open to the word of God." The old fool, talking about how a hard heart will hear the word of God, but nothing changes. Nothing can grow. And worry fettered inside Chris, remembering those conversations. Hearing him.

But it wasn't enough. Not soon enough. Not for him.

Outside, a vehicle approached. Chris moved behind the heavy sliding door. A door shut, and Chris flexed his hands. Counting to keep calm. Keeping his back pressed against the large door, his heart pounded. Chris tightened his grip on the gun in his hands. A surge of adrenaline coursed through his veins as Sebastian Daniels came inside. Beast.

He took a deep breath and stepped forward, pointing the gun toward Beast's back.

"Hey old buddy," he whispered.

Sebastian spun around. His eyes widened. "Chris? What are you doing here?"

Chris sneered, a cruel twist of his lips. "I'd tell you I came to help set up for the wedding, but I'd be lying, and I hate liars."

"Wedding?" Sebastian's gaze landed on the gun in Chris's hands. "I heard you were asking around about me."

"You are a hard man to find, but I knew you'd come back. Everyone always comes back to family." Soon, Beast's family would feel the same pain he did when Chris's brother and Audra were taken away from Chris.

"I hear you've joined up with my old family. I'm glad I'll still be able to call you brother." Sebastian's gaze remained on the gun.

Chris took a step back. "Brother?"

"Yeah. Brother." Sebastian held out his hands, palm up. "Family," Sebastian said again, lifting his gaze to look Chris in the eyes. Chris took a deep breath Looking a man in the eye and killing him wasn't part of the plan. He couldn't let anyone else have the job. They'd screw it up. No more screwups. If you wanted something done right, his father always said you had to do it yourself. His grip tightened on the gun. An accident. This was just all an unfortunate accident that would soon go away.

"I'm not your brother," Chris said, his voice calmer than the trembling going on through his insides.

"Sometimes family isn't about blood." Sebastian moved to the left, slowly, close to one of the occupied stalls. Foul beasts. He endured listening to the occasional bang of a horse's hoof against the stall doors and the settling of the barn. The place freaked him out with all its silence and random noises of horses and nature.

"You sound as messed up as the old men in that group you call a club back in Johnstown." Chris refused to think of Larry or the time the old man spent trying to convince him to live his life, according to Jesus.

"We all have our faults. Why don't you put the gun down, and we'll figure this out." Sebastian kept his hands where Chris could see them. No matter. Unarmed, armed. It wouldn't save him.

"You killed my brother. My *blood* brother."

Sebastian's face fell. "I-I'm sorry about the way things went down. You should have told me Pike was your brother. None of us knew."

"Yeah, because Pike wanted it that way. I had to work my way up the ranks. So he would acknowledge me." A tremor ran through Chris's hands as he spoke. Months of grief and anger, a bitter cocktail churning in his gut, clawed its way up his throat, forcing the words out in a ragged, desperate pitch. "Then I would have been his Beta. I would have helped run the club. But you killed him."

"He killed Audra."

Chris shook his head. "I don't believe you. You took his life and ruined everything!"

But before he could act, a voice rang out from behind him.

"Put the gun down!" A click of a firearm sent a shudder through Sebastian.

Startled, Chris whirled around. Cole stood at the back of the barn. "He's mine. You don't get to take back the hit."

Chris' lip curled. "I sent you months ago. I had to hire someone else."

"And he failed." Cole walked closer. His black cargo pants and black t-shirt were dusty and soiled with flecks of hay. Chris kept his gun pointed at Sebastian. Sweat beaded over his forehead, threatening to drip down and burn his eyes.

Chris hesitated, his mind racing. He hadn't expected the other hired bounty hunter to be here. Why did everyone have to go messing up his plans?

Cole held his gun pointed at Sebastian. "He's mine. That bounty is mine."

Chris grinned at Sebastian. "How does it feel to have people fighting over you to kill you?"

Sebastian met Chris's gaze head-on, his expression unreadable. "How much is my life worth to you?"

Chris shrugged, "A half a million."

"That's a lot of cash for an errand boy," Sebastian said.

"Work smarter, not harder. Isn't that what they say?" Chris glanced over Sebastian's shoulder, silently cursing as a woman with dirty blonde hair entered the barn. Frustration gnawed at him, but maybe having the sister—he assumed it was the sister—show up might play right into his hand. It was the best kind of revenge. A slow grin stretched across Chris's face.

Her eyes widened. "What's going on here?"

"Go back to the house," Cole told her.

"Looks like we have a party crasher," Chris drawled, keeping his gun trained on Sebastian.

"S-Seb?" The woman's hands trembled, holding a large glass of iced tea. "Is that you?"

"It's okay, Sam. Go back to the house," Sebastian said, not looking over his shoulder at the terrified woman.

Chris tilted his head and glanced between Sebastian and the woman. She backed up, but Chris waved his gun and pointed it at her. "Nope. I think she should stay."

Cold tea spilled down over her hand, and she dropped the glass to the ground.

"Let her go, Chris. She has nothing to do with this," Sebastian said.

"C-Cole?" Sam stammered.

"She's mine," Cole said, taking another step toward Chris. He held up his hand to hold back the bounty hunter. He could see it in the other man's eyes. The glint of worry was not easily hidden, and it gave him an idea.

"No," Chris said, pointing the gun at the woman. "She's mine. All this time, I've waited for the day to see you dead," he said to Sebastian. "But now?" He shrugged. "You also took Audra away from me. The son we would have raised together is being raised by another family. I think it's only fair that I get *her.*"

The woman gasped, her cheeks gone pale. Her wide eyes were adorable. Chris never owned a woman. Plenty of guys in the club had an old lady. Yeah. She would do. "Come here, sweetheart," Chris said. "You're mine now."

Cole growled, and Chris glanced over at the other man. "You get him and your money, and I get her."

"Touch her, and I'll kill you," Sebastian growled.

Wearing shorts and an old concert t-shirt with a pair of laced-up work boots, the woman stumbled back. "Don't," Chris said. "You run, and I'll kill him."

Sebastian's eyes narrowed on him. "Let her go."

"No can do, *brother.*" Chris motioned for Cole to join him. "If I don't kill you, he will." Cole took a few more steps closer. "And we can't have her spilling our secrets, can we?"

"Cole?" The woman crossed her arms over her chest.

"It's okay, Sam. I've got this," Cole said.

Chris snorted. *Sure, he did.*

Sebastian took a step forward, and Cole's gun pointed in his direction. "I don't miss."

"You're just too slow." Chris extended his hand toward her. His voice held a hint of amusement, masking the nervousness uncurling within him. "Come here, sweetheart, unless you want me to shoot your brother in front of you. It's brother, right? The resemblance is unmistakable."

Maybe this unexpected complication was in his favor, after all. This woman, with her fiery gaze and defiant stance, would bring a welcome challenge after he finished with Beast.

"Chris." Sebastian hissed a warning.

Tears crested over the woman's lashes. She walked toward him, slowly.

"Try anything, and I'll shoot her," Chris warned Cole. The humid air in the barn clung to Chris like a second skin, prickling his already dampening shirt. A sheen of sweat dribbled down the side of his face.

As Sam almost reached him, her foot snagged on something, sending her stumbling. A yelp escaped her lips as she collided with a nearby pitchfork. It toppled over with a clatter, startling a horse in the nearby stall. It reared up, and its whinny set off a chord of sound from the other horses in the stables.

Before Chris could react, Sebastian lunged. He grabbed a bucket, half-filled with brushes, and in a single, desperate motion, hurled it toward Chris. With a startled grunt, Chris lunged to the side. The thick rubber container whooshed past his head, missing by a hair's breadth. He stumbled, briefly off balance, and was forced to ditch the gun to shield himself from the flying projectile.

Cole grabbed Sam and pulled her to him, shielding her body with his own.

Frustration morphed into white-hot rage as Chris stumbled back, the impact of the dropped pitchfork handle sending a jolt of pain in the center of his forehead. The blow stole his breath, driving him back until he slammed against the rough wood of a horse stall. The world spun, a sickening kaleidoscope of hay and dust as he landed hard, slumping to the ground. Sebastian was on him in a heartbeat. Chris flipped and pinned Sebastian to the ground, but the victory was short-lived. A cold click pierced the air.

Chris's gaze snapped up, the world narrowing to the stark black circle of a gun barrel aimed directly at his stomach. His vision blurred, and blood seeped from his nose. He blinked as sweat burned his eyes. Her face was going in and out of clarity.

"Do it," he growled. "Do it!"

A moment later, pain exploded in his head, his hold gave out, and Chris went down with the scream of the woman who held the gun behind him.

25

Owen raced from the house, rushing toward Sebastian. The kid nearly tackled him to the ground as he latched onto him with an *umph*. Slowly, Caitlyn made her way toward him. The whine of approaching sirens cut through the crisp air.

Yeats weaved his way between the vehicles parked by the barn, making record time to get to Sebastian. "Caitlyn called. You good? Sam, okay?"

He looked at Caitlyn and lifted his chin. She waved. What was she waiting for? Owen clung to him, hugging him tighter.

"Yeah. All good. Thanks for checking on them," Sebastian groaned, his injured shoulder sending a fresh ripple of pain down his chest. Two cop cars pulled up alongside the barn, and a plain SUV followed.

One officer got out of the car and approached Caitlyn. Two more headed toward Sebastian and he directed them toward Chris, still lying in the barn, and they waited for the ambulance before taking him into custody.

Sam stood a few paces away. The sun falling behind the fence line in the distance. Her face twisted in a mask of shock and betrayal. Across from her, Cole leaned against the weathered fence post of the horse corral, his gaze locked on Sam.

"I'm sorry." Sebastian took a last fleeting look at Caitlyn before he went to see his sister, leaving Yeats to step up beside Owen.

"I envisioned this going an entirely different way," he admitted. He planned to come here in the morning, but the security alarm changed how he imagined this going.

Instead, they stood here, surrounded by the flashing lights of cop cars and ambulances with law enforcers and EMTs gathered in front of their family's stables.

She smiled through the tears. "I'm glad you are alright. I was so scared. I didn't know it was you at first." She leaned back, touched his brown locks of hair. "What happens now?" She glanced over at Cole.

"Are you pressing charges against this one?" Razek asked, gesturing toward Cole with a jerk of his chin.

His throat tightened as he looked at the pain etched in Sam's face. He never wanted to bring his sister pain. "He's an accessory to murder."

The words were a bitter pill to swallow, but the gnawing disappointment toward the man who'd been watching over his sister deepened. Cole flinched at the words, his face twisted in disbelief.

"He's been watching and waiting for me to come here," Sebastian said, a mix of fury and a deep, churning sadness accosting him.

A gasp escaped Sam's lips, a sound that shattered the tense silence.

The shock receded on Sam's face, replaced by a dawning comprehension that drained her face of color. "Is that true?" Sam asked, her voice trembling. A wave of desperate longing washed over Sebastian. He longed to reach out, offer comfort, and somehow erase the pain etched on her face. But before he could move, Yeats, ever the guardian, stepped forward to offer his solace. Sam recoiled, her movement swift.

"Is it true?" she demanded again. "You knew?"

Cole's shoulders slumped, his earlier bravado melting away. "I had no choice." His voice came out as a croak. He reached out a hand toward Sam, but she retreated farther, her eyes hardening with a chilling mix of fear and fury. "Sam, I would have never let him hurt you."

Another vehicle sped down the lane. Razek slid a pair of handcuffs into Sebastian's hand. He watched Sam and Cole. It was his fault. The secrets, the lies. The hurt raging in Sam's eyes.

"Sammy." Sebastian reached out a tentative hand, unsure if she would let him touch her. Sam's gaze met his, her expression giving him chills.

"Sam," Cole pleaded. "Babe." His voice cracked out the last word.

"Were you going to shoot my brother?" she asked quietly. Cole's lips tightened as Sam took that as a reply. "All this time. You were waiting for him. Why? What about your job? The kids. What about me?"

Anger simmered beneath the surface, and Sebastian covered his mouth with a hand to keep his thoughts from becoming voiced. The devastation etched on his sister's face raked him over a thousand hot coals.

Razek whispered something in Owen's ear, and the boy scuffed his shoe on the ground before heading away with a waiting police officer.

Cole hung his head. "I'm good at my job."

"And what exactly is your job?" Yeats moved closer to Sam.

"Killing people?" Sam accused, dismayed.

Cole lowered his chin. "I work in intelligence."

"How did you know I was here?" Sebastian asked.

Cole smirked. Lifted his chin in Owen's direction. "Your mother found some new photos in a scrapbook from the attic and Samantha put them in frames a few weeks ago. The kid recognized you from one of the photos." Cole's jaw tightened.

He glanced around at the cops inside the barn. Sirens sounded in the distance as the ambulance came down the farm lane.

"Cole." Sam's voice trembled. Tears glistened in her eyes. "You used me. All this time, I thought..." She broke off. Sebastian stepped forward, about to grab Cole, when Sam's arm went out in front of him. "No." She took the cuffs. "Let me."

Glancing at Razek, the chief of police shrugged. Sebastian handed his sister the cuffs. He reached for his gun, still nestled against his back. Cole kept his eyes on the movement. Sebastian aimed his gun at Cole to ensure the man didn't harm Sam, but his gut told him Cole cared about Sam. He couldn't, however, save her from this.

Sam walked up to Cole. With her back to Sebastian, he didn't let her see the gun he kept pointed at her boyfriend.

"Sam," Cole said again, in a way that made Sebastian feel bad for the dude. "I didn't have a choice. You better than anyone should understand."

"I understand," Sam said, reaching for his hand. He held out his wrists for her. "This is why you never could commit to a wedding date. Did you even love me, Cole?"

"Sam..." Cole's gaze lowered to the cuffs Sam wrapped around his wrists. Her shaking fingers worked to click each one in place. "When all this is straightened out, I'm coming back to you. All those plans we talked about—"

"Stop." Sam squeezed his cuffed hands. "Don't you dare use my hopes and dreams to manipulate me. If you loved me, you wouldn't have tried to help end my brother's life. I hope they lock you away for a long time." She dropped his hands, turned on her heel and brushed between Sebastian and Yeats.

Cole moved to go forward, but Razek grabbed him, and Sebastian held him at gunpoint. "Let's get this one out of here," Razek shouted as two cops came forward to help.

Samantha kept walking. Sebastian heard her sniffles and

went to go after her. Yeats put his hand out to stop Sebastian. He lifted his chin in the direction behind him.

Finally, Caitlyn made it the rest of the way from the yard, through the police, to get to them near the barn. Relief flooded her features as Owen raced toward her. "Mom! He's okay! Dan's okay!"

Owen clutched Caitlyn's hand as she intercepted Sam. Caitlyn spoke, head bent, and Sam turned her head to glance at Sebastian. Sam listened, her expression unreadable.

A flicker of hope ignited in his chest. Caitlyn's gaze flickered back toward him, a silent question hanging between them. Taking a deep breath, he met her eyes.

Caitlyn held his gaze for a long, searching moment. A slow smile tugged at the corner of her lips. Sam went with the police officer, who approached them. They would need her to give a statement like everyone else.

A warmth bloomed in Sebastian's chest, despite the chaos swirling around them. With Owen's hand in hers, Caitlyn strode over to him. Sebastian braced himself, unsure what to expect. Then she was there, right in front of him.

Razek took the gun from Sebastian's hand. "I think I'll hold on to this for you. When you're ready, let me know, and I'll give it back." Sebastian nodded, not taking his eyes off Caitlyn.

"You were never off the force, but I'm glad to have you back. I hear there's going to be a wedding here soon. Take your time," Razek said, clicking on the gun safety. "I'll see you back in Johnstown."

Before Sebastian could argue, Caitlyn said, "We'll be there."

"We?" Sebastian asked as she cupped his cheek. Sebastian leaned into it, closing his eyes as she leaned closer.

"We," she whispered.

"Me too," Owen chimed in.

Sebastian looked at Owen. "Can't argue with that."

"Nope." Owen said, "What Mom says goes."

"Then what does Mom say about making all this official?" he asked.

Caitlyn's eyes grew wide. "Daniels."

"Sebastian." His gaze lowered to her parted lips. "It's okay if you're afraid. We can wait. I got time. It's your choice."

Caitlyn glanced at Owen, then at Sebastian. "I know you are a good man, Sebastian Daniels, and Owen and I want to become part of your family."

"Forever." Owen bounced beside them.

"Okay," Sebastian said.

"Okay?" Her brow lifted.

"I think I can handle that," he said, watching Owen's lips quirk as he teased Caitlyn.

She tugged him by the shirt. The world around them faded away. The flashing lights, the angry shouts, the weight of betrayal—all of it dissolved into the gentle press of her lips against his. Soft and tentative at first, then it brimmed with unspoken promise.

Owen pulled away as Sebastian pulled Caitlyn closer in his arms. After he left her breathless, he asked, "Can you handle being married to a landscaper?"

"No." Caitlyn placed her hand over his heart. "Because my man is a law enforcer, and that's what I love about him most."

Sebastian covered her hand. "You love me?"

"Maybe." She gave him another quick peck on the lips. "Come. We should check on Sam, and I think we need to tell her about us, don't you think?" Her slender brow rose.

They walked toward where Sam stood talking with an officer. Sebastian's hand in Caitlyn's and Owen on the other side of him, they watched the ambulance leave with Chris inside.

"What happens now?" Owen asked.

"Now," Sebastian said, "we get ready for a wedding."

26

Haden and Holly exchanged vows under the old grapevine arch in Sebastian's mother's garden in the backyard. Two dozen guests under a tent turned into a hundred, and the weatherman's prediction of a hot July afternoon brought a light sprinkle of rain.

Sebastian stood alongside Rosco while Haden and Holly exchanged vows. Horses grazed out in the pastures beyond the tent, and the late afternoon turned into the evening. Emma sat with baby Isaac on her lap beside Charlie Brooks, the man who gifted him the Honda Rebel.

For the first time in almost a year, Sebastian breathed and relaxed. He listened to the music filtering through the barn speakers and watched his sister stay in the background. He introduced Caitlyn to Larry and Steve and their wives. During the ceremony, he lost track of Samantha. She dove into the details of coordinating everything for the wedding. He looked for her. In the kitchen of the old farmhouse, the caterer prepared finger foods and kept the cake chilled for the anticipated moment.

A knot of worry tightened in Sebastian's stomach as Caitlyn walked toward him.

"Did you find her?" he asked, his gaze lingering on the single braid cascading down her shoulder. He wanted to hold on to this moment, to savor the simple joy of her presence. But a primal fear gnawed at him. He loved her wholly and fiercely, and the thought of losing her was a terrifying abyss. All he could do was hold on as tightly as possible, hoping it would be enough.

"She's in the barn. You know Sam. She needs to keep busy. Let her have this time. She's stronger than you realize."

Sebastian balled his hands into fists, then unclenched them, the fight draining out of him. "It's my fault."

Caitlyn ran her hand up his arm. "You didn't make Cole lie to her."

"Seemed like a decent sort. I could have almost believed him."

"I did." Caitlyn glanced toward the barn. They stood in the grass outside the tent. Inside, his club brothers and friends watched as Holly and Haden cut their cake.

"He lied."

"He loved her. That guy, the one who wanted to kill you."

"Chris," he said, the sound of his name bitter on Sebastian's tongue.

"He held something over Cole. He forced his hand, but deep down, he loved your sister. I saw it when they were together. I saw it in his eyes. This was no job for him. Or if it was, he cared about Sam."

"Not enough to keep from ratting me out."

"It wasn't his intent to see Sam hurt." Caitlyn sighed.

"Maybe not, but he did." And Sebastian needed to make sure Sam was okay. He knew his sister. She might seem composed on the outside, but she would crumble as soon as this was over. This time, he planned to be there for her. No more running. He promised Caitlyn.

"You've got to let her deal with this on her own. You can't fix this for her. Cole's in jail, right?"

"He'll spend time, but not long." He gritted his teeth. Cole might get out in a few years with the right attorney. Sebastian intended to ensure he spent as much time as possible keeping Cole away from his sister.

"I need to check on her."

Caitlyn followed him as he headed around the barn. In the shadows near Stormy's stall, Sam stood in Yeats' embrace. Sebastian stiffened. "Figures," he muttered.

"It's okay," Caitlyn turned Sebastian to face her. "Let him be her hero one more time."

Turning his head to stare at the couple, Sebastian tried to swallow, his throat suddenly dry. Caitlyn tsked him. "Sebastian."

He loved hearing his name come from between her lips. "I'm her brother."

"And he's…. Thomas…" Caitlyn placed her hands on his face and turned his face back to look at her. "Who are you to intervene in the works of God?"

Sebastian opened his mouth, and Caitlyn pressed a finger to silence him. "I know you want to be there for her, but he's what she needs right now."

"I should have known Yeats would be there for her."

"You sound jealous. Be happy. You're safe. Sam may be heartbroken, but she's a grown woman. Give them this moment."

Taking a deep breath, he let his muscles relax. Not bothering to look at his sister and Yeats, Sebastian wrapped his arm around his woman as Owen hung out at the far end of the tent with a handful of kids his age, trying to burst a bunch of bubbles floating in the evening breeze. "I have a feeling our troubles aren't over yet."

Caitlyn followed his gaze to the gazebo, the girls giggling and dancing around Owen. She grinned and patted his chest. "Come on, we both deserve a slice of cake."

ABOUT THE AUTHOR

Growing up on a farm in Pennsylvania, Susan Lower yearned for adventure. A woodsy gal, Susan prefers camping over going to the beach any day. Still a farm girl at heart, Susan writes fast action reads filled with cowboys, heroes, and hope. She writes both western historical and contemporary romances, romantic suspense, and has been itching to one day write a mystery or thriller. Christmas is her favorite holiday, and she loves to write resilient characters struggling to overcome the complications of life while holding their values and strengthening their faith.

To learn more about Susan's books, sign up for her bimonthly email that includes exclusive excerpts, giveaways, and other goodies. http://susanlower.com/newsletter-sign-up/

ALSO BY SUSAN LOWER

Trade Secrets

Thunder Valley MC

Haden

Rosco

Sebastian

Hearts of Hidden Hills

Residence of Her Heart

Salvaged Hearts

Reckless Hearts

Holiday Hearts

Silver Wind Equine Rescue Romances

Forgotten Reins

Unbridled

Silver Stirrups

Brides of Annie's Creek

The Fruitcake Bride

The Thimble Bride

The Postage Stamp Bride

Cowgirl Mysteries

The Cowgirl Gets the Bad Guy

The Cowgirl Takes the Bounty

The Cowgirl Chases the Robbers